Patricia Reece

Rebecca's Anchor

Shadows of the Appalachians

Book 2

Patricia Reece

Outta the Holler Publishing
PO Box 1278   Bridgeport, WA 98813

www.patriciafayreece.com

DEDICATION

I dedicate this book to Christ Jesus.
Man can fail us, but HE will not.

ACKNOWLEDGMENTS

To my son, Tony, with his laughing brown eyes, who never ceases to bring me joy, Thank You.

Kathy Kennedy, my friend, had helpful suggestions on my manuscript.

Thanks go to Ginger Aster, my "beta reader".

I am grateful to my friend, Linda Bayless, for reviewing and discussing portions of the manuscript involving biblical sensitivity.

I appreciate Ken Raney (kenraney@mac.com)for a book cover well done.

..

CHAPTER ONE

Tuesday, December 5, 1780
Starlight, Virginia

Starlyn Peter Craighead must soon fight. Did a battle already rage, with his cousin Andrew in the middle? Starlyn shrugged into a coat, jaw clamped tight. Out a window, fingers of golden light traced a path through the early morning sky.

Never had he made a more difficult decision than travel to this faraway conflict. Shuffling slowly toward the front door brought back the time, as a young child, he stepped into spilled molasses.

"Starlyn."

"Yes, Father?"

"Can't go off like that. You'll freeze to death." Father held out a black military greatcoat with copper buttons. "Here, put this on."

Starlyn pulled back. "You always wear that when you travel."

Father rubbed the material between two fingers. "It is yours, now that you are traveling. Don't let anyone take it from you."

"Yes, sir." Starlyn reached out for a handshake but Father stepped close, grasping him in a hug.

"Be careful. Place your trust in the Lord." Father stepped back. "I am awfully proud of you."

Starlyn blinked, pulling on the greatcoat. The

material's smooth inner lining made it easy to thrust his arms through. It fit, falling comfortably below the knees. The worsted wool coat, more expensive than woolen, was sure to keep out wind or rain. Patting an inner pocket, where a hard object bulged, he pulled out a flintlock pistol.

"You forget about this?"

"No. I intended to give you that for upcoming business travels. A man needs protection during these uncertain times. Use it if you must."

Father accompanied him to the front room. Starlyn hugged his mother, bluish shadows below her eyes providing evidence she already worried. Did the decision to fight for their country's freedom put any of those silver strands in her chestnut colored hair? Sadness weighed on him.

He moved to Granda, who gripped him in a robust hug. "Be careful out there, Lad."

"I shall do my best, Sir."

Starlyn shook Jack's hand. Cobalt-blue eyes, the color of their father's, held a look Starlyn recognized, but there was not enough time to hear Jack out.

He started down the steps, stomach tight at the thought of being gone from home. Taking the reins of the tall dark gelding, he prepared to mount when the door flew open.

"Starlyn. Wait," Jack yelled.

"Better hurry, Mr. John Craighead," he called to his brother Jack. "I must get started." No warm house waited for him at the end of day, just a cold night ahead.

Jack rushed over to grab an arm. "I plan to marry before you come home. I have not told anyone yet, but…"

"What? Who?" It seemed like he should marry first.

Jack turned away, words mumbled, then came back to embrace Starlyn.

4

He pushed back on Jack's shoulders, looking into his eyes. He must know. "I didn't catch her name. Who is she?"

"Never mind. I will miss you, Star'n."

"Take good care of that tobacco crop till I get home." He recalled the contention over the last few months, before Jack finally agreed to take over the cash crop after their father interceded. Starlyn refused to make that the last word. "Shoulder your part of the family load. I'll see you after we win the war."

Jack turned toward the house.

Starlyn mounted, adjusted the thick gloves then kneed the horse. He must join the others going to fight against King George's army. Head low to avoid the December wind, he raised the collar of the greatcoat, and rode.

Several miles later, Starlyn slowed down. Thick trees lined the road, leaving no space for an opening. He would soon join two men from his area. They were both about his age. The three were traveling together part way to North Carolina. Despite their youth, the three were determined to fight this war for their families' freedom in their new country.

The sun came out, overlaying the forest with a golden cast, raising his spirits.

He slowed, watching for signs of trouble. The road, broken up from use, indicated it could be a bad time for patriots. The Tories arrested anyone traveling to fight against the Crown. Up ahead, a flock of birds took flight when a brown bear lumbered across the road. Starlyn gripped the reins until the bear disappeared into the trees.

Starlyn thought about the peaceful, happy look on Jack's face. He did not remember a time when Jack looked this happy. Where did his brother meet this young woman? Starlyn remembered evenings when Jack was gone. He would get a look at her and learn her name, after the war.

Up ahead, a large white oak marked the undefined path to a meadow in the forest. His blond, raw-boned neighbor, William, edged a horse onto the road. Starlyn followed him into the trees and dismounted.

A black haired man stepped forward. "My name is James. I don't recall who you are, but I've seen you around a few times."

"You also look familiar. I'm Starlyn Craighead." He turned to Willian. "What's your destination?"

"We're returning to our company, meeting them at Cross Creek. We'll leave you at Cape Fear Road."

"I'm going to join my cousin's North Carolina militia in Salisbury," Starlyn said.

"Tories passed by, not long ago." James nodded toward the road. "They're just looking for trouble—want to be seen as George's henchmen."

"Well then, we sure won't get there talking about it." Starlyn mounted, adjusting the collar of the greatcoat. "Let's follow that trail down by the creek. Most likely Tories travel on the main road."

He crossed the road, walking his horse down a small embankment toward a narrow trail, where they followed a rushing stream. The forest soon swallowed up the three among the biting smell of evergreen. Late in the afternoon the men rejoined the Carolina Road, traveling south to the Dan River.

Starlyn did not want to take on the deep, wide Dan. "That looks awfully cold," he said.

"I do not feel good about crossing this late in the day." James rubbed a glove over his saddle horn. "How about it, William?"

"I say cross over tomorrow, when the day is new."

"We will need wood." Starlyn dismounted.

"I'll get tinder," William said.

James tossed a rock. "The makings go there."

Each man did his job. Before long they gathered around a small fire, with James laying pieces close to the flames.

"Dry wood burns hotter," he said.

William smiled. "Don't put out much smoke, either."

Starlyn hobbled the horses then dug out food. When William pulled out a thin package wrapped in a bit of cloth, Starlyn looked down to hide his thoughts. James seemed better prepared for supper.

"William, I can't eat this much. It will rest heavy on my belly—make me groggy if we have a problem during the night." Starlyn rubbed his stomach. "My mother frowns on wasting good food. Care to take some off my hands?"

"Sure. I will help you. Glad to." Fingers trembling, William reached out for the portion Starlyn offered.

Hunger satisfied, Starlyn rolled up in blankets close to the fire. He got along fine with William and James, but tonight he missed the family. Even his hard-headed little brother's company might be welcome. The distinct, strong smell of evergreen filled the air as night creatures stirred under a slice of new moon. The sound of rushing water soothed him. Knees drawn close to the chest for added heat, Starlyn drifted into sleep.

He awoke to the sound of bird calls. Cracking limbs brought the forest alive, as larger animals moved in the distance. Then it grew quiet. Eyelids opened to slits, he was careful not to move.

"William, you awake?" Starlyn spoke softly.

"Yes. Several groups passed by on the road, real loud. A few Tories cut through, no doubt looking for men like us.

We need to get away from here."

"Yeah. There is bound to be trouble," James whispered.

Starlyn moved quickly to store the bedding before mounting to leave. The other two had done the same. He stopped far back from the water, studying the roiled-up river for a ford before motioning the others to follow.

He came to the river's edge but held back. Something troubled him about the angry body of water. James entered first, then William. Starlyn went in last as William's animal floundered, going sideways.

"Throw me the reins!" Starlyn shouted, moving up alongside William's horse. Grabbing the halter stopped the animal's downward motion, breaking the grip of the fast-moving current. Holding onto the reins as William fought to stay upright in the saddle, the righted animal struggled to swim while Starlyn led him toward safety.

Reaching the other shore, lower legs numb, he threw back the reins. Soaked to the waist, Starlyn's feet ached, with stabs of pain through the toes. They must stop, rub down the animals and feed them. Starlyn wanted dry boots but their horses came first.

They rode a half mile after leaving the Dan before the ache became unbearable. Was that a horse's snort in the distance? Did a Tory patrol already track them?

"Hold up, you two. I'm hungry. My horse needs some attention after that cold river." He knew smoke did not travel very far above a forest's dense trees. "We should go deep into the woods, among the thickest trees where a small fire does not show. It's safer. If there is anyone behind us, they may pass on."

"Let's do that." William rode closest to the road's

edge. "I am hungry enough to run down my food. Maybe kill it with my bare hands." Smiling, William entered the woods. Starlyn, then James, fell in behind.

They pressed through the forest, single file, until they reached a shallow branch coming off the river they followed.

"Someone start a fire." Starlyn threw his reins over a bush, then strode toward two large chestnut trees standing close together. Fallen limbs rested between the trees forming a windfall. From the amount caught there, encrusted with debris, Starlyn judged the windfall started years earlier.

He threw off the top wood, gathered a dry load then headed back, where William fed shavings to a weak flame.

"Make it small and tight. Don't want unexpected company." Starlyn dropped the armload next to William. "Where did you find the driftwood?"

"You are not the only one knows how to scrounge for kindling."

They gathered near the fire where Starlyn warmed his hands before going to take out a thick linsey-woolsey shirt from his pack. Removing his old coat, he pulled on the shirt before putting the greatcoat back on.

He checked the horse's hooves for small river stones, something learned while driving for his father. Starlyn used a knife to dig out two flinty chips, likely crushed from multiple wagon wheels crossing the ford.

He placed his boots close to the fire before they brought out food.

"We need to press on. The Moravian settlements are up ahead. We will continue past the first two." Starlyn continued, "After you two turn off, I'll travel on to the Salem settlement, where I'll stay the night."

William nodded. "I know this countryside well enough to ride it blindfolded. The road we take runs in the same direction as the Cape Fear Road, joining it at Abbots Creek."

Starlyn tore a hunk of bread in half, handing part to William. They talked as they ate.

"Starlyn, James and me save a few miles by going this way. Not to mention all of us travel together a little longer." William filled his mouth with the last of the bread.

"Are we ready to leave?" James said.

Starlyn nodded. "It's time to put on my boots."

James scattered the wood, kicking dirt on the coals.

At the Carolina Road, what Father called the Great Wagon Road, they turned left.

They rode in silence, alert for other riders. Two hours later they came to the turnoff. Starlyn halted for his companions to make their turn.

William drew abreast and reached out to shake Starlyn's hand.

"Hold on. I have something for you." Starlyn pulled out his older coat.

"I cannot take the coat off a man's back. That just ain't right."

Pride flickered across William's face while running a hand through his hair. Starlyn eyed the frazzled spots along the man's coat sleeves.

"Help me out with this. Father gave me the greatcoat. It gets too warm with a coat underneath. Wear this, then drop it off at my house when you go home."

William took the coat, sliding arms into it, and buttoned it up. He raised the collar.

"Take care of yourself, Starlyn. Don't let George's worthless men overtake you."

James rode past, touching his hat with the first two

fingers, flinging them out in a loose salute while making the turn.

As they disappeared into the distance, loneliness touched Starlyn.

His next stop, the third Moravian settlement at Salem, housed a productive, peaceful people who worshiped God. The Moravians never took sides. They were known for treating travelers well. There Starlyn would sleep safer than on the trail. He started the horse forward, driven by the knowledge he now rode alone.

A tingle crept up his back. He glanced over a shoulder. Three Tories stopped at the road William and James just turned onto. Two went their way. One came after him.

Starlyn kneed the horse to a gallop as he rode toward a curve.

"Oh Lord, don't let him catch me."

CHAPTER TWO

"Stop—I'll shoot," the Tory called.

Starlyn kneed the horse again, riding into the curve. A round screamed past him slamming into a tree. He veered off into the thick forest, dismounted and wrapped the reigns around a tree limb. Running toward the road, he crouched behind a tree.

The Tory slowed his horse, searching for the trail, but took off in a hurry traveling back in the same direct.

After the enemy disappeared around the curve Starlyn moved to the road for a look, hearing noise from the other way. A one-horse cart, loaded with farming tools and other metal items, approached. No doubt that scared off the Tory.

A young man about his age stopped the cart opposite Starlyn. "Everything all right with you?"

A row of brightly painted tulips, staggered with roses, ran along the cart's side. There was no denying this man's origin. "You're a Godsend, scaring that Tory off. Anything could have happened before I reached your settlement."

A little smile formed on the Moravian's face before looking directly at Starlyn. "They call me Mettle."

"Huh." Starlyn scratched an ear. "Don't think I ever heard that name before."

"It's because I build things out of iron and tin," the man said. "Isn't your father Reverend Craighead, from Salisbury?"

"No, that's Cousin Andrew's father. I'm Starlyn

Craighead."

"I recall Andrew's hair is lighter brown, with some green in his blue eyes. Well, need to get moving. Maybe I will see you again." The Moravian urged the cart horse on past.

Starlyn never knew a man to notice the color of another man's eyes before, but the Moravian worked in metal. Maybe he had learned the importance of paying attention to detail.

"How far to Salem?" Starlyn called out.

"Just one mile," Mettle shouted over a shoulder.

* * *

The aroma of baked bread hung in the air as Starlyn ate breakfast. The Moravians built the dining room separate for outsiders, away from their living area. Laying the napkin down, his hand brushed the maple table. A strong-backed Moravian with a good eye must have worked for that smooth, satiny finish. Starlyn ran the breadth of a palm over the table before rising.

He gathered up belongings from the building slept in the previous night. His horse received fodder early, in a protected stable. Starlyn considered the six-pence paid, for both their upkeep, money well spent.

Leaving Salem, he headed south on the road to Salisbury. Cold as it was, sunshine spilled over the day. He missed Andrew. After Uncle Alex moved their family, memories were the only thing left for Starlyn. Enveloped in the warmth of the greatcoat, reins clutched in a gloved hand resting on the pommel, he recalled their life together.

The family always said they looked more like brothers. Starlyn found someone like himself in Andrew. Over time, he honed manly skills on his cousin's know-how. After losing at horse racing, shooting or wrestling, he grew bull-headed. Andrew laughed at him. This placed them in hot competition once again.

The young ladies circled around his cousin like honeybees to a patch of wild flowers. Starlyn grew interested in Charity, who noticed plenty about Andrew but nothing about him. She pointed out Andrew's cowlick, swirled against the natural part, leaving his hairline in constant disarray. After she mentioned his cousin's eyes fringed with dark lashes, Starlyn stopped speaking to her.

He had spent a great deal of time thinking about their years together, and every day wished Andrew's family back in Starlight.

The sun settled warm on his face as the horse moved forward. He crossed the Yadkin River at the Trading Ford. Now Salisbury should be close.

The afternoon sun dropped low on the horizon. When he rounded a curve, a farm came into view. If the directions were correct, the log cabin belonged to Uncle Alex. Bone tired, Starlyn yearned for family and food in a warm house.

He reined the mount left through trees topped with snow. Urging the horse up a lane toward the house, the front door flew open. Starlyn almost did not recognize Andrew, who motioned him toward a large barn back of the house.

After Starlyn dismounted, Andrew fell upon him in an embrace before pulling back, red-faced.

Starlyn eyed his cousin. "You all right?"

"Don't ever tell anyone I did that—not very manly hugging my grown kinsman."

Starlyn gathered the reins. "Sure did miss you, too."

"We must take care of your animal." Andrew stepped over to the barn door.

Starlyn led the horse inside where they rubbed him

down then pitched fodder.

Back outside, Starlyn said, "Race you to the house."

"Let's go."

Starlyn stayed in front of his cousin, bursting through the door, Andrew breathing hard behind him. Did Andrew let him win?

Aunt Murna hurried forward, arms spread wide. "You must be hungry for some good food."

"I am starved. It was a long trip."

"Then I'll get it on the table."

She stepped aside as Uncle Alex came forward, hand outstretched.

"How is everything back home, Star'n?"

"Good. It's real good, considering the war."

Starlyn pulled a letter from an inside pocket of the greatcoat. "Father said to give you this right away."

His uncle took the correspondence and left the room.

Starlyn held out the coat to Andrew, who rubbed it between a thumb and fingers. "Uh-huh," he muttered, before hanging it on the wall from a wooden peg.

He followed Andrew into the common room. Uncle Alex sat hunched over an ornate, walnut desk, reading the parchment under candle lamp.

A spinning wheel occupied a portion of the room. A large stone cook-place ran the length of a wall. Flames licked up the center, casting a red-orange glow into the heart of the room. The table, a wide slab of walnut resting on heavy trestles, ran parallel to the cook fireplace. There Aunt Murna worked with a servant girl, warming food.

"Where's the rest of the family?"

"Right here, Star'n." William entered the common room.

Starlyn hung on as William pumped his hand,

astounded at the boy's size. At fourteen years of age, this lad might become someone to contend with one day. The thought of William tussling with Andrew over something they both desired brought a smile, until Starlyn realized that experience should always put Andrew on top. Starlyn cringed. He already received some of Andrew's experience.

Katherine entered the kitchen. Pretty as Aunt Murna, her luminous eyes matched the color of Andrew's. One day, Uncle Alexander would have quite a job keeping the young men whipped back until his daughter found the right suitor.

"William, go take care of the barn. Katie, I'm sure you can find something that needs done." Uncle Alexander rose from the desk. "Your brother leaves for war tomorrow morning. Starlyn needs to eat while we discuss important details."

Uncle Alexander gestured for Starlyn to sit at the table.

Aunt Murna filled a charger with beef and vegetables. Starlyn's stomach growled when she set everything on the table. "There's plenty left if you want more."

He silently gave thanks for the food.

"You're both joining the same militia company, I suppose." Uncle Alex leaned forward, arms folded. "The whole countryside believes the British are on their way here. Rest up—you may not get another good night's sleep for a while."

Starlyn finished the stewed apples, setting the bowl aside.

His minister uncle picked up the Bible. Peace descended on the table as he read First Samuel 17:37. "David said moreover, The Lord that delivered me out of the paw of the lion and out of the paw of the bear; He will deliver me out of the hand of this Philistine."

His uncle bowed. "Lord, we are as David, small, unprepared to fight such a great force, while our enemy is as the Philistine, Goliath. I fervently pray for deliverance from King George's hand. Nevertheless, Your will be done."

* * *

Starlyn's eyelids flew open. He dozed through the night, waking in fitful starts, only to fall back into sleep from exhaustion. He finally settled into that relaxed state of sleep, before a hand shook him.

"Get up, Starlyn," Uncle Alex said.

He moved to Andrew. "Son, breakfast is almost ready. Before long the men will arrive."

After Uncle Alex left, Starlyn rose to dress. He collected possessions laid out in an orderly fashion. He looked over at Andrew, who did the same.

"You think the fighting's going to get bad before the battles are over?"

His cousin gave that fearless laugh Starlyn remembered hearing from their younger days, always just before tangling in some competition.

"We'll give them a whipping they won't forget. I'm not afraid. Are you?"

Starlyn snorted. "No. I'm fighting for freedom— we're freedom's anchor. It can't get too rough for me."

Starlyn followed Andrew to the stairs. The smell of food hastened his steps down to the common room. They washed up at a sideboard by the back door.

Uncle Alex gave thanks for their food, asking for protection over them during battle.

Part-way through breakfast, Starlyn heard voices outside.

Uncle Alex slapped a hand on the table and rose.

"We've saddled your horses. They got plenty of the best feed."

Andrew went to kiss his mother's cheek as Starlyn quickly finished.

He rounded the table to hug Aunt Murna before following Andrew into the front room. Shrugging into his coat, Starlyn put up the collar for the cold ride. His stomach muscles tightened, remembering the decision to join up with Andrew. He had rather die fighting for their country's freedom than live a hundred years as someone else's person. It would take more than a stomach balling up for him to change course.

After settling the pack on his shoulder then picking up the saddlebags, Starlyn followed Andrew out the front door. Uncle Alex engaged a militiaman on horseback in conversation. The rest of the men sat high atop restless animals that snorted plumes of white breath, as dawn began to crack.

Shooting slivers of red, gold and orange lit the sky on fire. Despite the cold, Starlyn hesitated to move, not wanting to miss the spectacular display God surely gave to them.

Placing the saddlebags on his horse, he counted six men including the one leading their group. The dark stallion softly whinnied as Starlyn ran a hand over a muscular shoulder, stroking the animal's sleek coat. He mounted, pulled on gloves then waited for direction.

Uncle Alex cleared his throat. "Sergeant, can you tell me where they're going?"

The sergeant looked down at him, head slowly shaking.

His uncle ground the toe of a shoe in a tight circle as he said, "Knowing where they'll place their heads tonight will sure give me some peace of mind."

The sergeant pushed back his hat.

"If I intended to disobey my commander's orders, telling anyone our plans, then rest assured, Reverend Craighead, that would be you." The man looked into the distance. "But, I cannot do that."

Uncle Alex's foot stopped as he looked at the sergeant and smiled. "I'll pray the best for all of you. God knows you'll need it."

A man spoke up, long hair a shade darker than the tufts of blond beard he dragged fingers through. "Kings Mountain's just a start at running them out, if…"

"If, if?" Next to him, a little man said, "This time we won't just deal with Tory militia…"

Coughing softly, the sergeant interrupted. "Don't worry about that. Cornwallis, along with his troops, will just have further to run back home. But make no mistake—run they will."

As the sergeant gave orders to move out, above the confusion of riders commanding their animals, Starlyn heard his uncle's voice.

"God go with you."

CHAPTER THREE

December 8ᵗʰ
Rowan County, North Carolina

They left Uncle Alexander's house in the harsh light of a cold December morning. Starlyn rode abreast of Andrew at the rear of the troop.

"Do you know where we're going?"

Adjusting a hold on the reins, Andrew said, "We're headed toward Salisbury. We'll arrive there soon, unless the sergeant changes course."

In short order they entered Salisbury. Bright sunlight glittered off scattered patches of crusty snow, exposing the stark earth the small town sat on. A few men were out in the cold. The sergeant stopped to speak with two gentlemen crossing the road as Starlyn and the others looked around.

A man threw up a hand, smiling as he nodded, then turned to the boy with him. Starlyn imagined the man's words as he leaned down. "Look at the brave militia, fighting for our country. Some will die before it's over."

The sergeant broke off speaking to the two men.

"Let's go."

Their troop passed a small building identified as the Rowan County Courthouse. Andrew said Salisbury counted no more than two hundred citizens. The few they encountered seemed to welcome them. Starlyn was grateful. Too many Tories stood against the patriots.

After turning onto a road little more than a path, they stopped to pick up a man. They reached the edge of town when the sergeant signaled another halt. The last man to join their troop from Salisbury, Starlyn suspected, rushed out of the house calling to Sergeant Bone.

"My wife made something hot for the men to drink."

"Did you hear that?" Andrew spoke low. "Now we'll see what the sergeant's made from. If I'm right, we won't get any of that coffee."

Starlyn scratched his jaw. "If you're wrong, we'll go look for a commander who knows what he's doing."

The sergeant did not hesitate. "Can't do that—need to get out of here, quick. Hard telling who's peering out a window spying for the Crown."

The man mounted up, falling in behind Starlyn. Feeling closed in, Starlyn dropped back to the end of the line. Andrew joined him. He was unsure where Sergeant Bone led them.

Starlyn possessed no experience fighting the enemy, unless counting that advanced guard of Tories that once had chased Jack home. Father fired on the leader, who took off, the others riding hard to pass him by. Starlyn, though, had not fired a shot. Remembering that incident tensed up every nerve. He needed to learn something about battle.

He kept an eye on the trees as they traveled south on the Charlotte Road. If they came under attack, Starlyn intended to fight from the forest. They continued two hours, covering just over ten miles, when the sergeant slowed and threw out an arm.

Andrew said, "We're coming up to the forks of Crane Creek. Looks like he may stop."

Starlyn shrugged. "Yes, but I don't know why."

"That farm house in the distance belongs to Captain

Brandon," Andrew said.

The two men in front of them moved forward. Andrew beside him, Starlyn followed them onto a wagon road leading to a big log house with farm buildings scattered behind. A barn almost the size of the house sat to one side, with fields spread out beyond view.

Sergeant Bone faced the men. "Dismount. Stretch your legs while I get my orders."

Starlyn joined Andrew, who walked toward men gathered in a group. One stepped up to him, clutching a hat.

"Andrew, I didn't know your brother was old enough to fight. Looks just like you."

Andrew smiled. "Gentlemen, meet Starlyn Craighead, my cousin who came to join us."

Jamming on the hat, the man laughed. "'Gentlemen', he says. You can tell Andrew takes after his father. Reverend Craighead's rougher than a cob on the inside, but on the surface polished smooth as a river stone."

He shook Starlyn's hand. "I'm pleased to meet you."

Others nodded or threw up a hand to indicate the same.

The sergeant returned, mounted, and nudged his horse to a slow walk. The men followed him around a curve. Starlyn glanced back at the house, uncertainty growing. They came to a field set between two forks of a creek then followed a narrow path to the outer line of trees separating dense woods. Built against the trees were several lean-tos.

Sergeant Bone called a halt. Once everyone dismounted, the sergeant spoke.

"After Captain Reid joins us, this will be his company. The men back at the house are Captain Brandon's group." He looked toward the sky. "Some of you gather wood. It'll soon turn dark, we need a fire…"

"How long we gonna stay here, Sergeant Bone?" a man said.

"There will be few days to prepare before we start practice with Captain Brandon's company. It will take hard work to come out of this next battle alive. Talking's over. Let's take care of…"

Starlyn barely heard the sergeant's list. He watched several men who looked like seasoned fighters. He needed experience from tangling with one of them. It did not always take a bullet to bring a man down. A well-placed jab from a bayonet or a blow from a rifle stock also killed.

"I made it through my first skirmish." Andrew stepped closer. "You will too."

His cousin seemed to know his thoughts. Starlyn hoped Andrew was right, but taking no chances, turned to the only true Authority. "Lord, I will try not to bother You with unnecessary requests. Just lend me a hand this time."

Starlyn spun around when someone shouted "Here comes Captain Reid."

Several men threw hats skyward, whooping and hollering.

* * *

December 15th

Starlyn worked alongside Andrew before dawn, breaking camp. They had orders to clean the area, leaving nothing behind to indicate having been there. They also cleared the big field of debris, making ready to till come spring planting.

After his stomach complained from a meager breakfast, he was certain not to grow sleepy during travel. Starlyn did not expect to starve, but sure missed his mother's table.

They fell into the customary position at the end of the troop, as Captain Reid commanded their departure. They rode back past the farmhouse, where Captain Brandon's company led them forward continuing south on the Charlotte Road.

"What's all this slipping around, Andrew? I would like to face the enemy—get it over with." Starlyn grasped the reins in a gloved hand, working the other fist to increase circulation.

Lips pulled back in a grimace, Andrew said, "Tarleton's men have the best horses, along with supplies. Our ability to choose when we fight is most of our advantage. We must outsmart the King's army, or we lose the war. Then England will own us, and our descendants, forever."

"Well then, whatever it takes." Starlyn clenched a fist. "I want their yoke off my neck."

In the afternoon they stopped five miles north of Charlotte, at Colonel Alexander's mill.

The next morning, they took the right fork into the center of Charlotte. Starlyn noticed a brick wall three feet high, weaved into two tall rows of brick pillars, four in each row. They held up a rectangular wooden building with planks showing bullet splinters. Coming off each side of the second floor landing, where the front door opened, two well-built staircases descended to the ground.

Andrew pointed to the building. "My first enlistment, I fought at this courthouse under Captain Brandon. Got a taste of battle until we rode back toward Salisbury, fighting off the British the first few miles. About a week later, while other patriots ran up Kings Mountain mangling the Tories, we less experienced men held the horses. What a battle."

"That's the biggest house I've seen this side of

Williamsburg." Starlyn nodded toward a white house with multiple chimneys set among smaller simple homes. "Seems out of place here."

"That belongs to Colonel Polk," Andrew said.

The troop moved past Charlotte to join General Davidson along with more than a hundred men. Starlyn understood that Captain Brandon, Captain Reid, along with the rest of them, now fell under General Davidson's command.

Next morning, they all traveled toward General Morgan's camp. Starlyn's stomach tightened as they drew closer to what he and Andrew joined up for.

* * *

December 29th

Grindal's Shoals on the Pacolet River, South Carolina

Their group arrived at Morgan's camp. Starlyn blinked to clear away the image of so many men moving with the animals. Could that many fighters be gathered to wage war? Although accustomed to being around the militia, the soldiers scattered among the trees reminded him of a nest of ants.

Starlyn eyed the soldiers. "Maybe we should start doing something."

"We won't have time left over," Andrew said. "There are work details that require men who own horses. See the man wearing shoes? He's more valuable than the one with rags tied around his feet. The man with rags will do less work."

Starlyn's stomach churned seeing a deeper level of misery. The war had taken many lives. These men already survived the last few battles. He arrived with things others did not own. A horse, shoes, even good bedding.

Sergeant Bone rode up. "We need men. You four will

do." The sergeant pointed to Starlyn, Andrew and two others. "Join the six waiting with pack horses to forage for food. Whatever you find will help."

A light rain began as Starlyn approached the sergeant. "Sergeant Bone, how long must we wait before we exact satisfaction from Tarleton?"

The sergeant smiled at the outpouring of agreement from others. "Don't know, Craighead, but there's work to do. When not occupied, take care of your animals, or yourself. Be ready to fight when the orders come or Tarleton will get the satisfaction. Until then, get to work."

* * *

Starlyn washed his face with a worn cloth, rinsed it in a bucket of cloudy river water, relinquishing the cloth to Andrew.

The rising sun cast golden ripples across the darkened sky, turning the heavens into a splendid picture of what the day could be. Running fingers through his hair, lost in the vision playing out above, Starlyn did not notice Andrew had finished at the bucket.

"...been about two weeks since we arrived?" Andrew scratched his chest.

Startled, Starlyn replied, "It seems like that's about right..."

"Turn me loose. Ain't no spy. Ain't done nothing, I tell you."

Starlyn turned at the cry of outrage. Forty feet away, one Continental soldier held a horse's reins while two others worked to pull a man from the saddle. He fought like a wildcat. It looked like the man might get away, digging heels into the animal's sides. The soldier with the reins, legs spread apart, managed to hang on until the others grabbed hold again.

"For God's sake, let me go." Sobbing, the man screamed, "He's lying—lying through his eye-teeth."

The hair on Starlyn's neck stood up. They found a traitor in the camp? He looked at Andrew, who only muttered, "He would send us all into a death trap to help that bloody Tarleton win for England."

The soldiers managed to drag the spy off the horse. An officer took what one of them pulled from the man's pocket. After examining it, the officer tucked it away before pointing toward a tree standing out from the edge of the woods.

The two who pulled the traitor down each grabbed an arm. The man's body bucked, struggling to hold back, but they dragged him under the tree. Tying hands behind his back, they strung a rope around his neck—no easy feat, even for two men. The man with the reins held the horse steady while they placed the spy back in the saddle. One threw the rope's loose end over a limb, drawing it tight before knotting.

Starlyn watched the event, unable to turn away. The man screamed for help as they tightened the rope around his throat.

"Don't. Don't," he cried, as the officer slapped the horse's rump with a glove. The animal shot out from under, leaving the man swinging through the air, legs kicking and face contorted. It went on for less than a minute before the man stopped thrashing around. Soon the rope no longer moved and the body hung still.

Turning away, Starlyn tried to push down the sour taste rising in his throat. He had quelled the urge to grab the man, hold him up until someone could cut the rope. Of course, no one helped that young man. No one wanted to save a spy, a traitor who thought so little of his own freedom as to give it away, along with everyone else's.

* * *

January 15th, 1781

Up before sunrise, Starlyn helped Andrew stack wood they brought back from a fuel detail the previous afternoon. In the predawn light, a soldier rode into camp, horse moving fast. Dropping from the animal, feet in motion when he hit the ground, the soldier disappeared into the large tent General Morgan used to meet with the other officers.

"Uh—oh," said someone standing nearby.

Starlyn looked at Andrew. "He came in real fast. What do you think happened?"

"Don't know for sure." Andrew tossed a broken limb on the pile. "They only get in that big a hurry when it's important."

A quiver of excitement shot up Starlyn's back. "Something in my gut says trouble's coming."

As Andrew nodded, Starlyn wondered how soon before they entered the battle of their lives.

CHAPTER FOUR

Sunrise

Officers hurried in and out of the commander's tent, including Captain Reid. Starlyn watched them branch out in a high state of excitement, unable to figure out what happened. He hauled wood for the cooks, brushed debris off his greatcoat then hurried after Andrew, hungry.

Reaching for a bowl Andrew whispered, "Better eat fast. Something is sure to happen."

Starlyn lost all pretenses at manners while gobbling down the allotted fare. At Andrew's nudge he turned to see Sergeant Bone headed their way.

"Maybe now we will find out what the fuss is about," Andrew said.

The sergeant pointed to Starlyn, Andrew, then four others. "Captain says we're moving out. Help the officers' cooks break camp then load their wagons. You have ten minutes."

Sergeant Bone continued. "See Quartermaster Sergeant Billings for instructions. What're you waiting for, Tarleton's Tory green-coats?"

Starlyn rushed after Andrew, running toward the wagons by the river. There, two men readied barrels of food supplies as well as cooking equipment.

"Where's the sergeant?" Andrew said.

A man stepped toward them. "I'm Sergeant Billings. What do you want?"

Andrew pointed at the men coming up behind. "Sergeant Bone sent us to help the commissary pack up."

"You two get started." The quartermaster turned to face the approaching men.

Starlyn moved to the wagons, hearing the quartermaster instruct the other men.

A short, skinny man rocked a barrel from side to side, walking it toward several others grouped near two wagons. He started back, favoring his right leg then paused to gesture toward the other wagons. "I'm a cook. Will you help me get these barrels over there for loading?"

Starlyn said, "Which are the important barrels—the ones you use first?"

The cook pointed them out. Starlyn separated out several barrels, placing them elsewhere. He continued to work, as Andrew helped the cook move others.

"Give me a hand. We'll load faster working together." Andrew reached for one of the barrels Starlyn had set aside.

"Not those," Starlyn said. "They go on last."

A hand spread on the waist, in that way he had, Andrew said, "Why not? They're close as the others."

"They must go on last. They come off first."

"Huh. They all come off the wagon."

"Don't get stubborn, Andrew, we…"

"Hold it, he's right," the cook said. "If we get to these first, we'll start cooking from the flour keg and wet barrels of meat, while they unload the rest of the wagons. How long you want the officers to wait before they eat?"

The Quartermaster's head tilted in their direction, as Andrew said, "All right, Starlyn, let's get these loaded."

Part way through Sergeant Billings hurried to help them, lips pressed tight, as his gaze shifted around. The last barrel went on as the sergeant said to the man harnessing four horses, "Get that first wagon on the road, now."

Starlyn guided the barrels' placement with little more than a grunt as they hurried to finish. Did Andrew see his fear?

They barely finished the last wagon when Sergeant Billings shouted, "Get your horses and join your company. Fast, while you still can."

Running alongside others assigned to commissary, they found men holding the reins of several animals.

Starlyn's horse nickered as he approached. Mounting, they rode to catch the rest of Captain Reid's company, on their way to join General Davidson.

* * *

Their company moved forward along with the others. Starlyn settled into position for the ride. Sergeant Bone weaved through oncoming riders, headed back toward their group.

Andrew came alongside Starlyn. "What does the Sergeant want?"

"Don't know. Must be important."

Sergeant Bone stopped in front of them. "You men who assisted the commissary, go back to the wagons. Help them any way you can."

Starlyn turned his animal toward the forest edge to avoid the flow coming up from behind. The sergeant called out, "Hold on there. I want to speak with you."

He stopped to wait for the sergeant.

"Craighead, you seem to know your way around wagons. Keep a good eye on those for commissary," Sergeant Bone continued. "Major McDowell expects all the wagons to arrive in one piece."

"I'll do my best, Sergeant."

Starlyn crossed the road into woods so thick he had trouble seeing through the trees.

Holding on the reins, he settled into the saddle. The aroma of damp bark, foliage, and dank earth brought back times in the forests at home. Enjoying the smells, thoughts turned to Granda talking or laughing in that deep voice of his.

"Star'n, come this way. I'm over here."

Starlyn stopped. That sounded like his Granda, but it could not be. Ahead, almost hidden by a tree, Andrew waited. His voice was so firm, so deep, like the men in their family. Like Granda.

Gut tight, Starlyn pushed love for home back down, to remember after the war. He hurried to Andrew. "We'd better get to those wagons fast, or we're in trouble."

* * *

Riding behind the wagons Starlyn went slow to keep his horse from slipping on the cattle trace they followed. With mud a foot thick in places, the ten mile trip from Grindal's Shoals on the Pacolet River to their destination took longer.

They finally reached what Andrew called Thickety Creek. They set up camp on the banks of the small tree-lined stream thick with vegetation. Starlyn, Andrew and the others unloaded the wagons, grateful the provision barrels came off first. Before long, pots boiled. The aroma watered his mouth as he worked beside Andrew to finish unloading.

He hurried through a bowl of flour-thickened beef to take a quick look around. "I will find us a place to sleep tonight."

"I'll look for you after I'm through helping the cook," Andrew said.

Starlyn spotted a spruce tree wide enough to sleep under. If they angled their bodies close to the aged trunk, they might stay drier than out in the open. He retrieved his personal effects and shook out bedding on a dry spot at one side of the tree. He would lay uphill. Andrew soon arrived to claim the other side.

The four men who also worked the wagons chose a place under the tree.

"My back aches." Starlyn arranged the covers, grateful for the blankets.

"One of the roughest days I've had," a man said, pulling a pitifully thin, tattered blanket around the shoulders.

Starlyn sunk down in the covers, growing warm. As sleep crept in, his eyelids refused to close, unable to forget that frayed blanket. Sitting up, he peeled off a cover.

"It's gonna be a cold night," Starlyn said to the man as he held it out.

The man came for the blanket. Relief filled his voice. "I appreciate this."

Andrew reached around to poke Starlyn in the arm. "Now we can both sleep better."

The last thing Starlyn remembered was brushing off something crawling on his neck.

* * *

Andrew shook him. "Get up."

Starlyn rolled onto his back, staring at stars in an ink-black sky. "Say, if we get wood for the commissary to cook breakfast, maybe we'll eat sooner." He vigorously scratched.

Andrew stood. "You learn fast, my little cousin."

"Less than a year younger doesn't make me a little cousin."

They put away bedding, gathered wood to replace what the cooks burned, and deposited it at the officers' cook fire. Among the men in the crowd, the cook worked his way toward them, head going up and down each step he took. Two heaping bowls of food shifted in his hands.

"Eat while you can. It's a strange morning." The man's eyes darted around. "Never know what meal is your last for a stretch of time."

"We won't forget this," Andrew said.

Starlyn nodded. "Let us know if you need anything done."

After Starlyn took a bite, all resistance broke down. He ate so fast it became impossible to identify all the ingredients, deciding maybe it was better not to know.

Andrew grabbed Starlyn's arm as voices erupted.

"We've got trouble." Andrew pointed. "See that patrol? Something's wrong."

His cousin barely finished when a clear voice carried over the noise from breakfast.

"Turn out, men, and start loading wagons."

In the distance, with dawn cracking, Starlyn recognized the 'Old Wagoner's voice bellowing orders. General Morgan had arrived in camp. Starlyn mostly witnessed the General riding in, or leaving, wearing a blue cape trimmed in gold, over white buckskin clothing.

"Sergeant Bone's coming," Andrew said. "Captain Reid's right behind him."

Starlyn looked toward the captain as the company grouped around.

"Good morning, men," Captain Reid said.

"Morning, Captain," they replied, as the captain pivoted toward the sergeant.

"We need the same men who worked with the commissary yesterday to stay with them today. Have the rest form up. We're almost ready to leave. I'll return shortly."

Sergeant Bone pointed toward Starlyn, Andrew, and the other four. "You six load the wagons, get them moving. Anything they don't absolutely need—leave. The rest of you get ready to go. Be fast about it."

"We're leaving, Sergeant?" one man said. "I did not get to eat."

Sergeant Bone's neck veins swelled.

"Tarleton's army is only a few miles away. You inviting them for breakfast?" He looked around. "Go, go. What are you waiting for, the captain to return?"

Starlyn raced after Andrew to the officers' mess, throat stinging from the cold air. They were in trouble with little time to act. Tarleton was known for his cruelty to the patriots. If attacked, none of them might come out alive. He heard that Tarleton's Legion took no prisoners.

A driver waited on the wagon, holding the reins. Their cook dropped a barrel in the haste to load it. Sticking out a leg, Starlyn stopped the barrel as the cook limped after it.

"I've got it," he said. "What else you want loaded?"

The man bent over, grasping a knee. "Grab all the barrels you can. Empty pots, too. Kick full pots into the fire so they don't eat our food. Hurry."

Sweat gleaming on his forehead, the short man turned away. Icy fear raced through Starlyn's mind. The three no longer used care placing the barrels, but heaved them in the wagons along with utensils.

The first wagon pulled out as Starlyn raced Andrew to the fire, throwing over food pots.

"Not this one." Starlyn grabbed a piece of wood, sliding it through the pot's bail, hoping the handle held. "Here, grab hold. Too many men did not get to eat."

They managed to swing a second pot of food onto the tail end of the wagon, safely lodged, just as the driver cracked a whip over the horses.

Flinging the stick from the bail, Starlyn hurried away from the wagon in a run toward his horse. He rode after the wagons, Andrew's horse pounding behind him. Muscles throbbing for relief, he was grateful they accomplished all that work in so little time.

* * *

Starlyn followed the commissary group. Occasionally he and Andrew pushed a wagon through deep pockets of mud on the narrow, trampled road.

"We are headed for Broad River. Probably crossing over," Andrew said.

"The day's almost spent. Where do you think Tarleton is?" Starlyn gripped the pommel.

"Too close or General Morgan would not be moving us this fast."

A dragoon's sabre clattered as Starlyn followed along the tree line, close to the road. He felt safer knowing the dragoons guarded the army's flanks.

Sergeant Bone rode back to him and Andrew. "Keep these wagons moving. We'll set up camp in less than a mile."

"At the cow pens?" Andrew said.

"Pretty close." The sergeant moved on.

A half an hour later they were making camp. Order reigned as the army set up for the night. General Morgan and his officers arrived before them, their few tents erected on flat land between two gently-sloping hillsides.

Continental troops occupied one hillside next to militia encampments. Captain Reid's company, with Captain Brandon's company, set up on the other hillside surrounded by more militia.

Men gathered wood, started fires, or began cooking. After eating, Starlyn placed bedding on the ground next to Andrew's. Men in their company found places nearby.

At the nearest fire, Captain Reid motioned the company closer. "Tomorrow morning, you'll find breakfast already prepared. General Morgan wants you to eat for strength to outlast Tarleton's men." The captain gripped his sword's pommel. "Our assigned position is near the front. You will get first pick at the targets, so choose wisely. Follow your sergeants' orders. Fight bravely." The captain turned and left.

General Morgan, accompanied by Major MacDowell walked among the camp fires. Approaching, the General said, "Just hold up your heads, boys." Slamming a fist into his palm, the General continued, "Three shots—and you're free to fall back! When you return to your homes, how the old folks will bless you, the girls kiss you, for your brave conduct."

The 'Old Wagoner' said more, but Starlyn most remembered, "Three shots, and you're free to fall back."

When the general moved on, Starlyn headed for the covers, Andrew beside him. All night he drifted in and out of sleep, waking each time to the sounds of more militia arriving. The clear voice of General Morgan traveled through the camp, as he encouraged the troops.

CHAPTER FIVE

Wednesday, January 17
Hannah's Cowpens, South Carolina

Starlyn jerked awake, not sure why. He pulled the covers closer to keep out the cold. Unlike the previous evening's dark clouds, brilliant stars sprinkled a clear sky.

"Boys, get up!" General Morgan's voice roared through the camp. "Benny's coming."

Starlyn sat up as the camp came alive with figures of men moving in the moonlight. Andrew ground fists into his eye sockets.

"Benny's coming?" Starlyn yawned. "He talking about…"

"You know, Banastre Tarleton. You heard the General. Get up. Today we do battle with Benny." Andrew ran a hand through his hair. "You ready for Tarleton—or scared?"

"I have wanted this fight since I left your house." Standing, Starlyn reached down for the covers. "Besides, Granda says our family's too hard-headed to know fear."

Andrew retrieved bedding in one sweep. "All right, hard-head, let's get our belongings put away while there's still time."

Starlyn walked to the campfire where someone shoved a bowl of food at him. "Eat all you want, but do it fast. We're headed over to face our enemy."

He grunted, taking the bowl. The food went down quick. Who knew how long the battle would last. A hungry man only grew weaker as the day wore on.

"I guess they cooked breakfast last night, like the sergeant said."

"That Old Wagoner's real smart. Didn't figure out why the man put us running away, yesterday." Andrew glanced toward Morgan off in the distance, giving instructions to officers. "Turned out we did not run away from Tarleton. We hurried toward the best place to fight."

Men ate then left. Drivers working for the quartermaster took to their wagons, whips cracking as they drove the baggage to the rear of the battlefield. The men in Starlyn's company moved forward as Captain Reid and Sergeant Bone approached.

"Time to get in place," Captain Reid said as the sergeant headed toward the animals. "Put your horses behind that low hill over there, where the wagons are."

The captain turned back toward the group. "Get moving. General Morgan wants you ready before Tarleton arrives."

Starlyn glanced toward Andrew as they broke into a run. Finally, what they wanted. He looked skyward to fervently request, "We need some help."

Through the confusion of several hundred animals in motion, Starlyn managed to get out in front of Andrew, riding toward the wagons. Sliding off, handing the reins to one of their men collecting horses, he looked toward the captain.

Andrew joined him, muttering, "I want a chance to show I ride better."

"Any time you want, but…"

Captain Reid cleared his throat. "All right, men. If we

lose this battle, Tarleton won't go easy on us. Follow Sergeant Bone and remember General Morgan's instructions."

They hurried down the small hill, away from the safety of the wagons. Starlyn's gaze swept over the Cowpens. The overgrazed land had not completely grown back, the grass nibbled close the previous season. Little vegetation remained besides what ran along the stream banks.

Their rifles lifted, a flurry of excitement surrounded the men who rode past, toward General Morgan.

"That's our scouts Tarleton's men forced in. Benny's close." Andrew pulled up his coat collar. "It won't be long now."

"Line up here." Sergeant Bone swept the air with a finger. "Get ready to spread out across the field." His breath shot out, marking the air with white mist. "When the sharpshooters fall back behind us, you all become the front line."

A hundred and fifty feet in front of them, a group of fifty sharpshooters listened to their commander's instructions. Starlyn's attention returned to Sergeant Bone.

"Aim for the men with the epaulets. Make every shot count."

"Does that mean shoot the officers?" a man said.

The sergeant nodded. "That's exactly what it means. I'll be here with you."

As another scout galloped by, Bone's voice dropped to a strangled whisper. "Kill every one of them you can." Voice raised, he continued, "Now spread out. It's time for General Morgan to crack his whip over Benny."

"I guess we're the General's whip." Starlyn glanced at Andrew, who nodded.

Legs stiff, Starlyn moved into place. He patted the

ammunition pouch hanging from a shoulder. Andrew hoisted his gun upright, face strained. This was not friendly competition, like back home. What if they did not come out of this alive?

Spread out across the slope behind them, regular Continental soldiers lined the hill. Dark blue tri-corn hats matched dark blue jackets over white vests, with white trousers.

Behind the Continentals, closer to the wagons where the slope dipped down, General Morgan, along with a few officers, prepared to direct his army. Starlyn had passed them earlier, coming down. Somewhere between General Morgan and the wagons, more Continental cavalry, along with mounted militia, waited for the command to enter the battle.

The air practically crackled like just before a thunder storm. Every muscle in Starlyn's body seized up; preparing for what came next. The only way out of this was to fight his bloody way through. He stood ready to do that.

"Here they come," echoed from the ranks of the sharpshooters. Starlyn, along with militia brothers, raised their voices pitching it over their shoulders to the Continental infantry. It rolled over the cow pens like thunder. Starlyn heard the faint sound of drums and fifes as redcoats appeared on the distant roadway. A small bunch of Tarleton's mounted green-coats brought up one side, brandishing weapons.

"You know the General's orders," Sergeant Bone shouted. "'Hold your fire till you see the whites of their eyes.' Wait for my command."

Starlyn figured the skirmishers and sharpshooters heard orders to hold their fire, too.

General Morgan gave the orders putting Captain Reid's company near the front, just behind the sharpshooters. The General's plan from the night before rang in Starlyn's ears. "Just hold up your heads, boys. Fire three shots, then fall back behind the regulars and stand proud."

The British cavalry moved up fast. Beyond them came Tarleton's green-coats. A group of soldiers wearing dark blue caps, the rims speckled with red and white, waited in the distance.

"The men wearing those blue caps are King George's Scottish Highlanders," Andrew said.

Starlyn swallowed. "You mean we'll fight other Scotsmen? God help him if I get my hands on one."

Andrew grunted agreement.

As the rising sun scattered rays of gold across the field, the crack of sharpshooters' rifles filled the air. They shot at redcoat infantry and some of the cavalry. The militia held their position as the sharpshooters fired their rounds, redcoats dropping like apples in a wind storm.

Soon the sharpshooters fell back, making Starlyn's group the front line. Redcoats continued to advance and, behind them, the Highlanders waited. Tarleton's Legion lay beyond, in their green coats with black plumed hats.

The enemy advanced at a fast pace. Fear swept over Starlyn, the taste of cornmeal and rancid beef rising up to sting his nostrils.

"Lord, stay with me." He waited for orders.

"Fire now!" Captain Reid's voice filled the air.

He shot his first round. Finished reloading, he looked up as a redcoat leveled a weapon at Andrew.

"No!"

He moved to close the distance when, from the side, a Tory green-coat advanced uphill toward him. Starlyn dropped to one knee, killing Andrew's redcoat.

He worked to reload as the green-coat aimed his rifle.

Death was coming. Then Starlyn thought he may have already passed on— something so strange happened.

A man hurried toward him, fleeing from a large, dark shadow that chased after. The man drew even with the green-coat, flipped around then came between them to face Starlyn. The Tory's rifle discharged into the big man's back.

In that moment of life or death, Starlyn stared up at the light shining from the man's face, the light too bright for Starlyn. He looked down, and waited for the man to fall from the gunshot. Nothing happened.

The man swung around to face Starlyn's enemy, sweeping a leg behind the green-coat's knees, dropping him to the ground. He then turned away, long strides covering the distance. Starlyn wondered what the dark shadow was, and why did it now flee from the big man?

The act bought Starlyn time to load as the green-coat struggled to rise, attempting to reload. Starlyn fired a third round, dropping the green-coat, then hurried toward Andrew.

They moved off to the left, following other militia circling the small rise behind them. There he reloaded as they waited for instructions.

The incident on the field troubled him. When the big man turned, sweeping the Tory off his feet, Starlyn thought he saw something protruding from the man's back.

"Stay close," Captain Reid said. "Follow me."

The captain led them around the other side, back toward the battle.

As they cleared the knoll, confusion rose over three differently dressed enemies. One man asked, "Which ones we supposed to shoot at this time, Captain?"

"Get the indigo caps with red and white checks, then everyone else."

While the bullets flew past in both directions, Starlyn

bent down on a knee, getting off a shot that dropped a Highlander. He reloaded, hardly able to think in the swell of screams. The field thinned as part of Tarleton's men turned and ran, some on horseback. Many of the enemy threw down their weapons to lift their hands. Others dropped to the ground.

A group of militia cavalry went after the enemy. "Tarleton's quarter!"

Two officers rode by. "Tarleton's quarter? Stop them before they kill all the prisoners like Tarleton does."

All firing stopped. Starlyn rested the stock of his gun on the ground, grasping the warm barrel to lean on as he tried to make sense out of the death and confusion. The first man to reach the fleeing enemy put a bayonet through one's back. Officers on horseback reached their men, stopping them from killing the rest of Tarleton's troops trying to surrender.

Andrew approached, a disgusted look on his face. "I guess they're just giving Tarleton's men a taste of what Tarleton took pleasure in doing to their patriot brothers in other battles."

"Kind of looks like that to me, too. But it isn't right." Starlyn switched hands on the barrel.

Andrew nodded, "We're not animals, to act like that. We're men, made in the image of God."

The mounted militia brought back the enemy as Sergeant Bone gave instructions to gather weapons and pile them down by the road.

Starlyn went back for overlooked guns, strewn beside bodies on the ground. Picking up the weapons, he heard Major McDowell tell Captain Reid, "After the equipment's gathered, form your company at the base of the knoll for a burial party."

Starlyn shuddered. How much more killing must he do?

CHAPTER SIX

The sun touched Starlyn's face, as active muscles provided warmth from spading the ground in the crisp, cold day. He wiped at sweat as men placed bodies into the holes, looking away after recognizing one as his handiwork. The battle lasted one hour—yet they buried enough dead to ensure Starlyn bad dreams.

Sinking the spade in the ground, dirt flew. Starlyn stopped to catch his breath then shoveled again.

"Starlyn Craighead."

He faced Captain Reid. "Yes Sir?"

"You're needed for special detail." The captain pointed toward their company.

Starlyn hurried to Sergeant Bone to hear the orders.

"During the battle, we took thirty wagons from Tarleton's men. General Morgan's Continentals, along with the Virginians, marched prisoners out this morning, taking twenty five wagons." The sergeant pointed down the road. "The last five traveling with General Davidson just became your responsibility."

A man called out, "Where they at?"

The sergeant continued. "If you own a horse, get it. The wagons are down in the woods, off the road."

Ten men on foot walked with the sergeant. Starlyn accompanied his cousin to their horses. Many men had died—some patriots—but most wore King George's red or green. Was the tide about to turn against the patriots? He and Andrew were safe now, but for how long?

He rode to the wagons then walked with Andrew to the sergeant.

"Starlyn, take a few men to go through the wagon's freight. Get a good look at the important stuff. Don't take much time."

"Yes, Sergeant." Starlyn pointed toward Andrew and four others.

As they worked through the contents, he found a large amount of high quality foods. They would eat better for a while. There were several casks at the back of one wagon. Starlyn crawled over barrels of gunpowder and lead balls, to investigate.

"Come see this, Andrew. I do believe Tarleton indulged, maybe even his men, with rations of rum."

Andrew called back, "Come look at what's in the last wagon, Cousin. Better hurry. They're already into it."

Jumping down, Starlyn turned to see two of the men wearing red coats. "What are you doing with those? Take them off before we get in trouble."

"Can't. You'll have to rip it off me." The man's eyes glistened as he backed up. "I'm warm for the first time in weeks."

Looking down, Starlyn searched for a way to deny these men the chance for something as essential as coats. He just could not find the heart to tell them no. Being warm seemed a small thing to ask.

"Wear them until I ask the sergeant."

* * *

The sharp blast of a bugle split the air. Starlyn leaned down from a wagon, taking a wooden box Andrew held up.

"Hurry, Andrew. It seems like an officer disperses

new orders every time that bugle sounds." Starlyn reached for another box.

They worked in silence until Andrew said, "We're through, and none too soon. A captain's speaking with Sergeant Bone."

Jumping off the wagon, Starlyn waited for his next order. Not feeling so young or inexperienced any more, he recognized this loss of innocence as the bitter price paid for their country's freedom. After the war he would return home a changed man. His gaze went to the sergeant headed their way.

"We need drivers, Craighead. You take care of that."

Starlyn swallowed. Sergeant Bone just expected him to know the right drivers, coming from a freighting family. Maybe so, but what if he failed?

The sergeant stepped closer. "No need to drive, having your own horse, but when we get started stay close to the wagons. We don't want to lose any."

Andrew walked over as the sergeant left. "You don't look so good. Something wrong?"

The battle he just went through, and the weeks of travel, weighed on Starlyn. "I need ten drivers. Fast. Think our company has that many good enough to not ruin a wagon?"

Thumb stroking his jaw, Andrew nodded. "They don't all need to come from our company. Not much time. We'd better hurry."

"We? Are you volunteering to help me?"

"You're my cousin. I'll always help you." Andrew smiled. "Don't worry. We'll do it right."

"Then let's get to it." Starlyn said.

Starlyn found four men who might be good drivers.

Andrew rode through the trees and dismounted. Moving fast, Andrew reached him.

"I found four drivers coming off burial detail. They're on their way. Along with two more who aren't wearing enough clothes to keep out the wind."

Scratching his head, Starlyn said, "What'll we do? Give them coats from the wagon?"

"I don't know, but you had better decide. The sergeant's coming." Andrew cut his eyes right. "The drivers are here. What do you want me to do?"

"Take all six back to the wagon. Give each a coat. Maybe the sergeant won't refuse them."

As Andrew rushed toward the men, Starlyn barely turned around before the sergeant closed in, worry creasing his face. "We're running out of time. Did you find enough drivers?"

"Well, yes. I managed to find ten drivers. They seem like a pretty fair lot."

The sergeant cleared his throat. "Where they at, Craighead? We don't have all day."

Starlyn reached down to scratch a knee. He straightened up as men wearing green or red jackets flowed toward them. "Here they come, Sergeant Bone. They need warm coats, so I gave them some we found."

The lines in the sergeant's face deepened. "Why did you do that before speaking to me?"

"Well, Sergeant Bone, I, I..." Starlyn's chest tightened as he searched for something to say.

Arms crossed, a foot thumping the ground, the sergeant said, "I want an answer."

Starlyn had to tell the truth. "These men know how to drive a wagon, but some of them are cold. I gave them the coats because we must get on the road quick. Do you want me to confiscate them?"

"No. You made a good decision. I'll speak to Captain Reid." The sergeant glanced away then shook his head. "One thing, though. They better lose those jackets going into battle or their own men might kill them."

The sergeant walked away, toward others milling around.

Andrew brought the drivers, and spoke in a low voice, "Well, how'd he take it?"

"Sergeant said I was correct." Starlyn turned to the drivers. "About wearing those coats into battle, we'll shoot anything in red or green. When the fighting starts, take them off. Sure ain't worth dying to be warm."

He singled out five men. "You're driving first. Take a second driver, pick a wagon then get those teams hooked up."

They all ran toward the wagons when the sergeant bellowed, "Get going. We're moving out."

* * *

Wednesday, January 31
Catawba River, North Carolina

Starlyn reined his horse left, out of the path of men moving forward. The sun stood directly overhead, a few thin clouds strewn across the sky.

Leery about straying too far ahead, he let the wagons catch up, falling in behind the last one. Andrew rode out of the trees, moving into position beside Starlyn. They traveled without speaking until his cousin broke the silence.

"Seems we've been on the move for the last two weeks, stopping only to eat or sleep at a different place each night."

"At least you have an idea of where we're headed. I

don't." Starlyn grasped the pommel, glancing toward Andrew. They must stop soon, before daylight ran out.

Back home, Father would be entering the barn with Granda to tend the animals. Their hanging candle lamp's soft glow would smooth out the rough corners, giving the barn's coarse edges a golden appearance. He almost heard the familiar sounds of the cows and horses as Granda's soft voice settled them down, carrying traces of the Scottish tongue. Did they miss him as much as Starlyn missed home?

"Are you listening?" Andrew said.

"What's that again?"

"We're heading north. Beattie's Crossing isn't much...Oh, here comes Sergeant Bone."

"He's in a hurry," Starlyn said.

The sergeant moved in behind them. "Andrew, spread the word we're almost at camp."

"Right away." Andrew rode toward the wagons up ahead.

"Pay attention, Craighead. The five wagons, with our regular two, belong at the edge of camp." The sergeant shifted in the saddle. "Make sure the drivers understand that."

"We staying with the wagons?"

"Captain Reid's orders. Make sure you follow them." The sergeant reined his horse along the tree line toward the front.

Starlyn glanced up wondering how much daylight remained. His back ached for some rest. Food sounded good, too.

The lowering sun hung like a giant red ball, scattering long golden rays over the surrounding hillsides, shimmering off the river they followed. All the beauty the golden circle cast down to earth made the rest of the winter countryside uglier when that glow disappeared over the horizon.

Starlyn rode alongside the seven wagons, repeating the sergeant's instructions for the drivers to stay together. He returned to the last wagon, eyes on the others as Andrew weaved in and out of the group, occasionally glancing back.

Starlyn's memories flooded in from their childhood. Like Andrew urging him on to win, after a bigger boy hit Starlyn out back of the church. Then quick as they came, the memories stopped.

After Andrew returned, Starlyn said, "Glad you're back."

"What do you mean glad I'm back? Did this war finally get to you?"

Starlyn did not hesitate. "Guess I never said I'm glad you are my cousin."

"I feel the same about you." Andrew tilted his head.

Chills prickled Starlyn's back. There was no time to think about childhood memories now. They were headed into battle.

CHAPTER SEVEN

February 1st
Beattie's Ford, North Carolina

Starlyn's militia group arrived at Beattie's Ford in the late afternoon along with other companies. His drivers lined up their wagons on the outskirts of camp. The officers went to meet with Generals Davidson and Morgan.

Sergeant Bone came directly back, reaching the company before Captain Reid. "Gather around here, men. Pay attention. We have a change of orders."

Captain Reid stepped in close to Sergeant Bone. "Get ready to move. We're leaving in twenty minutes. Sergeant, make sure the company stays together, along with Craighead's wagons."

The sergeant nodded. "Yes, sir."

Reid spoke again. "When Captain Crawford's company starts out, fall in behind them."

* * *

Starlyn's company arrived at Cowan's Ford at dusk, with little time for the drivers to arrange the wagons. Men started fires and assisted the cooks, while others gathered fuel or cared for the animals. They had barely recovered from the rush to Cowan's Ford, when Sergeant Bone called them together.

"Captain's on the way to give us orders. Pay attention. They're important." The sergeant looked back over his shoulder.

Captain Reid's long stride covered the distance.

"Men, soon as the Catawba River started to recede, General Morgan raced for the Yadkin River with his men and all those prisoners." Reid coughed. "We militia will stop Cornwallis from crossing the river here at Cowan's Ford. The men from Mecklenburg shall guard the river against the British crossing. If they try, we will help Mecklenburg's men turn them back." After Captain Reid finished, he left.

Andrew leaned closer to Starlyn. "General Davidson just arrived."

Later, the lame cook waved both cousins forward to get their supper. Food bowls in hand, they moved to an aged oak tree. Under its heavy limbs, Starlyn sniffed the heaping contents, hunger squeezing out a growl. Taking a bite, the taste of meat flooded his mouth.

"We're fortunate to get wooden bowls. Did you see the men's faces behind us when the cook handed out tin plates?" Starlyn gripped the bowl, planting a fist at his waist.

"It's pewter, Starlyn."

"Yes I know, but wooden bowls are easier to handle away from the table." He also appreciated the eating utensil. The last men served did not always get a spoon.

Starlyn tried to stay awake long enough to finish the meal. He must find a place to sleep close to the wagons. It could rain.

Steady fires dotted the hilltop, land descending to the embankment half a mile below. Andrew found a place close to him, along with other Rowan County men.

Would King George's army try to cross here? Men stood guard near the river as others walked the hillside watching for any sign of the enemy.

* * *

Starlyn jerked awake, cracking his head on a wagon wheel. Finding no signs of blood, he settled deeper in the covers' warmth, head throbbing. Gazing into a black, starless sky, the new moon visible only by a faint trace around its circle, he searched for what woke him.

In sleep he had struggled with a dark foe, unable to get on top. Awake now, mind shrouded in dread, something seemed wrong. Low fires left the camp without much light. The sound of stillness roared in his head—far too quiet. Starlyn eased out of the covers, stood and went to shake Andrew's shoulder.

"What?"

"Get up Andrew. I've got a bad feeling. Something's not right..."

A gun shattered the silence.

"The British! The British! They're in the river—coming across!"

Starlyn grabbed Andrew's arm, hefting him upright. Around them, men threw off their blankets, reaching for weapons. The camp turned into a mass of bodies moving in all directions. The flash of British artillery exploded from down the river.

"Form up, men." Sergeant's voice carried above the mayhem, cutting through the confusion. "Move now."

Rifle in hand Starlyn ran toward the voice, heart beating like an ambitious blacksmith pounding out metal. Andrew kept pace as they dodged other militia members hurrying to answer their officers.

Sergeant Bone stood ram-rod straight. "Blasted fog. Get over there—give them some help. Keep low." The sergeant turned toward the ford. "Now, right now."

They arrived behind the cavalry, whose steady fire thinned out the enemy's front ranks, slowing them. A British officer on horseback appeared, shouting instructions, starting his men forward again. A patriot cavalryman reloaded then fired, dropping the officer into the river. Several British in the water pulled him onward.

Starlyn fired, stopped to reload then fired again, but they continued to come.

"Star'n, come on," Andrew called, motioning to retreat. A volley of lead buzzed past Starlyn's ear. He backed away from the riverbank, fired another round then ran toward the ridge, stepping behind a tree to reload.

General Davidson, along with another officer, rode their horses down near the water's edge. The officer yelled, "Fire away. Help is at hand."

Just then, a musket ball knocked General Davidson from his horse. Even as the cavalry rode in, Starlyn knew that the general was dead.

"Up the hill! Up the hill!" the officer shouted.

Sucking in air, Starlyn scrambled with other patriots toward the ridge, some turning to fire as they went. The cavalry covered their retreat as the British advanced, bayonets attached. He searched for Andrew, who could already be at the top.

As Starlyn hurried up the hill, a thin, jagged sliver of gray opened across the night sky. About thirty feet ahead, Andrew came into view, stumbling along. Clyde, a man from their company, held his cousin upright. Rushing, Starlyn caught up with them.

"What happened?"

Clyde pulled back, hand covered with blood. "Must have taken a round to the chest."

"Stay with us," Starlyn said. "We need your help."

He stepped in close. Andrew threw an arm around his

neck. Starlyn grabbed a hand, circled Andrew's waist with his free arm, while Clyde took the other side. They towed Andrew up the hill.

"How bad you hurt?" Starlyn said. He eyed the dark, wet stain that spread out from Andrew's chest.

Breathing hard Andrew said, "I need help. Hurry, Star'n. I'm growing lightheaded. I...I think I'm going to puke."

"Go on."

Starlyn gripped his cousin's hand tighter as Andrew projected a stream. Once through, Starlyn used a coat sleeve to wipe his cousin's face. Then he gripped Andrew's middle again, taking him up the hill with their comrade's help.

Where did the strength come from to dig in and haul his kinsman to safety? With the General dead, they were on the run, leaving each person to get out the best way they could. On top of the plateau, they swung left.

"Help us get to our horses."

"All right," Clyde grunted, getting a tighter grip on Andrew. "Let's go."

Starlyn's mind whirled. He pulled out an idea, tossed it aside, only to search for a better one. He must help Andrew.

"Is this close enough?" Their comrade's voice reflected fear.

"Maybe we'll see you later." Starlyn doubted he could have purchased help like this. When the man nodded, Starlyn said, "Thank you. I won't forget this."

He clasped Andrew tighter, half dragging him to the rear of the wagons. Their friend, the cook, emptied one out.

"My cousin's wounded. I need to get him out of here."

The cook looked at Andrew's chest. "He must lie

down to have any chance of living." The man shook his head. "We're at a disadvantage. George's army—they're coming after us."

"What are you doing with that wagon?" Starlyn got a better hold, raising Andrew.

"I'm taking a wounded officer out of here, along with two others. I will take your cousin along, but he must go to Salisbury. If I hurry, I might get out in front of the others. It's going to be a rough drive."

"He's going. Salisbury is home. Maybe you could take him to Alexander Craighead. Let us get him into a corner of the wagon then I'll get the horses."

After the cook helped, Starlyn went to hitch the team. The cook arranged the wounded men then came to help Starlyn.

"Say, is his father the Reverend Craighead?"

"Yes."

The cook continued, "It'll be a privilege to take him to the Reverend. He helped my uncle when men got after him. The Reverend held them off long enough they figured out my uncle wasn't their man. Yeah, I'll take him all the way home."

A cavalryman approached. "Hurry, there's not much time."

"Tell them I'm coming." Under his breath the cook said, "Hope there's another driver to go with me."

Starlyn barely heard his words over the sound of gunfire and confusion. The cook gave him a two-fingered salute before crawling up on the wagon to take the reins. Starlyn gathered the bedding, stopping to watch men from their company run to hitch the other wagons.

"We need these for the wounded," a driver said.

Starlyn hurried for the horses, surprised to find both still there, considering the rush to get away from the enemy. Securing the bedrolls, he mounted, leading Andrew's horse.

His cousin lay in the wagon with nothing to keep out the cold. Blood ran from the chest, spreading across his coat. Andrew might die from exposure. Starlyn kneed the stallion. Freighting experience took him through the mass of men, animals, and wagons hurrying away from Cowan's Ford.

Starlyn understood why the cook wanted out so quickly. Soldiers filled the road. Farm wagons joined the run, some piled with household goods, young children or small animals. Cows were tied off the back, or being driven by older boys or women.

Riding around a wagon filled with wooden crates, some holding chickens, Starlyn slowed. "Where are all these people going?"

The driver looked at Starlyn, thatched hair sticking out.

"Those British and Tories already raided our land, taking most of our food." The man patted a crying woman who sat next to him. "They're gonna kill us one way or another. Either a musket ball or eating our last bite."

"We'll run them out soon as we regroup," Starlyn said. "Just stay ahead of them."

Catching Andrew's wagon, he motioned the cook to the side. "Here's Andrew's horse. I need to cover him."

The cook nodded. "Better hurry. If this officer dies, it's my fault for stopping."

Starlyn hurried to the wagon. He crawled in then shook out the blankets over Andrew. "This'll warm you."

"Not cold, Star'n. Don't feel nothing but tired, so tired."

Starlyn straightened Andrew to look at his chest. A

wound that severe might kill him.

"Andrew, you have to fight to stay alive. You'll soon be home with your father." Tears ran down Starlyn's face as he cradled Andrew's head close to him.

"Star'n...Star'n," Andrew plucked at Starlyn's coat. "Father...tell when his heather blooms...I'll waiting for..."

As life ebbed out of Andrew's body, Starlyn recorded the words in his heart.

"Nooooo!" Starlyn shouted as Andrew gurgled, but he was gone.

Something inside Starlyn went with him. If he lived, he would carry Andrew's words back to Uncle Alexander.

Two cavalry officers rode up. One grabbed the reins from the cook. "Are you crazy? You are holding up Captain Crawford's transport to help. If he dies, you won't get away with that."

The cook turned back to Starlyn. "Still alive?"

"No," Starlyn said.

"Get out of here." The cook whispered. "I'll take his body to the Reverend. Horse, too."

"I cannot leave him like this."

The officer turned toward Starlyn. "Get down from the wagon now! That's an order."

Starlyn moved to the edge trying to think up an argument, but the commander threw the reins toward the cook. The officer batted his hat against the lead horse's flank. The animal jerked, throwing Starlyn off the wagon.

"God, no."

He got up off the ground, scrambling to get on his horse.

Fist shaking in the cold grey morning, Starlyn shouted. "If it is the last thing I do, I'll get you redcoats for killing my cousin."

He would not quit the fight. Andrew was dead. Nothing changed that. Turning back to look for the company commander, Starlyn shouted again.

"They'll pay a mountain of lives for taking yours, Andrew. I promise that."

CHAPTER EIGHT

Starlight, Commonwealth of Virginia
June 1st, 1781

The scent of sweet flowers filled the air in Rebecca Thompson's small rural community of Starlight, nestled in the western hills of Virginia.

The War for Independence had taken its toll. Today, though, a small remnant of young men from Captain Callaway's militia company marched down the street. They returned home from fighting the British and bedraggled as they appeared, some wounded, the men smiled. Rebecca joined the crowd gathered to welcome them home, most cheering or shouting encouragement. She leaned toward her friend, Sarah McClure.

"Didn't Jack have a brother fighting with the patriots? Maybe he'll return home today."

"Rebecca, you don't recall Starlyn?" Sarah's thick-lashed eyes studied her. "Years ago, after getting in trouble for sitting on Jack, you noticed his brother, Starlyn. Remember? You said he would be your husband one day."

"Well, I wasn't the only one in trouble for that tussle, Sarah. You helped."

Shoulders snapping back, hair white as a snowcap swirled around Sarah's face. "You were worse, not getting up like you should. Jack liked you even then. Else, he would not have let that happen."

Rebecca pursed her lips. "What you said about Jack's brother, Starlyn. I don't remember what he looked like, nor do I recall saying that. Remember our age, just five. I think you made it up."

"No, I did not." Sarah flew at her, wagging a finger.

Rebecca backed up, offering her a smile.

"Wasn't Jack so handsome, and Lydia beautiful, when they wed?" Sarah said. The disagreement subsided and they moved closer to the crowd.

Rebecca searched for the reason Jack Craighead chose Lydia Brown, when he really wanted her. Why did she fight so hard against that, always pushing him away? Handsome, Jack always reminded her of someone.

Their friend, Lydia, asked Sarah to invite Jack over to socialize several times. Jack had married Lydia, it seemed, because she was always after him. He just could not outrun her.

"Rebecca you're going to look beautiful in the blue and yellow paisley dress your mother stitched up." Sarah giggled, grabbing arms to swing her around, chanting, "Eighteen. She's going to be a lovely eighteen."

"Stop! Stop that. Everyone's staring at us." Rebecca's face grew hot from embarrassment. Why did Sarah do that to her?

"All right, Rebecca, but you're acting like an old wash woman who never has fun." Sarah's shoulders gently shook, hand covering her mouth.

"Well, Miss Sarah, how do you know the color of my dress? Mother's just finished it." Rebecca stepped back. "Don't dare say I told you. I'm quite sure I did not!"

"Uh-oh! I must be more careful what I say," Sarah mumbled as she moved to the right, gracefully gathering her skirt to step over a puddle. "Father let Mother purchase the cloth when they traveled to Richmond last month. Father said no girl should come into womanhood in anything but a pretty dress."

Rebecca peered through narrowed lids.

Sarah sighed. "I wanted to surprise you, that is all."

Rebecca nodded. "I knew my father could not afford the money for England's cotton cloth. It's far too expensive, Sarah. Especially with very little coming over during this war."

"But my father has the money, Rebecca. We are friends, well, almost since we started crawling. We're like sisters. You cannot refuse a dress from your very own sister." Sarah's fingers fluttered around her hips, as she leaned forward at the waist. "Still my friend?"

Rebecca smiled at Sarah's common, scrub-woman stance. "Yes. You'll always be my friend."

Sarah swirled in a brief curtsey. "Come on. We shall go by the dressmaker's. I want to see what she's stitching together—perhaps a new style from France."

Rebecca tilted her head back, laughter in her throat, as they kept the same brisk pace. She knew they looked remarkably different. Her own dark hair and blue eyes contrasted with her friend's hair, shining white in the sun, with large eyes the most unusual color of grey. Rebecca envied Sarah her beauty.

Entering the dressmaker's shop, Rebecca moved to a tray holding buttons, ribbons and bows in various colors. Then she noticed some blue in a corner. "Let's go look at that cloth."

"Hold still, Bec." Sarah picked up a ribbon then guided Rebecca to the mirror on the wall. "I want to see how this looks on you."

Sarah had used her childhood name, bringing back memories for Rebecca.

Gathering loose wisps of hair, Sarah tied the red ribbon around the thick mass at the base of Rebecca's neck, making a bow. She turned sideways for a better view of her dark hair against the red ribbon.

"It looks charming." Sarah winked at her, sending Rebecca into peals of laughter.

Leaving the shop, Rebecca said, "That's a beautiful blue gown the seamstress worked on."

"No doubt being stitched for a lady who could well afford the price," Sarah said.

They strolled along, coming to the fruit trees in bloom.

"Sarah, Reverend Malcolm West is a handsome man. No doubt he is a man of the Lord." Rebecca smiled as her friend's cheeks turned pink. "Is Malcolm going to marry you? What does he say about a wedding date?"

"How am I supposed to know? Malcolm does not act like someone who wants to become my suitor. For all I care, he may never be. I do not think he is that interested, anyway." Sarah clasped her hands.

"You must not speak so harshly about him." Rebecca shook a finger. "Those men of God take plenty of time to make up their mind. They want the right woman. Malcolm may want to make sure you're the one, only you do not see how interested he is."

"The man should not take too long, lest he find himself officiating over my wedding to someone else." Sarah pursed her lips.

Rebecca knew that if given the opportunity to be courted by her right man, Roger, she would make her feelings known. Otherwise, Roger could grow interested in someone else.

* * *

"Are you going to wear your new dress to services?" Mother said.

"No, I'm saving it." Rebecca lay down the hairbrush. Sarah was a good friend. "It's the prettiest dress I've ever owned."

Rebecca's family arrived at Blackwater Valley Presbyterian Church. The congregation finished their greetings before families found their seats. The sanctuary grew quiet as the preacher took the pulpit.

Rebecca glanced around. Roger sat with the rest of the Woodson family. Where was Priscilla? For the last six months, Roger had taken the seat at the end of the pew with Priscilla enthroned in the favored position between him and his family.

She tapped a finger on a knee. Might Priscilla be ill? The girl appeared hearty enough, not having previously missed a service. Priscilla usually kept a shoulder pressed against Roger through most of the sermon, making it difficult to see if something ailed her. Would Sarah know?

Rebecca glanced across the aisle, where Sarah sat at the end of the McClure family pew.

"Psst."

Sarah turned, blue dress a splash of color against the pew's brown tall backrest.

"Where's Priscilla?" Rebecca mouthed.

The palms of Sarah's hands turned up, wrists fringed with lace. She shook her head.

Lips pressed together, Rebecca patted her hair with a hand as she shifted attention toward the front. Today she looked only at Roger, thankful he chose to stay home with the local Bedford County militia. He had looked so important training with the other men, so handsome.

If only Roger Woodson belonged to her.

CHAPTER NINE

The sun's rays flowed through the window, tempting Rebecca to go outside. She had an invitation to visit Sarah McClure for the afternoon, but should stay busy until her friend arrived.

"Mother, what else do you want done while I wait?"

"There's nothing pressing. I would like you to come home early. Your father expects to eat on time, and after scrubbing the upstairs, I shall need your help getting supper on the table."

Mother's shoulders slumped as she spoke, reminding Rebecca of a wooden scrub brush stood on end, bristles collapsed inward.

"Won't you put it off until tomorrow? We'll clean the floors together," Rebecca said.

"No, I'll scrub today. Tomorrow's our washday." Mother rubbed her lower back. "Why don't you wait on the porch for Sarah?"

Rebecca leaned in, kissing her cheek. Outside, she took a seat on a three legged stool. Soon a pair of white-socked horses pulling a surrey stopped in front of the house. Their chestnut-colored coats gleamed in the sunlight. Sarah's father stepped down, hurried around to take Rebecca's arm, and guided her onto the seat beside Sarah.

Mr. McClure returned to the front seat as Sarah leaned over, whispering in Rebecca's ear. "A spring cold kept

Priscilla out of church. But there's more."

So that was why. What else did Sarah know?

Rebecca hesitated to speak with Sarah's father present. The two rode in silence the rest of the trip. Mr. McClure guided the buggy to a stop in front and came around to help them down.

Excitement washed over Rebecca, eager to hear more about Priscilla.

Sarah started toward the house. "Let's go see Mother. I want a piece of cake."

In the common room Mrs. McClure greeted Rebecca with a hug. "I'm so pleased you came."

"Thank you for inviting me," Rebecca said.

She took a seat at the table next to Sarah while Mrs. McClure served slices of spice cake and milk.

Rebecca finished the cake, listening as Sarah's parents discussed the war. She glanced at Sarah who jerked her head in that 'let's go' gesture they used around others.

"Mrs. McClure, you are such a fine cook."

"Gracious, that's a lovely compliment. You're like a daughter to us, Rebecca. Now tell me, how are your parents?"

"Very well, thank you."

The desire to speak with Sarah mounted. She smiled then rose from the table, following her friend into the front room reserved for guests. They took seats on a camel-backed sofa. Rebecca blew a long breath, grateful for some privacy.

"How's Priscilla's cold? Taking those terrible tasting cures like I did last year?"

"Yes." Sarah pushed back hair. "The worse medicine tastes, the better it works."

Examining a fingernail, Rebecca said, "Well, I recovered. Most likely she will, too."

"Never mind the cold. Priscilla may still miss some

services. I overheard Mother tell Father the family has problems."

What was that—Priscilla not there to sit with Roger at services? Rebecca's heart fluttered, eager to learn everything Sarah knew.

Sarah yawned as if indifferent, smoothing out the lap of her forest green dress.

"Sarah McClure, there's more to tell. Don't put me off or leave anything out."

"Well, I suppose I could tell you…"

Peals of laughter erupted from her friend. Rebecca joined in, clutching the sofa's wooden armrest.

Their laughter faded and Sarah wiped her eyes.

"Mother told Father Priscilla's aunt took ill. Someone must travel to Williamsburg to care for her."

Hands clasped together Rebecca said, "Do you think Priscilla's mother will go?"

"No. Her father does not want his wife away so long. That leaves Priscilla or her younger sister. It will be one of them."

"Did your mother say which one?"

"No. Mother's not sure they've decided yet. I think they'll send Priscilla."

Rebecca shifted forward. "Why? Why do you say that?"

"Well, Priscilla's the oldest daughter with the most knowledge about medicinal remedies. The British no longer occupy Williamsburg, so she can travel with only a servant." Sarah's forehead wrinkled. "Their mother favors the younger girl, and may not want her baby gone."

What a blessing the girl's mother felt that way. "Oh Sarah, that's fortunate for me. Roger Woodson is so handsome. Why, he can just have any girl he…"

"Mm-hum. Wouldn't surprise me if she left tomorrow," Sarah said.

Rebecca stood to adjust her skirt. In the corner of the room, opposite the rock fireplace, sat the harpsicord Sarah used for lessons. Mrs. McClure played it at the last social. That evening, their plans finally worked to help Lydia catch Jack Craighead. Up until then he wanted Rebecca, who had considered it, but Jack never called again, giving her no reason to make a decision.

Rebecca's thoughts shifted. "Let's go see if your father is ready to leave. Mother wants me home early."

In the common room, Mrs. McClure handed Rebecca a small package. Removing the string she unfolded the cloth to find a lengthy piece of robins-egg blue ribbon. Rebecca ran a fingertip over the glossy surface. Father could never afford to buy something this beautiful.

"It's so pretty, Mrs. McClure. Thank you."

"I purchased yellow ribbon for Sarah last month. I thought of you and chose this."

Leaving, Rebecca hugged her. The woman seemed more like a close aunt than just Sarah's mother.

After settling into the seat, Rebecca barely said a word on the ride home. Sarah only smiled. The steady clip-clop of hooves sent Rebecca's thoughts to her future. She wore unstylish, mostly well-worn dresses while Priscilla owned the best. Was there enough time to capture Roger's attention before Priscilla returned?

The team stopped in front of the Thompson's house. Rebecca grew impatient waiting for assistance from the carriage, when Sarah's father came around the side to take an arm. Once down, Rebecca clutched her skirt to rush toward the front door, only turning back to wave at the sound of

Sarah's musical laughter.

She hurried inside, forgetting to thank Mr. McClure—such bad manners.

In the common room Mother stirred a kettle. "Could you sew bows on my dress with this ribbon Mrs. McClure gave me?"

Mother's face softened. "What a dear person, thinking of you."

"Mother, you sew everything so well. I think Mrs. McClure knew you would put this to good use."

"There's still work left for tonight." Mother smoothed the ribbon. "Wash day's tomorrow. When do you need it done?"

"By the end of the week, if you can. I'm wearing the dress to services this Sabbath."

Mother smiled. "I'll be sure it's ready by then."

Back in June Rebecca turned eighteen and had worn the dress several times. The ribbons were sure to give it a new appearance.

* * *

Rebecca cast shy glances at Roger, with hope of being courted. Did he notice her?

Each night, before bed, uncertainty grew stronger. Pulling a brush through her hair in a long stroke, Rebecca thought about Roger's noble appearance. A few strokes later, brush switched to the other hand, she put voice to a thought tugging at her mind.

"Mrs. Rebecca Woodson."

She envisioned him on bended knee, saying "Rebecca, I've waited so long. Say you'll become my bride."

* * *

"Rebecca, don't grow concerned. He'll ask you to

marry him. You'll see."

Rebecca recalled the rush of confidence during their walk, when Sarah spoke about Roger.

Sarah said it again. "Do not let this bother you. Before it's over, you'll marry Roger."

When they stopped to watch a yellow butterfly float toward the meadow, Rebecca stuck Sarah's words deep in that hopeful chamber of her heart.

* * *

August 5

As they prepared to leave church Rebecca's face grew hot when her father approached Roger's family. Recently, she started speaking to Mr. and Mrs. Woodson when entering or leaving services.

Outside they waited for Father, who guided the horses to where they stood. First he assisted Mother then Rebecca.

"Something happen with the Woodsons, Will?" Mother said.

"No, no, just time we get to know Roger better. Rebecca smiles and he smiles back." Father urged the horses forward. "Roger's invited for the afternoon. He will stay for supper."

Her heart soared with expectation before she thought about the differences between their families. The Thompsons' old, two-story frame house in the small town, on a sliver of ground, contrasted sharply with the Woodsons' large brick home on spreading land.

Arriving home, Mother started cooking. Rebecca assisted until Roger arrived then led him to a resting place on the front porch. They sat directly beneath the spreading limbs of the sycamore tree, across the road from the watchful eye of old Mrs. McCracken with her tattered cat, Missy. Rebecca waved at the elderly woman.

"It's a fine day." Roger's finger brushed against Rebecca's arm, while placing hands in his lap.

A spidery tingle fanned out over her shoulders. "Yes, it's most lovely!"

Hearing Roger referred to as a 'potato-hole Woodson' had captured her interest from the beginning. People who knew the story envied his family history. Rebecca fidgeted, thinking about this.

"Is it true what they say, Roger? I mean, uh…about the 'potato-hole' legend?"

"Yes. That's absolutely the truth. I descend from the physician, John Woodson, and wife, Sarah. They arrived here from England in 1619."

Rebecca looked down. If only Roger's family became her family, too. She gazed into his face as he spoke.

"During that 1644 Indian uprising, Doctor Woodson made a run for home. They killed him close to the house. His wife had Thomas Ligon, the shoemaker, inside, crafting the family's winter shoes."

Rebecca nodded as Roger spoke.

"Sarah Woodson and the shoemaker barricaded themselves inside the house. When the Indians came for them they fought back hard, desperate to live."

"Oh, Roger…"

"Quite something. Between Ligon's gunfire, Sarah scalding one Indian, before braining another with an iron roasting spit, they survived. Fearing the worst, Sarah hid their two children, saying later she had hoped at least one might live."

She leaned closer, "That was so brave."

Roger nodded. "Sarah put one boy among the

potatoes in the floor storage hole and the other under their overturned washtub." She told each child, "Stay there—don't make a sound."

She listened, as desire for Roger grew.

"Sarah, the children, and the shoemaker lived through the attack. That's good for me, otherwise I would not be here."

Roger peered into the distance before he turned to her.

"It has become legendary to descend from the 'potato hole Woodson' or the 'washtub Woodson'." He leaned in a little closer. "I'm a potato-hole Woodson."

Rebecca gazed up at him. She intended to marry Roger Woodson. His bloodline was sure to enhance the Thompson-Woodson descendants. Happiness spread as he took her hand.

Now, if only Priscilla stayed away long enough for this to happen.

CHAPTER TEN

March, 1782
Starlight

Rebecca slipped into a cloth coat before stepping out to the porch. Despite the cool weather, the first sparrow of the year made its appearance. Yesterday, a deer eating green shoots in the field ran off when the outside door banged. The graceful movement of the animal's legs as it fled blossomed into such beauty it captured her attention.

Leaning against a post, breathing the crisp air, Rebecca recalled a visit to the McClure's the previous summer. Her desire for a relationship with Roger Woodson led her to confide in Sarah. She did not talk about her willingness to take whatever he offered, if only friendship.

Priscilla, who sat with Roger during services, went away to care for an aunt. Rebecca pushed forward in an attempt to know him better. She almost grew ashamed of the brazen, forward manner, until it brought some results.

Many changes took place after that. Priscilla came home long enough to get permission to live with the aunt and gather some possessions. Rumor was fondness for a young man in her aunt's community brought on the desire to move.

Father invited Roger to visit them. Occasionally, Rebecca now sat with the Woodson family during services. Matrimony must surely be next. He spun Rebecca's heart out of control, bringing thoughts of his good name becoming hers. Mrs. Roger Woodso…

"…becca—meet you at the carriage." Mr. McClure moved to stand beside the horses. When had they arrived? She did not see or hear them until Sarah's laughter penetrated the silence.

Hurrying, Rebecca said, "I'm awfully sorry. I didn't mean to be so slow."

"No need to concern yourself about that, Rebecca." Mr. McClure patted a shoulder before taking an arm to help her up.

Rebecca settled next to Sarah, who smiled before leaning over to say in that definite way she had, "Gaining on Mr. Woodson, are we?"

Rebecca nodded. Being friends so long, Sarah practically knew her thoughts. She made the trip in comfortable silence.

Handing their coats to a servant, they entered the common room. The wide walnut sideboard, covered with a white cloth, held serving trenchers filled with various foods.

Reaching for a saucer off the shelf below, Rebecca took a slice of Mrs. McClure's spice cake. The servants baked, but no one made this cake like Sarah's mother.

Placing the saucer on the table, Rebecca pulled out a heavy chair, sat and took a bite of cake. Chewing on a plump raisin, she listened as Mr. McClure spoke.

"It's already six months since we surrounded Cornwallis, forcing their surrender. Between the French fleet, our army and militias, there was just not any way out for them."

"How long now before the men come home?" Sarah said.

Mr. McClure glanced at his daughter, muttering something about respect before he continued.

"We contained King George's men in all the port cities they occupied. It's obvious we won. It may not take over six months before they sign a treaty." He snorted air. "Those bloody redcoats will soon go home. Many of their Tory henchmen already look for other countries to infest."

* * *

April
North Carolina

The British evacuated Yorktown in October. Starlyn, now with the Randolph County militia, traveled to Wilmington, still being occupied by the enemy. Wilmington's foreign troops left by the middle of November, making it the last time he laid eyes on a British soldier.

Starlyn, along with fifty militiamen, hunted down Tories throughout the winter. Loyalist Colonel John Elroy and two men found paroled patriot Captain Johnson in possession of a firearm. They shot him in the head, but the captain's friend escaped to raise the alarm.

The militia executed Colonel Elroy along with one of the men, unable to find the other.

After that incident Starlyn left for home, determined his work finished. Traveling the Philadelphia Road to Starlight, he intended to stop at Uncle Alexander's house in Salisbury. Bitter wind swept Starlyn's soul, knowing he must face Andrew's father with the message entrusted that morning Andrew died.

* * *

Starlyn urged his horse onto the path that went by their house, toward the barn in back. The same place he met up with Andrew, so long ago, before they started out. Given the knowledge his cousin faced certain death fighting the British, would Starlyn have still gone?

Yes, no matter what. He could never let Andrew die alone, even if…

"That you, lad?"

His mind traveled back to before their journey started. Coming out of the barn, his uncle looked like Andrew. Starlyn's mind cleared, staring into Uncle Alexander's face.

"Star'n, I hardly recognized you." His uncle grabbed hold of the halter, stopping the horse. "You all right, Lad? I did not mean to startle you."

"Yes. I'm on my way home, but I wanted to see you." He slid off the horse, grateful to stretch, his gaze on an area not previously fenced. "It's about Andrew. I must speak to you."

"Come with me." His uncle walked toward a gate in the fence, movements slow.

Starlyn followed. A tombstone sat in a corner, under a maple tree. The oblong strip of dirt in the shadow of the stone, certainly once level, now rested below the bordering earth to faintly outline the grave.

He started to turn away, but Uncle Alex grasped a shoulder, urging him forward.

"There may come a day when we carefully bury our family according to space, but my son was first, not only in birth but in death." Starlyn leaned closer to hear the last few words. "We found no need for a graveyard until Andrew died."

"He was not alone at the end." Starlyn stared at Andrew's name on the tombstone. "I covered him with a blanket."

"Well—then did it end for him?"

"No. I told Andrew the wagon headed home to you, but it seemed he did not hear. His face glowed like sunset on a river, staring into the distant sky as if watching something." Warm tears flowed down Starlyn's face. "He called my name, grasped my coat then pulled me closer. 'Tell Father when his heather blooms, I'll be waiting.' Then he died."

"God bless you Star'n." Uncle Alex embraced Starlyn before stepping back to wipe at tears.

They hovered over Andrew's final resting place before going into the house.

After supper, Starlyn attended his uncle's church meeting where he became a believer.

The next morning he started home, wearing Father's great-coat over tattered clothes. During the ride he pondered the uncertainty of recovering from the scars of war. The new country might prosper, but only because of the courageous fighting throughout their nation. The personal losses from their victory were many. In his spirit Starlyn nearly became a beaten man, without hope.

Well, until the night Uncle Alex introduced him to his Savior.

* * *

Starlyn Peter Craighead arrived in Starlight, hardly thinking about anything on the final day except Uncle Alexander's news that after he left for the war, Granda died. Starlyn did not go to the cemetery on the hill, needing more time to accept Granda's death on top of Andrew's.

He fought hard during the war, not thinking about his own actions, even though others did. After storming the British redoubts with such precision, they started calling Starlyn 'Spearhead' instead of 'Craighead.' The redcoats could not stop him, and he rarely missed—not so much a brave man, just a driven man.

Andrew still lay dead, Starlyn killing only half the

enemy he intended to make pay for the murder of his best friend.

* * *

The first service Starlyn attended, a dark haired young woman with blue eyes glanced his way. Something about the eyes stirred a memory, not clearly recalled, but associated with a pleasant feeling.

She sat with Roger Woodson, a man Starlyn harbored an unpleasant opinion about. Not that Roger caused problems, but the man was too proud of himself. He descended from English ancestry, something that galled Starlyn, what with Andrew dying at the hands of King George's army. That, as well as a rumor the Woodsons might sympathize with the Crown.

After they returned home, Starlyn said, "Father, is the young woman who sat with Roger his wife?"

Father raised an eyebrow, a smile appearing when he glanced out the window. "Why don't you ask your brother?"

Starlyn turned when Lydia came through the door, carrying a covered pan. Jack followed, gaze shifting between Starlyn and their father.

"Something you want to know, brother?" Jack said.

Starlyn blinked, though not surprised Jack somehow knew ahead what came. As children, Jack evaded Starlyn's clutches simply by reading his face, although deserving whatever Starlyn eventually gave him.

"Who sat with Roger today? The lady seems familiar."

Emotion flickered over Jack's face. Starlyn hesitated. What crossed his thoughts?

"Rebecca Thompson. The one I wrestled with as a child. Remember? You broke it up." Jack reached for the pan, but Lydia hurried toward the common room and Mother. "No, she's not married to Roger, at least not yet."

Starlyn scratched his head. "Oh, she's one of the two girls who wrestled you down?"

Giving Starlyn a disgusted look, Jack walked in the direction of Lydia.

The incident came back to Starlyn. Not quite Jack's size, yet she flattened him. That girl didn't get off Jack until Starlyn threatened to move her. Then he noticed the soft glow on her face.

"I'm going for a walk." Starlyn said.

Outside, he started up the incline toward the graveyard on top, timber bracing the small hill on each side. He stepped over already-tall weeds on the rutted path. The sun warmed Starlyn's face, reminding him of happy days spent with his Granda.

* * *

Rebecca never got to know Starlyn, but the memory of that day came back. All the Craigheads attended her family's church. Just back from the war, Starlyn looked more handsome than when standing next to Jack, on that long ago day. Sarah said Rebecca had vowed, at the time, to one day marry him. Those words rang familiar, but there was no time for Starlyn. Rebecca's thoughts were on Roger.

Two weeks later, Starlyn arrived at church with his family. He took the pew with them but stared back at her so long, Rebecca's face grew warm. After leaning toward his father, Starlyn strode down the aisle.

"I'm just back from fighting the Crown. I need to be around a beautiful lady. May I sit next to you today?"

"I suppose so." She fingered her lacey collar as she wondered what Roger would do about this.

Rebecca looked up to see Roger starting down the aisle. No doubt he realized someone occupied the place next to her.

"This is my customary seat," Roger said. "I believe you need to look for another."

"I've found my seat. I won't move. Perhaps it's time you find another place to sit for services." Starlyn gave Roger a curt nod.

Heat filled Rebecca's face at Starlyn's reply. She glanced sideways, surprised at his confidence.

He shifted position toward her then lowered his voice, "I hope Roger finds a seat."

Roger returned to his family's pew, only to frown back at them. Feeling a twinge of disloyalty, she wondered if Mother and Father might favor Roger over Starlyn.

Later, during their ride home from church, Father said, "Didn't ya feel like Roger shoulda been sittin' with us today, daughter? Ya hardly know that Craighead lad."

CHAPTER ELEVEN

Rebecca Thompson intruded on Starlyn's thoughts during services. He positioned himself to see the face, hear the voice, of the woman he intended to marry. Did she know the Lord? This was something he desired in a bride.

One Sabbath evening, as they sat on the front porch of their family home, Starlyn said, "Da, I love a woman who wants another man. I don't know how to hold her attention long enough to tell her how I feel."

Moonlight picked out threads of silver woven through Father's hair, gazing at Starlyn from eyes framed with shiny spectacles.

"Go on."

"I need..." A tremor crept into Starlyn's voice, not there since he had become a man. "I will do what it takes to make Rebecca Thompson my wife."

* * *

Thomas Craighead heard the yearning in his firstborn son's voice and entertained some thoughts of his own. He leaned closer.

"If you love Rebecca, don't let Woodson walk away with her."

"I...I don't know how to stop it."

His son's obvious misery, fists clenched, told Thomas he must help.

"Yes, you do. Find a way to break up this budding

romance. Move quickly. Don't let anything stop you."

Starlyn nodded. Heads almost touching, they discussed the problem, their low voices flowing out into the quiet Virginia night.

* * *

"Hey! Stop that. What are you doing?" Eyebrows pinched together, Roger jerked at the horse's reins, trying to take them back.

Wrapping the reins around one wrist, Starlyn used the other hand to grab higher. He glanced back at the men who stayed around after services.

"I have a proposition for you."

"Turn my horse loose or you won't get anything." Roger tried to break free.

"I'm interested in Rebecca Thompson. I want you to leave her alone."

"I will not do that. Now turn loose."

Starlyn held tight as Roger made another attempt to free the reins.

"The men think we will settle this like gentlemen." Starlyn steadied his legs, getting a better hold on the bridle. "They think we're working out a way to do that."

Roger's shoulders straightened. Chin up and lips tight, he stared keenly down his nose at the group of men.

Was that a flicker of interest rising in Roger's eyes, or was it just hope? Starlyn shook off the doubt. Roger always relished a challenge, it seemed.

"What do you think is fair competition?" Starlyn said.

"To determine who walks away from her? Well, I suppose if it's competition for Rebecca's hand, then bare knuckles or nothing."

Starlyn forced a smile, remembering the rumors about Rogers's experience in that area.

"Dueling seems more definite, don't you think?"

"And give you the advantage, Craighead? No. Bare knuckles or nothing."

Starlyn hesitated long enough for Roger to snatch the reins from his hands, almost running him over as he cut his horse back toward the group.

"What about pistols at twenty…?" Starlyn broke into a run. "Hold up there, Woodson."

"Get it worked out?" someone said when Roger reined in.

Starlyn hurried up after Roger dismounted, head shaking.

"Come on, Potato Hole," a man said. "You afraid to make this deal?"

"What've you got to lose?" another called out.

Grateful for the men's prodding, Starlyn stepped closer to Roger. "Well, you chose bare knuckles. Going to back down now?"

"No, but you will regret this. I'm going to pound you into the ground."

Starlyn grunted, sealing their deal with a handshake before the witnesses.

As Roger rode off Starlyn whispered, "All I need to do now is win this fight."

* * *

The struggle between these young citizens caused Starlight's community concern. Men grouped around the two at services. The elders held their tongues during the turmoil, fearing any opposition could split the church.

Both men had agreed on September, the following month. Those not taking sides were the women of Starlight. They did not know and attributed all the excitement to the upcoming visit of General Daniel Morgan. Chance set their contest on the date of the General's arrival. Some wondered if the two still intended to do this with the war hero in town.

* * *

Felix McKnight worked hard for a measure of respect from his master, Thomas Craighead. A mere servant, he wanted to please Thomas at every opportunity.

He had brawled in the inns of his homeland before finding a way onto a boat headed from Ireland to the colonies. Felix considered the departure a timely bit of good luck, arriving in Virginia just before the outbreak of war stopped most shipping.

Oh, how Felix loved a lively brawl, winning far more fights than he lost. As the energy mounted before each bout, he talked to himself for courage.

"This is for sweet Moira," he declared. Thinking of his love for her he snapped a quick left jab then a right cross straight from the shoulder. Felix clung to a feeling of honor in fighting fair that permeated his very being.

After a win, he chose elegant steps to dance a jig, sometimes accompanying the dance with a favorite Irish song, purging leftover energy. Did his opponent's friends think Felix had already broken into the forbidden whiskey while, infuriated, they pulled their man from the floor?

Although born in a shanty, Felix McKnight possessed a nobler heart, perhaps, than one 'higher born'. He moved fast, embraced fearlessness, only to revel in the opportunity to work his body far beyond its abilities. While little known to many, the fighter possessed a romantic heart. Moira held no doubts when he sang "My Lovely Moira Rose".

Then came that fateful day when Felix said, "He can't be dead!"

Crouching down in disbelief, he looked for himself.

The unfortunate incident that killed opponent Leamus Quinn in Londonderry sent Felix fleeing for his safety. The boat soon left, headed far away from Moira Rose.

Pure chance placed him as a servant in Thomas Craighead's household. While standing in line with other indentured servants disembarked from an English ship, Felix's cramped muscles loosened when a stately man said, "No, I insist on this indenture. He's my man."

Not much older than the master's son, he possessed experience in a vastly different area.

Felix sought out Thomas. "Sir, I can help young Starlyn thrash that Woodson with what I know."

After some discussion, Thomas said, "Are you positive about this?"

"Yes, Master Thomas."

Felix strolled away, smiling. That snobbish Woodson needed a good whipping. As excitement shot up, Felix exclaimed, "I won't get the chance to show Roger what I know, but Starlyn will."

Cracking good humor boiled over inside. With Felix's help Starlyn might take Woodson's lovely lady. Deep in his Irish heart Felix thought it fitting. He resented the Englishman with his elaborate silver spoon.

That evening, Thomas, Starlyn and Felix huddled around the table in the common room talking late into the night.

* * *

Starlyn disappeared every afternoon for the next two weeks. At first he thought Felix might beat him to death. The man so thoroughly enjoyed their bouts that Starlyn looked ahead for places to hide—should he not hold his own with such a good brawler. Then stubbornness set in, making it impossible to give up.

"You're late again, lad. Fear of my fists becoming stronger than your lovely lady's smile?"

Nose in the air, Starlyn said, "You don't scare me, Felix!"

He almost tripped scrambling away as Felix put a row of thumps across his skull. Starlyn's feet danced long strides outside Felix's reach until the dizziness cleared and the pain in his head passed.

"Rebecca having your children," Felix taunted, "or Roger's?"

"Enough from you!" Starlyn moved in, fists at the ready.

"Come on, lad. Get outta the peat bog."

They grunted, punching only inches apart.

"That's it," Felix hollered, that crazy gleam in his eye. "Move forward, lad, you got me."

Starlyn stepped into Felix's right fist. He came to, then slowly rose on one knee, head swirling.

"Get away!" He slapped Felix's hand to the side then stood up, unsure about continuing.

* * *

Each time they met, Felix did what Thomas expected. At times, feeling a streak of sympathy for Starlyn, Thomas' words came back as though his master stood there watching.

"Teach Starlyn more than he needs to know, as if he were your flesh and blood. That way you won't let him fail."

Remembering that, Felix reached into that Irish humor to laugh. Even while quickly putting everything he ever learned about brawling into this young man Starlyn, his beloved master's son.

* * *

The day arrived, promising to be hot and humid, the

air already dusty from the gathering crowd. Starlyn and Roger were scheduled to 'go a bout', as the men of Starlight paid their respects to "The Old Wagoner," General Daniel Morgan.

Thomas found a table in the Blue Horse saloon. He welcomed Daniel, his good friend and the man Thomas credited the most for winning the war for independence.

As the day warmed, the ale flowed freely. Some men's comments turned to speculation about the big event. The noise grew louder as excitement, mixed with the curls of rich tobacco smoke, increased. Bulge-eyed Big Hiram, owner of the tavern, signaled his boys to close the grillwork where they dispensed the spirited liquor.

When the General inquired about the commotion, someone said, "It's Starlyn Craighead's fight. He's Thomas's son."

"God Bless that Craighead lad. He fought under Pickens at Cowpens," the crusty Old Wagoner exclaimed. "He's sure to handle himself."

Then, as if someone fired a round calling the men to arms, the tavern's floorboards groaned from the weight of nearly forty men who stampeded toward the back door. Out of the Blue Horse they poured, into the warm day. Thomas Craighead and General Morgan followed, along with the two men who accompanied the General to Starlight.

* * *

Starlyn wiped hands down his trousers. He was not afraid for the men of Starlight to see him fail. He only feared losing the opportunity to court Rebecca. She made all the difference. The pitch of the crowd shot up as Father escorted the General toward the group. Courage surged through Starlyn at the sight of the two men. They meant the most in his life, along with Andrew and Granda.

Roger stood legs apart, arms crossed, a superior sneer showing. A vocal group of the man's supporters stood close.

"Don't fear him, Roger," one said. "Starlyn didn't experience sporting pugilism like we did in New York."

"You'll wipe the ground up with him," another yelled.

Roger and Starlyn moved toward the middle as the men circled them. The crowd jostled for position when Starlyn landed the first blow, unexpectedly rushing Roger. He followed it up with a short left jab to Roger's soft underbelly.

"Ugggh" escaped as his opponent belched wind.

"Get that ugly Englishman." Men cheered Starlyn's bold move as Roger struggled to regain his breath.

Then, quicker than Starlyn expected, Roger came back with both fists positioned.

"I'll fix you! She's mine, you ignorant Scotsman."

Roger's insult broke Starlyn's concentration. It may have been easy to duck the fist that exploded in his face, knocking him down, had Starlyn paid attention to the long reach of Roger's arm instead of his words.

Starlyn swiped at the blood on his face then looked up to see Roger descend on him. Fending off the blows he gained footing, seeking distance from his opponent. Then Roger came again.

Starlyn stepped back, stomach drawn up in a gut-wrenching knot. With the knowledge of no place to hide, he spread his legs in a solid stance.

"Not going anywhere," Starlyn whispered. "I'm going to win."

Then he heard a commanding voice from Cowpens, booming familiar words.

"Face about, Lad! One good blow and the victory is yours!"

The General's words traveled over the crowd, triggering memories that Starlyn could not avoid—painful memories from a battle still fresh. Those words strengthened his determination not to lose this victory, either. He squared his shoulders, flexed arms then quickly headed for Roger, meeting him part way.

The afternoon sun blazed hot as he pounded on Roger, unwilling to back up. Cheers filled the air each time the Englishman went down. Soon perspiration mingled with dust, turning everything into a stinging blur, but Starlyn swiped at his eyes and kept coming.

Roger caught Starlyn off guard with a mule-kick, dropping him to the ground. He wrapped an arm around Starlyn's neck in a headlock. Roger worked himself behind, flipping Starlyn onto one side with an arm, cutting off air. Starlyn could neither move nor breathe. It was only a matter of time before he passed out.

"I'm going to tell my bride you cried," Roger said, "and you begged me not to hurt you."

When Starlyn struggled to get away, Roger continued. "And we'll laugh about this. We'll celebrate my win on our wedding day. Then…"

Roger didn't finish because Starlyn did something so out of character he cringed in shame. He twisted his head to the right, clamped down on Roger's inner forearm, taking such a powerful bite it broke through Roger's skin, almost removing a plug. Roger screamed like a wildcat caught in a hunter's trap, but Starlyn hung on, biting deeper. Then with renewed vigor, he bit anywhere he could on Roger's arm.

With his teeth embedded in Roger's flesh, tongue trying to avoid the taste of human blood, Starlyn said from a corner of his mouth, "I'll eat you alive if you don't let go."

As Roger turned loose, Starlyn pulled back looking for the chance to get away.

"It's over, Craighead. I'm going to kill you!"

Starlyn rolled out of Roger's reach and scrambled to his feet, getting a brief glimpse of men bowed over in laughter.

"Get another bite!" someone hollered.

Tired from rolling around in the dust, blood dripping on the front of his shirt, Starlyn was not beaten yet. He rushed Roger with renewed vigor.

The blow Starlyn dealt Roger knocked him back with more ease than expected. Then Starlyn rushed in on Roger as someone in the crowd hollered, "You can take him!"

The pummeling knocked his opponent to the ground and it was Starlyn's turn to get a hold on Roger. He chose the scissors grip, a move perfected on Cousin Andrew. Methodically working strong legs on Roger's waist, Starlyn took away a little more of Roger's breath with each squeeze.

He then switched to a headlock, squeezing until Roger grunted, "Enough."

The beaten look on Roger's face satisfied him, but the crowd wanted more.

"Give some more of what he deserves."

"Finish the man off."

It crossed his mind to extract more pain from Roger, but Starlyn had no stomach for such cruelty. This man only wanted a chance to win Rebecca.

Starlyn gingerly came to an upright position. Swiping his forehead with the back of a hand to remove the caked-on dust, he wiped it onto his breeches.

"What did you say?"

"Enough—you won."

Starlyn reached down, grabbed his hand, and helped

Roger to his feet.

* * *

Felix stood back from the crowd watching the encounter between the two men. Chin up, shoulders back, his heart beat faster when it became give-and-take for Starlyn.

Once Starlyn began giving more than he received, Felix's chest swelled with pride. Master Thomas' son sure gave Woodson a sound thrashing. His heart beat with pleasure, almost as though winning that fight himself, after working so hard to teach the lad the fine art of brawling.

Felix watched every move with interest. He would relive it over and over, this important favor done for his master's son. Felix had not taught Starlyn how to graciously act like a man. It became obvious he already knew this when he reached down to acknowledge the worth of his opponent, the loser.

* * *

The enthusiastic crowd of men shouted or whistled in an uproar of excitement when Starlyn passed by. The marks left on both men's faces might easily be explained away. The women of Starlight could overlook these details due to excitement over the General coming to town.

The event, though, quite possibly might change the life of one woman in particular. This was Starlyn's hope.

CHAPTER TWELVE

September 1782
Starlight

"Rebecca Belle Thompson, fill this with blackberries before working on your belly. Now hurry, girl. Half the day is already gone."

Mother held out the wooden bucket. Rebecca cringed at the blackberry stains, a reminder the last time it did not come back full. The plump juicy berries tasted so good it was difficult putting them in that bucket.

Hurrying through early morning ground fog, Rebecca arrived at the berry patch and followed a small path into the middle of the briars. She picked from plump, black fruit, avoiding the thorny spreading limbs that snaked outward to claim new ground.

The late morning sun burned hot for autumn, attracting small buzzing insects that attacked her sweaty neck. After filling the bucket, fingers gently tugged off large juicy berries to eat. Rebecca first blew them off, remembering the death of a child some blamed on tiny green spiders found on berries last year.

Something scurried past her feet, sending a chill and the thought that few survived a timber rattler's bite, so common this time of year. Rebecca grabbed the bucket, hurrying from the patch. If bitten, the run for help pushed the venom through the blood stream quicker.

Once home, the sweet smell of cooking blackberries

filled the house as she helped Mother turn them into jam. Rebecca smiled at the thought of almost eating more berries than last time, despite Mother's warning.

"I'm taking a rest, Mother. So should you."

Rebecca went to sit on the porch, pushing damp hair out of her face. Mother hardly ever sat down, always working so hard. She removed the apron, using it to fan away the heat.

Next, the bedding needed checked. After a while, Rebecca rose and started through the house, hanging the apron over the banister before going to the second floor. Turning right at the top landing, she passed her parents' sleeping room on the way to the last door on the left.

They used this room for sewing, along with storage. The trapped heat almost stifled her. The smell of dust, along with a peculiar odor, emanated from woolen winter clothing that hung on wooden pegs during summer. She picked up a cleaning cloth from Mother's sewing table to dust off the large trunk that sat on a braided cotton rag rug.

The rough patchwork design making up the walls and ceiling of the room, formed by strips of wooden boards, soothed her. Going to the small unevenly glazed window, she pushed it open. One arm on the sill with her head stuck out, Rebecca peered down at a bird's eye view of their well-worn house.

The large old sycamore spread its broad limbs, providing good shade. Their centered front porch always caught a breeze. Old Mrs. McCracken's place stood directly across from the Thompsons, where the elderly lady liked to sit. Her cat, Missy, had snatched more than one bird from the Thompsons' bushes.

Rebecca tracked black and orange feathers, strewn around the blueberry bushes in the uneven three-cornered yard.

"You're in trouble, Missy."

Close by Father had piled a mound of pebbles for the cat that wanted his sweet singing orioles. Not big enough to do any damage, it did not seem to matter. Father threw them close to the four-footed intruder who came to take his joy.

Mother said their two story house needed a good whitewash. Father's words rang clear. "I got more important things to spend my money on, Mary, than painting this house."

She went back to the trunk, opened the lid, and sat on a rough-hewn stool. Leaning forward, skirt spread over knees for a wider lap to work on, Rebecca reached for a quilt. Worn but still intact, needing little attention, it was folded then placed on her right.

Mumbling, "Umm, umm," when assessing the large amount of repair needed on the next one, she dropped it down on the left.

She had reached the bottom of the trunk when footsteps hit hard on the stairs, moving quickly up the hall. It sounded like Father. Why such a hurry?

Standing, Rebecca ran hands down her skirt before shaking out the hot air trapped in the folds. Pushing aside hair with a forearm, she blew upward to cool her brow before picking up the quilts needing repairs.

Her mother's voice filled the hallway, sounding sharp. Who did Mother scold like that? Despite knowing it was not polite to listen, curiosity prevailed. Quilts clutched, Rebecca quietly stepped toward their door and leaned forward.

"What do you mean they brawled over our Rebecca?" Mother said, in a scandalized tone of voice.

The mention of her name started a flutter in Rebecca's breast. A feeling of excitement crept inside.

Rebecca wanted to hear more.

Father cleared his throat, a sign he was put off by Mother's indignation.

"How did this come about, Will?"

"Mary, all I know is they made an agreement and shook on it."

"William Thompson, you ought to be ashamed! You should have stopped them."

"Can't a man talk around here? Besides, I don't know exactly what the deal was." In a soothing voice Father began again, "Just let me tell ya…"

Rebecca shifted weight, the loose floorboard forgotten until it creaked. Father ceased talking.

"Hush," Mother said.

Rebecca rushed back into the sewing room, dropping the quilts.

She listened for their door to close then cautiously crept back into the hall. Would everyone around town know there was a fight?

"A bloody fight it were," Father said. From experience, along with the sound of the floorboards, Rebecca knew he hopped around vividly reliving the event. "It looked like Woodson might win the bout. I put me money on him, I did." It grew quiet, then Father exclaimed, "I even put extra. But that hardheaded Craighead just would not quit."

When it grew quiet, she imagined fists punching the air as Father actively worked to include all the details, much as he had done in the past.

"Every time Woodson knocked Craighead down, well…" Father stopped.

Rebecca was sure a head-shake followed. Then Father continued, "Craighead just got back up to come at Woodson again."

After a silence, Father said, "We wanted ta stop the fight, but Master Thomas said not to."

"'No,' Thomas said. 'You ought to let them go. The lad can handle it.' So, we let 'em go."

Father continued, "Craighead sure enough wanted to win that fight, he did."

Was there a touch of pride in Father's voice? Rebecca imagined his chest swelled out.

She suspected this might end in a more heated discussion than her father wanted. She envisioned Mother's lips pursed, chin scrunched up, before saying, "You should not a done that, Will."

Did Mother's finger wag disapproval at wagering? After clucking her tongue to indicate it was finished, Mother might turn it loose. Rebecca had seen this happen before.

Mother gave in to Father's animated account of the story, as usual, when he continued on. Only exclaiming, "Oh, Will!"

After their voices dropped low, Rebecca moved quickly, not wanting to get caught in her shameful act. Clutching the ill-gained information close, she left the quilts in the sewing room then quietly tiptoed down the hall. The jam must be put away, then later the quilts retrieved after Mother and Father came downstairs.

Father said Roger had lost? What in the world did that mean?

CHAPTER THIRTEEN

January, 1783
Starlight

Thomas Craighead entered the common room. He took the hands of his wife, remembering their courtship years before. Sophrona hid those hands, with the curved baby fingers, behind her back. Until the day Thomas captured them and thoroughly examined each finger before kissing her.

Back then Sophrona's father, Peter Hackett, almost succeeded in replacing him with another man. What if they had not married, Starlyn or John not been born? Thomas shuddered to think about that. Now their eldest son must not lose the chance for happiness with Rebecca.

He gently rubbed Sophrona's two crooked fingers, saying, "Starlyn's in love with Rebecca Thompson. I'm afraid the strong desire to marry her is powerful enough to ruin him, should he fail. We must see she feels welcome in our family."

"Yes. Our love for Starlyn will make that easy to do."

Thomas left the room, wondering again about his wife's perfectly curved littlest fingers. No one could explain their origin. Only that through the generations a family member had been born with fingers like Sophrona's. Neither of their sons' hands looked like hers. He had stopped puzzling about them, only ever so often rediscovering the trait.

He pushed the mystery aside. Starlyn needed his attention. If in his power, Thomas intended to see that his son brought Miss Rebecca Thompson into their family.

* * *

On April 15, 1783, in the Presbyterian Church both families attended, Starlyn married Rebecca. Thomas's younger son, Jack, handed Starlyn the wide golden band embedded with an emerald. Thomas had insisted Starlyn's grandparents would have wanted their eldest grandson to place grandmother's ring on his bride's finger.

With Jack and Lydia already in their own home, Thomas encouraged Starlyn and Rebecca to live with the family after the wedding, for as long as they chose.

* * *

Late September

"Rebecca, where are you?" Starlyn called, voice loud for a soft-spoken man.

Leaving a servant to finish the dough, she hurried from the common room, down the hallway of Thomas' house. Starlyn stood next to the stairwell, eyes shining so bright Rebecca laid a hand on his forearm to check for fever, leaving a trace of flour.

"What, Star'n? What's wrong?"

Hair on his head stuck straight out the back in that funny little tuft, instead of lying flat. This sometimes happened when Starlyn grew excited. Raking fingers through his hair somehow seemed to finalize the way her husband felt about a matter. Rebecca suspected the act put words to his thoughts when making an important decision.

"I just looked over that sixty acres. It borders Father's, which will belong to me some day," Starlyn said.

Her husband seemed to immediately regret his words.

"Didn't ever mean it to sound like that, not the

reason I want it bordering Father's land. I love my father is why..."

"Star'n, I know that. You only meant, being the first-born son, you will inherit it one sad day."

He nodded, taking her hand. "Soon as I hitch a wagon, let's go take a look at it. Bring a blanket. It may get cool."

"I'll just go rinse my hands," Rebecca said.

She removed her apron, wiped the flour off his forearm and walked toward the common room.

Starlyn brought the wagon to the front. "You look tired. Maybe you should stay home."

"Oh, no. I want to see that land."

Starlyn clasped her shoulders from behind, thrusting upward. She settled on the seat.

He shook out the blanket over her lap then climbed up, taking the reins. They did not travel far before he stopped the wagon.

The two strolled a sunlit knoll to an opening that led into the dense forest. His arm encircled her waist, bracing each step on the uneven ground as they passed between two large trees. A few steps into the woods, they entered a small clearing, where a ray of sunlight shone down on a fallen tree, barren limbs jutting from the end. Starlyn stripped a heavy sprig of leaves from a bush, using it to brush off the log. Tossing the branch aside, he guided her to the log before sitting beside her.

"I want to build our home on this land." Starlyn pulled her small hands into his.

"It's lovely and so peaceful." Rebecca shifted toward him. "Will we truly live here?" She echoed the hope in her heart, sure her face shone bright with love for him.

"Rebecca, I could move a mountain, if only it ensures you look at me like that again. Yes, my family possesses the means to purchase this land. Father will deny me nothing. Yes. Yes. We will own this land."

Starlyn turned toward her. "Tell me, Mrs. Craighead, what sort of home will I build, where you shall reign over our children and servants alike?"

"I would like it big." Rebecca tapped fingertips together. "And maybe with a second floor?"

"I already possess the building plans for just such a structure," Starlyn said "It may take several years to finish."

"I can hardly wait to see it," she said.

"Come, let's walk some more before we go home." Starlyn took her hand.

Rebecca stopped to admire small, blue wildflowers. Starlyn picked one and she stuck it above an ear. Then the blossom fell.

"Your blue eyes held a trace of lavender next to the blossom. Shall I pick you another?"

"No," Rebecca said.

"Then perhaps it's time we start home."

* * *

Starlyn went to the office where his father conducted their freighting business. The maple desk gleamed in areas not covered by stacked parchments. Before the war, Starlyn used a portion of the desk to manage the tobacco crop. Once home from fighting, he took back the crop from Jack, and now used another room as his office.

Father glanced up. "Come in, Lad. No need for an invitation."

A fist at the waistline, Starlyn strode to the desk. "Rebecca and I visited Mr. Guttener's land."

Father placed the quill in the inkpot. "Then tell me.

What did Jacob Guttener's land look like? How does it compare to the asking price?"

"The man seems as tightfisted as anyone I ever did see, asking fifty dollars an acre. Though I must say, Mr. Guttener is as congenial as the land is beautiful. Tall, mature trees a man could make into anything, from a house to fine furniture." Starlyn sat down in one of the stuffed chairs separated by a small table. "I hesitated to press him on the price until I'm ready to negotiate."

"Star'n, you'll have an acceptable amount of funds for bargaining. It will take work to keep the price affordable." Father's piercing blue eyes peered over spectacles. "Whatever deal Jacob offers, do not let the man hold a contract, or you'll never get his hand out of your money purse."

* * *

Starlyn worked evenings designing furniture. He paid close attention to the details then acquired wood to build each piece. Occasionally he stopped to think about a design for a cradle. Love filled his heart at the thought of going through life with Rebecca and their children.

One Sunday afternoon Starlyn took her out to the workshop, where a 'lady chair' waited.

"Oh, Starlyn, that's beautiful. It looks like the New England banister-back Sarah's mother has."

"Granda Craighead built it for my grandmother. The vertical slats are made from prime pieces of maple." Starlyn paused, remembering Granda. "Father says we may have it."

Rebecca pointed to a place on back of the chair. "There's something here. What's this?"

"After he finished, Granda carved our Craighead mark on the back." Starlyn ran a hand over the smooth wood, bright from age. I brought it out for you to sit on when I build our furniture."

She looked beautiful sitting in the chair Granda had brought all the way from Baltimore County.

"Are you feeling well?" Starlyn said.

"I'm hungry. I would like some of your mother's cake."

He extended an arm and they walked to the common room, where they sat at the table across from Father.

Mother took Father's empty saucer to the sideboard, returning with cake for them.

"Star'n, do you still intend to make an offer on Mr. Guttener's land?" Father said.

He gazed at Rebecca then turned to Father. "Yes, we're quite interested in that land. It's beautiful and it borders your property."

"Well then, I'll get the promissory note ready while the land's still available. We will go over the details whenever you like."

* * *

Monday, October twenty-fifth, 1783

The next morning after breakfast, Starlyn went to the office. Rebecca brought in mugs of coffee, handed one to him and the other to his father, before sitting in the chair next to Starlyn.

"Tell me then," Father said to Rebecca, "what do you think of the land?"

Starlyn watched her struggle as if forming thoughts before she said, "It's the most tranquil place I have ever been, besides church and here."

"Well, Lad, shall we go over the terms of the loan?" Father tapped a parchment on the desk.

"I'm not concerned, Da. Any way you write it will be fine with me."

Father nodded. "Rebecca, what do you think about that?"

A smile touched Rebecca's lips. "Father Thomas, your son is right. I would not think to question his opinion about how you term the loan."

Now Starlyn smiled. Rebecca may not have addressed him as 'Father Thomas' if her parents had not already moved to Petersburg to help a relative with farming.

Father picked up the parchment. "Lad, I am the holder of the note. I have also placed Jack's name on it."

Starlyn scratched an ear. "This is our loan, Da. Why is my brother's name on it?"

"Well then, Lad, it is family money. There's a clause making Jack the beneficiary if I die before it's fully paid. Any balance due will become part of my estate and a portion of Jack's inheritance. As the eldest, everything becomes yours, but I've made allowance for your brother to inherit a certain portion. Therefore, it's important to place Jack's name on the note along with mine."

Starlyn nodded. "But Da, I don't expect to inherent everything. I do understand it's our custom for the eldest male to inherit the land. Younger sons move out to make their own way."

"Well then, Jack will get whatever family mementos you wish, but the bulk of my estate is yours. Now let's finish this."

Starlyn stood and looked over his father's shoulder.

Father pointed to 'Monday, October 25, 1783.' "Is today's date alright with you?"

"Yes, it is."

Father moved a finger to 'January 25, 1794'. "I've made this the due date. We can choose a later time if you like."

"No, I earn a tidy sum running our freighting business. Besides, I do not want to stay in debt longer than necessary."

"If the sum of three thousand in gold satisfies you, then sign here."

He reached for the quill and signed, noticing Father used John's given name on the note—not Jack.

"That amount is enough to offer Mr. Guttener fifty dollars an acre, if I need to."

Father signed, sprinkled the parchment with fine sand and set the document aside to dry.

Starlyn took Rebecca's hand after they left the office. "What's troubling you?"

"It's so much." She looked down. "I'm not used to being in debt."

"You must not worry, Rebecca. As you know, Father is a just man."

"Yes, but of course you're right," she said.

CHAPTER FOURTEEN

April 1784

Starlyn poured over the house drawings. A Craighead home, he must bend to the task of completing it.

The previous year he purchased sixty acres of timberland from the jovial, but shrewd, Mr. Guttener. The front side bordered a quarter mile of Father's property. Their home site sat in a small meadow on a rise that lay slightly off center. The back side gently descended toward a strong, sweet-tasting spring.

Starlyn grasped the edge of several drawings draped over the crook of an arm as he looked ahead, giving instructions to James, the leader of the workmen.

"Remove all the trees lining the meadow front..."

James looked past him. Starlyn turned to see Rebecca, skirt clutched, as she stepped fast on the uneven ground. Why did she interrupt him in the middle of work?

"James, I'll be with you shortly," Starlyn said.

Rebecca rushed up, grabbed his sleeve, face set in earnestness.

"Starlyn, will you leave the yellow poplars? They belong there." She smiled, face sweeter than the first taste of honey.

He brushed a hair from her face. "We need to clear a road. The soft tulipwood is for the inside structure, even for some furniture."

"Oh, but Star'n, they're far too beautiful where they are."

Thrusting fingers through his hair, Starlyn sighed then called to James.

"Take down the other trees but leave the poplars. We'll look for a stand elsewhere."

Majestic trees, they grew pods that blossomed into butter-colored tulips, in contrast to the green leaves. The ones Starlyn left would fan around to come down the other side of the building site, standing tall like sentinels.

* * *

September

Starlyn came up beside Rebecca, who stared at the rock pile.

She smiled. "Seems like a big bunch of rocks. That enough—or do you need more?

"This will just get us started. We'll need enough field stones to make the foundation then lay bases to set the fireplaces on. I'm putting in a root cellar which also needs a foundation."

He guided her toward the building site, and pointed to some drawings he held. Sliding a finger over the sheet to the foyer's entrance, he moved it left to tap the large corner room.

"This shall be my office."

He tapped the parchment near the front room. "We will have a stairway, accompanied by a substantial balustrade to the upper floor. I shall put sleeping rooms up there, along with a sewing room."

His finger trailed the lines of a hallway where rooms came off, to a square marked as the dining room. Starlyn tapped the large, remaining section of the first floor. "This will be a large common room, with a small room coming off the side. I'll use the entire outer wall for the cook fireplace."

Rebecca pressed closer and Starlyn smiled. He had made her happy.

In mid-September, between freighting assignments, Starlyn continued to work on the house. Rebecca seemed to enjoy autumn, but occasionally stayed home complaining about aches or pains not clearly identified. In October, when color touched the trees, his wife stopped traveling to their building site, often suffering from an upset stomach.

"Mother, is Rebecca ill with something?"

"I'm not sure, Star'n. Your wife has asked what's wrong with her, but I hesitated to say anything." Mother's eyes held a distant look.

Could Rebecca have an illness that would kill her? He shunned that thought of losing her. Starlyn avoided conversation with Mother about Rebecca's illnesses.

* * *

Late November

One day, several weeks later, Starlyn came home to find Rebecca humming as she mixed dough.

"Starlyn, wait while I find a servant to finish this. I won't be long."

He took a seat at the trestle table, enjoying the warmth from the fire in the cook place. From behind, gentle fingers gripped his shoulders.

Starlyn slid around to face Rebecca. "Is something wrong?"

"No Star'n, though I must talk to you."

"Well then, what?"

"Let's go sit in the front room," she said.

Once there, his wife sat on the sofa as he added logs before coming to sit with her.

Rebecca shifted toward the fireplace, where red-orange flames swirled around the logs. She rose, going to Sophrona's desk positioned in front of a window, where she opened a drawer and returned with an object.

"Isn't this beautiful? Your mother allows me to use the desk for correspondence as well as sewing. It's so quiet in this part of the house."

"Oh, yes. I see how you appreciate that. What have you there?" Starlyn reached out to take a beechnut colored bonnet. He balled up a fist and stuck it in the little hat. "Say, there's something missing here. If you expect this to fit me, you'd better add plenty more material."

She giggled before snatching the bonnet off his fist. "No, I think it's exactly the right size for the owner. Expect to see him or her around the middle of June, this coming year."

"You mean you're—you're..."

"Yes. I am with child."

* * *

Late April 1785

Starlyn walked past the brick kiln toward his workers, who gathered near a huge tree. The sycamore stood down from the back of the house, in the direction of the spring. It reached a hundred feet tall, measured nine feet through with broad leaves sprouting from thick limbs.

"Don't cut down that tree. Leave it standing." Its size and form charmed Starlyn.

"But it's mature, Mr. Craighead. The hard wood makes for some fine furniture."

"No, that grand old tree will provide plenty of cool shade."

Turning from the tree to look for Rebecca, Starlyn recalled a conversation about their family.

"The house must be overrun with our children," he had said.

Rebecca preened dark tresses, contentment filling her lovely face. "They shall be well fed and happy."

That day Starlyn decided she must not always be tired. She would have help.

He found Rebecca, then taking a hand walked her back to the worksite. There, several men ran a pug mill to produce the clay for bricks. Once formed, the bricks dried in the sun before they were fired in the kiln.

Starlyn pointed out a corner brick with their names etched on it.

Rebecca bent down for a closer look. "Oh, Starlyn, such a lovely thing you did."

Later that day, he contemplated their child's birth. The hour had grown late for completing a cradle. In the evening, right after supper, he worked with the good wood Father insisted on providing.

The following evenings Starlyn walked the floor considering details, then carved two elegant wings sweeping away from the middle panel of the tall headboard, giving the appearance of floating. Before finishing, he added a surprise for Rebecca, the idea coming from the boy still left in him.

* * *

June fifth

"It's a lovely day," Starlyn said, "Care to walk with me?"

"Yes, I'd like that." Rebecca grunted, shifting from side to side as she lifted off the sofa.

He took an elbow, guided her through the front room then out the door. The table Father built Mother so long ago still stood on the back porch, sturdy as ever with a few marks to show its age. Starlyn smiled at his name crudely scratched in the table. Father had called him outside after discovering that mark. "Is this your handiwork?"

"Yes, Father, but I assure you that won't ever happen again." Starlyn had looked down, waiting to hear the punishment.

Father said something unclear.

Starlyn looked up. "What was that, sir?"

"The next time you decide to leave your mark, start with a sharp knife, scratch it out then take your time carving the words."

A warm feeling had surged inside at Father's forgiveness.

They reached the first step, and he took her arm as they started down. Mother's lilacs filled the air with a sweet floral smell. The aroma from the rose bushes they passed reminded him of tea. As a child, Starlyn played among the plants his mother brought from Baltimore Town to Virginia. Most all had survived over the years.

Rebecca's soft hand in his, they walked toward the trees in the distance, the ground thick with bluebells. Back then they almost came to his neck. Today the flowers floated around his knees. He had always liked the color.

"Umph," Rebecca muttered.

"What's wrong?" Starlyn said.

"It's probably just a strained muscle. Your mother said working my legs will help me deliver the child." They walked until Rebecca bent down, cupping her extended stomach.

"Is everything alright?"

"I think it's time to turn back. What I felt has shifted up from my legs." Rebecca straightened up, face red.

Starlyn took her arm as they struck out for the house.

They entered from the front porch.

"I want to lie down," Rebecca said. "I'm going to the bed."

"I'll wake you for supper."

Strolling to the common room, he sat next to Mother. "Rebecca had difficulty during our walk. Do you think the child is coming soon?"

"She's close to travailing. She may give birth in the next week."

"There's no time to spare. I must finish the cradle."

* * *

After staining the wood, Starlyn brought the cradle from the workshop into the house. He went to the front room. Rebecca sat at the desk sewing something for the babe but folded the garment and came to stand close.

"There's something I want you to see," he said.

They entered their room. The sharp suck of breath told him she discovered the cradle.

"Oh, Star'n. I cannot believe how pretty it is."

She hurried over to glide a hand across the maple wood.

Starlyn's hard work, using sand with a smoothing block, had brought out that satin finish.

"Look at the secret place we have." Starlyn rested a hand on the side of the cradle.

He guided Rebecca's hand beneath the cradle to a small wooden latch then turned it. A panel of wood dropped down. "Feel for the opening, then put what you want into the space provided between the flap and the boards."

"It's almost in plain sight, yet I would never have found it. It's a perfect place to hide important things."

His chest swelled with pride. "That makes all the hard

work worth it."

"Ummm." Rebecca rubbed her stomach. "Think I will go to bed early. This ache seems different."

"Then are you doing alright?" A knot twisted his stomach.

"Yes, I think so."

* * *

June thirteenth

Rebecca admired her husband's mother. The woman still held her beauty, along with a calm bearing perhaps well-seasoned by life's difficulties. She wanted to grow closer to Sophrona, but Lydia, Jack's wife, had married into the family first. Sophrona treated Lydia like a daughter. Even more so after Lydia's mother died from what the doctor thought to be a heart condition. Still, today Rebecca needed a mother's help.

She rose from the table. "Sophrona, something is wrong."

Her mother-in-law set the breakfast dishes back down. "What is it?"

"I think that I'm in travail."

"You should go lie down."

"First I must change. My skirt's wet."

They started down the hall. Inside the room, Sophrona helped her into a loose shift.

"The pain is growing worse. I'm scared. Will I die like Mrs. Mitchell?"

"Don't you worry. Everything will be fine. Starlyn must know."

"Hurry. I need you with me." Rebecca reached out for her hand.

Her mother-in-law's face lit up in a smile before leaving.

* * *

Sophrona clutched her skirt, gliding through the house to the common room, where a servant swept the floor. Heart pounding, she recalled the death of her first child, then the second. This must not happen to Starlyn's wife. Sophrona did not dwell on the babes' deaths, but remembered that help came from the Lord.

"Run to the freighting shed. Tell Starlyn to come quick!"

"Yes, Mistress." The servant hurried toward the door.

It seemed only minutes when Starlyn rushed in. He took an arm. "Mother, sit down. What hurts?"

Sophrona pulled back to stare into her son's troubled face. "Not me, Star'n. Rebecca. She's in travail."

"How soon?"

"Don't know, but I must get back to her." Sophrona turned toward the servant who went after Starlyn. "Bring hot water, blankets, and don't forget my medicinal herbs."

"But Mother, I'll stay home. Let someone else take this freight. I want to be here."

"Don't worry about that, Starlyn. Finish your delivery. This being Sophrona's first, it could go way into the night before the babe arrives." She swirled toward the door, calling back to the servant. "Now hurry, Selma, bring me what I asked for."

Twisting the knob, Sophrona pushed the door open.

"Please don't leave me again. I can't stand being alone in such pain."

Sophrona's heart filled with tenderness for this young wife Starlyn loved. The look of fear on Rebecca's face closed the gap that existed since Starlyn moved her into their home. For the first time, Sophrona felt like she had another daughter.

"Starlyn knows the babe is coming. You'll work hard, but do not worry. We'll deliver this child, God willing."

Rebecca's eyes rolled back in her head as she grabbed Sophrona's hand in a bone-crushing grip.

"God, help me with this pain. It is killing me!"

CHAPTER FIFTEEN

Evening time

Starlyn drove the team hard, delivered the freight load then headed home. Arriving as the sun dipped in the west, scattering golden rays over the treetops, his body ached in new places. He strode to the house and stepped over the threshold into the common room.

"Where's Rebecca? Everything alright?"

"She's still travailing, Master Starlyn," a servant said. "Should I pour coffee?"

"Not yet. Tell my mother I'm home."

The woman disappeared down the hall.

Starlyn sat at the trestle table but soon rose to pace the floor, fingers poking hair off his forehead.

The servant hurried into the room. "Mistress said to come quick. The babe is born."

Mother stood at the door, smiling. A babe lay in Rebecca's arms, wrapped tight. Its little face looked layered with a whitish substance, eyes swollen shut.

"You feel all right?" Starlyn said.

The soft smile and shine in her eyes answered that question.

"Thomas?"

"No. Jane."

Their first child was a girl, not a boy? Starlyn pushed down the disappointment to embrace the thought of a daughter.

"Well then, Charity Jane, just as we said."

His wife smiled, nodding, as he leaned over to kiss her then their tiny daughter.

* * *

1786

Rebecca mixed dough, careful not to move. Janey crawled along the floor. The child gripped her skirt to pull up and take a wobbly first step. She fell back to sit directly down on the floor with a thud. After that day, Janey used Rebecca's skirt or anything close to pull herself upright. Slowly she teetered from one object to another, never letting go until fat little hands gripped the next.

One afternoon, their daughter let go of a bench to head for the doorway. Rebecca turned from the cook place to see Janey disappear down the hall, making a small gurgling sound.

"No, Janey."

The child propelled herself forward. When stout little legs stepped faster to stay upright the fear almost snatched Rebecca's breath away. She hurried down the hall to stop Janey.

"That's a good girl. Come to me." Starlyn reached down, grasped small arms, swirling Janey in the air, accompanied by her laughter. He pulled the child into the crook of an arm. "I did not know our daughter could walk. You never told me."

Rebecca snorted in exasperation. "She couldn't walk that well until just now. This is the first time—must have heard you come in."

Starlyn repositioned Janey in his arm and pulled Rebecca to him.

"My two favorite ladies."

Happiness tugged at Rebecca as she moved in closer.

* * *

Starlyn walked the building site with Felix, the friend he credited for the win against Roger.

After that fight, when Rebecca ignored him, Starlyn thought about how Felix might handle being spurned by the woman he loved. Starlyn had mustered the courage to say, "If you aren't interested in me, Rebecca, just say so. There are plenty of other women not so eager to push me away."

"Well, I don't know," she replied. "Just give me time to think on it."

Two weeks later Will Thompson had dropped by the freight shed. "We'd like you to join us after services, this Sabbath."

"Rebecca, or you?"

"No, no Starlyn, you're wrong about this. Rebecca asked me to invite you."

"I don't think she's really interested in me—maybe in Roger. Tell your daughter that I will try to find the time to come."

Sabbath morning, during services, Rebecca's gaze had rested on Starlyn often enough that he thought about courting her again. He lurched when she smiled directly at him. He had decided to arrive on time.

"Sorry. What did you say?" Starlyn leveled his gaze at Felix.

"I asked if you had all the bricks for building. I hope your lumber is drying out. I want to see your house ready for winter." Felix stepped closer. "Autumn is usually warm enough to put in the windows."

"Yes. We shall have everything it takes to make my wife a fine home."

* * *

Rebecca dropped the added weight from being with child, her gait comfortable as she walked through Sophrona's sweet smelling flowers with Janey beside her.

"No, don't touch that." Rebecca grabbed Janey's stubby little fingers reaching out for a honeybee on a blossom. "You must not touch the bees. They will bite you."

Her daughter pulled loose to wander toward the lilac bush as Rebecca finished up. "Janey, time to take the flowers inside."

"She's a lovely child." Sophrona ran a hand over the girl's hair. Janey settled into the sofa, moving close to Starlyn's mother. "I'm sewing this girl a new dress with long sleeves. August is hot, but soon it will grow cooler."

Rebecca studied Janey's hair, so dark like Grandmother Thompson's. The child had Grandmother Craighead's grace and slim build, with Starlyn's large blue eyes.

Starlyn entered the room. "Here are my ladies."

"How's the house coming along?" Sophrona said.

"We have about two months' work left. It should be finished by the end of September."

Sophrona smoothed Janey's hair. A trace of emotion settled on the woman's face, pricking Rebecca's heart.

"We won't be far away, Sophrona. Sometimes we'll need you to take care of Janey."

"Janey so enjoys mornings with Granda Thomas," Sophrona said. "Yes, maybe even stay overnight."

The joy on Sophrona's face made her happy they became good friends after Janey's birth. Their child loved Starlyn's parents. Rebecca loved them, too.

* * *

Starlyn left the wagon with a servant and started

toward the house, the sun warm on his back. He would pack tomorrow's loads after supper. He moved stiffly up the steps, grateful to be walking after so much driving. Their house was almost ready, mostly because of Father's list of craftsmen who assisted with the work.

On the road before daylight, Starlyn was exhausted. The elderly lady at the last delivery wanted the freight placed inside a shed. He reached into a pocket to stroke two thick, smooth coins the woman had insisted upon adding as extra payment.

"You look pale, Mother. Feeling alright?" Starlyn kissed her cheek.

"Yes. I've been helping your daughter mix a cake."

Janey yanked on his hand. "Fer...Fer...It's fer later."

Starlyn took a deep whiff. "Spice cake. Just what I wanted today."

As Janey turned back toward his mother, Starlyn started for the hallway.

"Supper won't take long," Mother said.

He found Rebecca in the front room. "Put this with the rest of our savings."

She rubbed the gold coins. "Where did these come from?"

"I moved a woman's delivery into a shed. I refused the coins, but she would not let me leave until I agreed to take them. I did not want to disrespect her. What was I to do?"

"Take it, of course. Only a grateful person would insist on paying you this much."

Father called from the door, "Your mother says it's time for supper."

"Good. I'm hungry." He followed Rebecca into the

hallway.

* * *

A few days later the family sat down at breakfast. After the blessing they ate in silence, except for compliments about Mother's food.

Father stood and started for the door, then turned back to say, "Could I see you when you're through?"

"Yes."

Starlyn finished then strolled to the office. Father sat at the desk.

"You must be close to finishing the house. How soon will you need the glass for the window panes?"

Starlyn rubbed his chin. "With all the work going on, I have not thought about anything but the dimensions."

Father slid a sheet of parchment across the desk. "What size are the windows? How many are there?"

"Since I'm putting in seventeen windows of various sizes, I need a total of 235 panes, each 8 by 10."

"You intend to make allowance for the rough roads they'll travel?"

Starlyn ran a hand through his hair then reached for a quill. "I'll add enough panes to cover breakage during transport as well as accidents while glazing."

Laughter lit up Father's eyes.

"There's a load going to Hillsborough tomorrow, Star'n. I'll tell the driver to drop your order by Courtney and Watts store. Another freighter's headed to Halifax in a few days. It's not that far out of the way to pick up the glass on their return." Father stood, walking to the window. "I'll send Felix on the Halifax run to make sure the glass gets packed well enough to arrive in good condition."

"Can you do without Felix that long?"

"Six days is no problem. Give the joiner the

dimensions to start on the window frames. There should be time to join most of the window sashes."

Starlyn moved to stand by his father. "Think he will get it done? I'd sure like to get moved in by mid-October."

"Felix will help with the glazing. After the sashes are in the frames there is plenty of time to place them before the move."

* * *

Wednesday, August sixteenth 1787

Starlyn entered the common room, going to the trestle table, as Father set down a mug.

"How did they do, Lad? Break many of the lites?"

"Felix said five got cracked."

Father grunted. "Ordering extra was smart. There will be enough panes to replace any the joiner breaks. Felix may need to replace a pane or two, as well."

Starlyn smiled at the thought of Felix breaking a lite, more than worth the price paid for the extras just to watch. It sometimes happened, squeezing one into the 8 by 10 space. If it did, Felix would cringe hearing him say, "Get out of the peat-bog, lad"—something Felix often said when training Starlyn to fight Roger.

"I'm going back to work, Father. The time will go. Those doors won't get hung by themselves." He stood, grasping a shoulder muscle, hoping bedtime came early tonight.

CHAPTER SIXTEEN

April 1787

Rebecca took Janey's small hand and stepped through the door onto the porch. Spring sweetened the air as the sun warmed her cheeks. Janey pulled away, going to sit down on the stairs. Turning around to face the steps, the child began a slow backward descent down.

Skirt floating, Rebecca sidled down the stairway past their daughter. She wanted to walk Janey down, but hesitated. The child must learn independence. Still, their daughter need not fall. Rebecca stayed in upright position below, carefully backing down the steps.

On the ground, Rebecca stepped out to gaze over the land. The tree line had slowly receded as Starlyn took down timber to plant crops. Glancing back toward their house, her breath caught at the sight of rose-red brick, rising tall in the pale-gold sunlight. Starlyn intended to add the second floor. She had thought more like her Thompson family's plain wooden dwelling. This two-level home looked like a mansion compared to the house Rebecca grew up in.

They acquired two indentured servants the previous month, a middle aged woman, Parthia, along with Elijah, a sturdy man showing good freighting skills.

Parthia stepped out from the common room. "Shall I mix the dough?"

"I had rather you watch over Janey."

"Yes, Miss Rebecca."

Once the servant reached the ground, Rebecca went up to the common room. Deep into combining ingredients for bread, she jumped as a tingle ran up her neck. Caught in the rippling emotions of love, Rebecca turned to the touch of Starlyn's lips. The overpowering smell of him bunched a knot in her stomach. She pushed away then whirled around, searching the room for servants.

* * *

"Father wants my help when I'm over there managing the tobacco crop. Between that work, our crops and hauling, May looks like a full month." Starlyn placed the napkin on the table.

Rebecca filled his coffee mug. "We could eat the midday meal with your parents."

"Mother insists on more time with Janey." Starlyn eyed the old work shoes he wore. They must be replaced.

"Our daughter needs the love your mother gives her. Maybe even let Janey stay the night?"

"Jack will bring Lydia over, especially for Sabbath supper." Starlyn reached over the table to touch Rebecca's hand. "I know how you enjoy her company."

Rebecca's smile improved Starlyn's mood. He hungered for time with his wife, meager as it was. After working the fields, the tobacco crop, along with managing the freight-line, Starlyn looked forward to Janey visiting her grandparents overnight.

He started toward the door, mind now on such things as building that new freight shed.

* * *

June First, 1788

Rebecca helped Parthia hang the iron cooking pot on the trammel. They filled it with water along with chunks of meat. Rebecca swung the pot over the cook fire.

"Put the vegetables in the pot in time to get tender." She paused to take off her apron. "Have the Sabbath meal ready for the table when we get home, along with fresh bread. Remember the spice cake."

"Yes mistress. Now don't you worry none. We'll take care of it."

She hurried to the sleeping room to change into a brown dress with a full skirt. The white ruffle at the throat and wrists matched the delicate stitching of the thin wrap that covered her shoulders.

"Look, Mother. See my beautiful dress?" Janey slowly turned for her.

Rebecca smiled in pride at the perfect fit of Janey's blue silk dress. She leaned down to kiss her daughter's soft little cheek. "You're lovely. Now let's go find Father."

She took Janey's hand as they started down the hall toward the sitting room, where Starlyn waited.

* * *

After supper, Starlyn went to the back porch. Rebecca soon joined him. They sat together in silence, both lost in thought until she spoke.

"There's news you may want to hear." Rebecca laid a soft hand over his.

"Oh, what's that? Something you learned from Lydia after services?"

"No, something I told Lydia after services."

"Well then, what was it?" His thoughts went to the freighting schedule, instead of on Rebecca's answer. "What's that? Lydia is with child…"

"No. I'm with child."

Starlyn clasped her shoulders. "You're sure of that?"

"Yes. He should arrive in December."

"You're positive it's a boy, then?"

"No, Star'n, I'm not. But I think perhaps so." His wife's head tilted back in laughter.

How Starlyn loved her joy. They talked until the sun splashed rays of gold over the porch. When the western sky turned red, Starlyn took Rebecca's elbow to stand. A last look as he closed the door showed the red melding into the night sky.

* * *

Monday, December third, 1788

Autumn's beauty had left a stark contrast to the barren tree branches that whipped around with the winter wind. The last six months went fast for Rebecca, belly growing bigger each day.

She shivered from the cold air seeping around the outer areas of the common room, grateful for the heat pouring from the cook fireplace. Placing an empty glass on the trestle table, Rebecca worked herself into position. Knees locked and feet spread wide, she pushed down on the table bench, struggling to rise. After taking a few steps, pressure squeezed each side, circling to the front, belly growing to a peak as pain clawed at her mind. Rebecca was in travail. Placing an arm under her stomach, she called out, "The babe's coming."

A servant helped her back to the table.

"Quick, find Parthia then have Elijah take the buggy for Sophrona." Shuddering in pain she said, "Hurry, this one's coming fast."

Soon Parthia helped her to the sleeping room and into a cotton shift.

She lay on the bed, feet on a pillow, cloth gripped in each fist as Sophrona hurried through the door.

"Parthia, bring me hot water, a pan, two old quilts and a bucket."

"Yes, Miss Sophrona." The servant hurried out the door, pulling it closed.

* * *

Starlyn crossed the porch, opened the door then stepped inside. The common room was empty, except for a servant who hurried to take his coat and hang it in the scrub room. The look on the woman's face, when she returned, brought tightness to his chest.

"Where's Janey? Something happen to her?"

"No, Sir. Janey's with your father. Miss Rebecca's in travail. Your mother is with her." The young woman wrung her hands.

"Is my wife alright?"

"I don't know." The servant looked down.

They had indentured this young woman, Alice, two months previous when being with child slowed Rebecca. "Well, don't you think it's time to find out? Go on. Go."

"But, but your mother may scold me or punish me for interrupting."

Starlyn forked his hair. "Go tell Mother I'm home and I'd like to see Rebecca as soon as possible."

"Right away, Master Starlyn." Did her face smooth out as she started toward the hallway?

Alice returned. "Your mother says you may come see your wife."

Starlyn went to the sleeping room. He hurried over to push back the damp, twisted hair from Rebecca's forehead. A babe, tightly wrapped in a blanket, made soft sounds.

Starlyn rubbed Rebecca's cheek with a thumb. "Does Janey have a sister?"

"No, we have a son." Rebecca smiled gently as he

took her hand.

He studied the twisted little face, its eyes swollen shut. Rebecca looked so tired, evidence she worked hard to deliver this babe. "Shall we call him Ransom Andrew Craighead?"

"Star'n, I think that's a perfect name."

He studied Ransom's thick shock of hair plastered to his small head. Starlyn looked at Rebecca, who snored softly.

"He's a fine looking lad, Mother."

"Yes, and looks a little like your cousin Andrew did. No doubt he's a Craighead."

Starlyn kissed his mother's soft cheek. "Thank you for helping my wife deliver our son."

* * *

Sunday, July 22nd, 1792

As Rebecca put on a wide-brimmed hat, a glimpse through the door showed Ransom chasing his sister. Going on four years in December, their son's shoulder length hair floated out behind, blue eyes squinting, and looking enough like Rebecca's father to moisten her eyes. Four years earlier she received news that her father died after a runaway team rolled the wagon. Mother lived only a week before passing. They had seen their granddaughter, Janey, a year before the accident. This gave Rebecca some consolation during grief.

"Ransom, don't chase Janey. Do you want your sister to stumble? Maybe ruin that pretty dress?"

He slowed to a stop as that charming look settled on his face. "No, Mother."

At the bottom step Rebecca called to the children. "Come wait for your father."

They traveled up the road to Thomas and Sophrona's house. Starlyn helped her down, swung Janey to the ground then reached out to catch Ransom, who jumped. Starlyn took

Rebecca's arm as they trailed their children to the house.

Thomas opened the door. "Your brother hasn't arrived. Let's go to the common room for something cool to drink while we wait, Lad."

Starlyn and Rebecca took a place at the table. He softly drummed fingers as he said, "Father, it's almost nine years now since we borrowed to buy that land. Today we have the balance."

"That's more than two years early," Father said. "I hope it wasn't a hardship."

"Not terribly." Starlyn reached into a pocket, pulled out a leather pouch then counted out gold coins on the table. "Seems like this should pay off the note."

"You're right, lad. That takes care of your obligation."

Ransom burst through the door. "Uncle Jack's here."

"Star'n, I'll take these funds to my office. Later today, I'll return the note you signed." Thomas rose, picked up the gold and left the room.

After Starlyn went to speak with his mother, who stirred a pot at the cook fireplace, Rebecca's thoughts settled on the note. The oppressive weight of being in debt had caused them to put just about everything they could spare toward paying it off. Only the children had received good clothes or shoes. A seamstress must stitch new wardrobes for both her and Starlyn.

"You looked so deep in thought I hesitated to interrupt you." Lydia's face lit up with a smile. "Whatever were you thinking about?"

"Four new dresses, shoes, and other pretty things I'm in need of."

Lydia held up four fingers, mouthing the number as Rebecca leaned close in, voice low. "I want to tell you about this dress—well actually more like a gown…"

Jack clasped Lydia's shoulder. "You must not be thoughtless. Mother cannot supervise cooking, enjoy the children, and set the table, too. We'll starve before she's finished." Jack glanced toward Starlyn. "Let's wait on the porch. It's far too hot in here."

Rebecca stood, smoothing out her skirt as she went to Starlyn. "I'll send one of the servants out with something cool to drink for you three men."

Two hours later a servant removed a large piece of beef from the flames, which Sophrona started roasting long before they arrived. Parched, Rebecca picked up a mug off the sideboard, filling it from the pitcher. Sophrona came to pour a glass of water, then stepped aside.

Rebecca turned toward the sound of breaking glass, liquid spreading on the floor. Slumped over, Sophrona gripped the sideboard. A thin layer of moisture covered her brow, face devoid of color.

"My chest...so tight...can't breathe."

Rebecca placed an arm around Sophrona's waist. "Someone get Thomas!"

Lydia helped her walk their mother-in-law to a seat at the table. Rebecca sat next to her, waiting for Lydia to wet a cloth for Sophrona's face.

Thomas hurried in, Starlyn and Jack behind him. "What's wrong?"

"Sophrona could not breathe." Rebecca stood, handing the cloth to Thomas.

Her father-in-law sat next to his wife and wiped her brow. "Fronnie, you feel alright?"

"Don't fuss over me. I'm feeling better now." Sophrona's voice sounded weak.

Starlyn urged Rebecca away from the table. "How

long before supper is ready?"

"We have most of it finished."

"We're going straight home after we eat. Mother needs rest. She won't get any if the children are here."

Starlyn returned to the table. "Mother, won't you come outside with us until it's time to eat? The cool air will refresh you."

CHAPTER SEVENTEEN

Sunday, August the 5th 1792

"Father expects everyone this afternoon. Servants are preparing the food." Starlyn lowered his gaze. "We'll only stay long enough to eat. I don't believe Mother has recovered, yet."

Rebecca ached at the pain in his voice. "Are the children too much for her? We can leave them with Parthia."

"No, Mother wants to see the children. I'm going to hitch the horses. I do not want us to be late for services."

* * *

Starlyn guided the family into the Presbyterian church Granda Cyrus helped design years earlier. He took a seat next to Father, the children sitting on the other side of Rebecca.

"I expected Mother here today," Starlyn said. He glanced toward Rebecca who nodded at Lydia and Jack coming toward them.

"She wanted to rest up for the children," Father said.

"But then she's feeling alright?"

"I believe just a little tired."

It seemed to Starlyn that services hardly began when they stood to sing the closing hymn.

Outside he said to Father, "We're stopping by the house with instructions for the servants. We'll come directly from there."

"Well then, I'll tell your mother."

* * *

Rebecca was thankful for the comfortable dress she had changed into. How did her husband's childhood home stay so cool the hottest days of summer? At times even the common room cooled down.

"You are lovely as a flower," Starlyn kissed his mother's cheek.

Sophrona's fingers fluttered near the broach at her throat. "Oh Star'n, even as a lad you were charming."

Rebecca hugged her mother in law. "Your broach is pretty, too."

Jack entered with Lydia. Rebecca moved back, making way for them to greet Sophrona.

The family had settled down in the front room. A servant entered, going directly to Sophrona. "Supper is on the table, Mistress."

"Let's eat and enjoy each other's company." Sophrona rose, accepting Thomas' arm as they walked to the common room.

During supper Starlyn said to his father, "Felix available anytime this week?"

"No, he's riding with a freighter headed to the seacoast. He goes there regularly to visit the ships' captains sailing from Ireland."

"Well, perhaps another time," Starlyn said.

"There are other men to help. Something you need done right away?"

"No, it can wait."

After supper they were well into Sophrona's creamy rice pudding, one of Rebecca's favorites, when Jack set down his spoon.

"Mother, I'm sorry we must leave shortly. Are we getting together next Sabbath?"

"Yes. Let's all do that."

Starlyn leaned toward his mother. "We also must leave. I'll come over in a day or so to visit you."

A chill spread across Rebecca's back.

* * *

Later that evening

The sun set, as their household settled in for the night. While Rebecca reached for night clothes, Starlyn fell into bed bone tired.

In the early hours of dawn, he awoke to a pounding on the door. The last thing Starlyn remembered was the cotton shift clearing Rebecca's head and shoulders before sleep overtook him.

The pounding grew louder. He hurriedly dressed, then rushed down the stairs and opened the door to a muffled voice.

"Master Thomas says hurry. It's your mother."

The distance to Father's house seemed impossible to cover, as he rode under a threatening sky. Part way there the heavens opened, driving cold needles of rain down his face. The ground already turned slick as he rode up to the front door.

Once in the house Starlyn rushed to his parents' sleeping room, where his mother's grey face greeted him. "Star'n. Oh Star'n, be strong for your father and tell John I love him…"

"Save your strength, Mother."

Thin fingers that gripped his wet shirt dropped to the bed.

"Father. Father?" Jack called out from the hall. Father rose from the sleeping room chair to go meet him.

"Mother, are you all right?" Starlyn said. The brief

sound, like a child's rattle, told him it was over. Jack arrived too late.

Starlyn swallowed, pushing back bitter tears. He had planned to visit the next day, but now that could never be.

"Mother, I came quick as I could," Jack said, rushing into the room. He took her hand, then dropped it and backed up.

Starlyn reached out. "She said to tell you she loves you."

Jack knocked his arm away. "If the servant only came for me first, I would have been here before my mother died."

Starlyn tried to comfort him, but Jack turned away. He did not stop when their father said his name, only called over a shoulder, "I'll see you tomorrow morning at the graveyard."

* * *

June 7th, 1793

Rebecca peered out the window. A heavy feeling grew inside as her husband mounted up and rode away. She knew where he was going. Last winter Starlyn made visits to the hilltop every fortnight. First he stopped by to see Father, he had said, then walked on up to their family's graveyard. Rebecca suspected he cried, or maybe spoke aloud some comforting words from the Bible while standing at Sophrona's grave.

His visits had slowed down to every month. Like early last year, Starlyn cut blossoms from his mother's flower garden. He made sure to take roses and lilacs, his mother's favorites, for her and his grandfather's graves.

Rebecca went to the common room to stir a large pot of turkey soup hanging from a trammel. A sip of the broth indicated she should add the vegetables.

"Mistress, Felix McKnight is at the door asking for

Master Starlyn. What should I tell him?"

Rebecca smiled as Parthia shifted from one foot to another, unsure what to do.

"Bring Felix in here. Don't keep him waiting at the door." Starlyn would regret missing this visit.

Felix entered the room ahead of Parthia.

"I'd like to speak with Starlyn as soon as possible."

"He's not here. Could be at Thomas', or the graveyard. I'll tell him you came by."

"Well then, I'll just let myself out."

Just before supper time, Starlyn entered the common room.

"Earlier, Felix came by for you," Rebecca said.

"Seems like Father said he went to the sea-coast to visit a ship's captain."

"Well maybe, but he's back now."

"Must be important," Starlyn said. "I will just go find him."

A servant checked the soup vegetables for tenderness while Rebecca cut a crusty loaf into slices the thickness Starlyn liked with soup. He soon returned home.

"I found Felix at Father's." Starlyn ran fingers through his hair.

She turned for a stack of bowls, calling over her shoulder, "Everything alright?"

"Well, I'm troubled, is all."

Something in his voice caused Rebecca to look back. "What is it?"

"Felix has obligations to a child without mother or father."

She picked up the bowls. "What? What child?"

"We'll talk later. I'm hungry. Besides, he's coming by

tomorrow."

CHAPTER EIGHTEEN

The next morning during breakfast, Starlyn remembered there was explaining to do. They both went to bed without talking the evening before, too exhausted.

"Felix should arrive by mid-morning. There is something I must tell you."

"Yes, something about a child."

Starlyn nodded. "Felix traveled with a freighter to pick up a load in Petersburg. He went down to the wharf to meet the ships, discovering one of Father's good friends, Captain Samuel T. Smith."

"What does that have to do with a child?"

"He found this young girl on the ship and brought her home to Father."

"That doesn't sound right. What's a little girl doing on a ship?"

"Rosie's mother died on the voyage. The man who was to indenture her refused to pay the passage, much less indenture a motherless child. The captain agreed Felix could take the child home to Thomas, to see if he would guarantee safe placement."

Rebecca took a pinch of salt from the salt cellar, sprinkling it over her food. "So how did Felix know your father would do that? If Thomas says no, will Felix return her?"

Now was the time to tell it all. Starlyn swallowed

hard. "I assured Felix we would consider accepting this child's indenture if Father does not."

"Starlyn, if we ever thought about accepting this child, I assure you it would not be as an indentured servant. Not one so close to our children's age. This little girl must have equal standing with our children to call this her home."

* * *

Saturday afternoon, June 8

The breeze stirred Rebecca's hair as the four of them stood on the porch's edge enjoying the summer morning. Felix McKnight's wagon rolled down the lane, bringing the child closer to their house.

Felix stopped the horses, helped the little girl down then started up the path. Only five years old, she wore a long sleeved green dress hanging down to creased shoes, far too big. Her plump little hand clutched his sleeve.

Confusion settled on the girl's tear-stained face when they walked out to greet her. Janey reached for her hand. Reddish-brown curls bounced when the girl jerked back. Her eyes narrowed, as if in distrust—before her face lit up with a smile too bright to ignore.

Rebecca compared their daughter to this stout, round-faced child Felix called Autumn Rose O'Reilly. Could Rebecca accept the child? Give Rosie, who found herself far from home and alone, a mother's love?

"Starlyn, you and Felix can sit at the back porch table while I get us something to drink," Rebecca said before entering the house.

She filled mugs with coffee, placed them on a tray with a platter of cookies, and went to the back porch. Rebecca gave Starlyn a mug, then Felix, before taking a seat.

"Well then," Felix said, "what are we do about Rosie?"

"I am not sure," Starlyn said.

He turned to Rebecca. "What about this Irish lass Felix brought home to Father?"

"Why did Thomas not want to keep her?" Rebecca offered Felix the cookie platter.

Felix shifted closer toward them. Ransom chased Janey around the house. Rosie trailed behind squealing in laughter. He took a bite from a sugar cookie, then a sip of coffee before speaking.

"Master Thomas said at the least she needed a mother in the home. He did not want to raise a five year old girl."

Starlyn held back a smile. Despite now being a free man Felix still referred to Starlyn's father as 'Master Thomas'.

"I want us to give this child a home, Rebecca. She could become like a younger sister to our children."

"We'll do whatever you want."

The children circled the back yard again. Rebecca called them over for cookies. First Janey, then Ransom, each took two.

Rosie filled both hands.

"We're only supposed to take two," Ransom said.

"They're mine." Rosie clutched the cookies to her chest, small chin stuck out. "Mine."

"Yes, they are yours," Rebecca said. "No one shall take them from you."

The lesson on manners his son gave this determined little girl did not get past Starlyn. Somewhere, maybe more than once, the child had gone without. He cringed at the thought their children never experienced hunger like Rosie might have. Their children received everything they needed, even getting most of what they wanted.

Tapping fingers on a knee, Starlyn said, "Felix, maybe

ask Rosie what she thinks about living with us."

Felix reached out a hand toward the child finishing some crumbs trapped between the fingers on one hand. "Want to stay here with Janie and Ransom?"

Rosie moved close enough to place elbows on Felix's leg, face resting in her hands. "I want my mother—wanta go home."

The three exchanged glances, Starlyn not sure what to say.

"Rosie, come see me," Rebecca reached out for the child.

The girl stumbled over to bury her head on his wife's shoulder. Tears came, with Rosie's little body convulsing as Rebecca's arms encircled her. "You can stay with us or go back where the ship's captain will find another place for you to live. Janey and Ransom want you here. Will you think about staying with us?"

"All right. I will stay if you want me to."

"It has been a long day for Rosie," Rebecca said. "Did I see a trunk in your wagon?"

Felix nodded. "I'll retrieve it."

Starlyn rose. "It looks like a big one. Let me give you some help."

"Bring the trunk up to Janey's room." Rebecca stood, taking Rosie's hand then turned toward Starlyn. "I do not want this child sleeping alone in our big unfamiliar house."

CHAPTER NINETEEN

Rebecca gazed out the window on the hot day, thankful for shade from their trees. Two years earlier the family watched Felix McKnight drive his wagon down the lane bringing Rosie. Since then, the child had started calling her Aunt Rebecca. Janey and Rosie still slept in the same room. Rosie fit into their household like she belonged there.

"Aww—turn me loose right now!"

Hurrying toward the front, skirt hem brushing the floor, the screams grew louder. It must be Rosie. Rebecca went out the door as Starlyn came around the house. They found Ransom holding her in a head lock.

"Turn loose, Ransom," Starlyn said. "You're going to break her neck."

"But, but I can't. She will hit me again and this time I'll hit back."

"Ransom, let go," Starlyn said, a fist resting at his waist.

"Why are you hitting him?" he said to Rosie.

The child stood, sweat droplets on her forehead. "Cause, cause Ransom said Aunt Rebecca cannot be my mother."

Body stretched forward in indignation, Ransom said, "No I did not. I said Mother was not Rosie's mother."

"Do you want to call me mother?" Rebecca said.

"Uh-uh. But if you're not a mother to me, I'll just

have to leave." Rosie's bottom lip primped up, eyes brimming.

"Don't cry over that." Starlyn patted her on the head. "Rebecca's a mother to you—just not your mother. Now don't be so rough with Ransom."

"Yes, sir." Rosie started toward the house.

"Rance, I'm proud of you." Starlyn clapped him on the back.

"It hurts when Rosie hits. I just hope she doesn't try my patience."

Rebecca watched Starlyn fight a smile, wondering how long he could restrain it.

* * *

Saturday, May 24, 1796

Summer, fall and winter had passed as the family pulled Rosie into their comforting embrace. She talked about her brother dying before they set sail on a ship crossing the big water. Rosie also told them her mother was cold when they pulled her away. She spoke of a woman holding her back when they dropped Mother into the big water.

Lately, though, the child hardly spoke about any of that.

Spring's sunshine warmed the earth bringing flowers that produced lovely scents.

"Jack, you going to help me move this into the house or complain all day?"

"Your idea for me to come along. Besides, I don't think this should belong to you."

"Never mind." Starlyn shook his head. "Rebecca, where are you? Come see what Father gave us."

Starlyn stared at the site of her beauty as she entered the front room. "Father gave us Grandmother's Welsh cupboard. The rose-covered plates you like so well are in the wagon."

Rebecca smiled as she smoothed back hair.

"Show us where you want this." He leaned down, grasping the cupboard. His thoughts cleared, realizing Jack had spoken. "What's that you say?"

"It's just not fair for you to own them. They should belong to me."

"Granda gave them to Father, his firstborn son. Father gave them to me—his eldest."

"That doesn't make it right. I'll get them one day, just wait and see."

Chills moved up Starlyn's backbone. He arched a shoulder to shake off the feeling.

* * *

June 1797

The Craigheads paid the captain for Rosie's passage to Virginia. Starlyn had petitioned the court for a special indenture. The court agreed. Rosie would live with them until the age of eighteen. Rebecca had insisted Rosie not be a servant but a family member, and now was pleased she had. They would not use her as an indentured servant, so the court insisted the child receive training on how to make a living after departing their home.

"After I stopped by the apothecary I spoke with Margaret Moore about Rosie's apprenticeship." Starlyn handed Rebecca the medicinal slips Abb Moore made up for her.

"Is Maggie interested in instructing her?" Dressmakers produced a steady income. Maggie was one of the best. Rebecca's shoulders tensed up. What if the woman did not want to take on Rosie?

"She's interested enough, but insists Rosie has to be

eleven years old before starting."

Drawing in a deep breath, Rebecca softly blew it out. "Maybe over the next twenty-one months, contending with Rance, she'll grow some patience for the apprenticeship."

"I hope so. I found them buckling up again yesterday, wrestling. If the lass does not find some patience, there could be trouble." Starlyn laughed then shook his head. "It's a good thing Rance will outgrow Rosie in time, or that young lady might get the best of him."

Rebecca's thoughts went to Janey, a mild daughter compared to this child Starlyn wanted them to raise. She was sure he made the right decision.

"I must work on the delivery manifest while there's time. We're backed up on orders." On the way out, Starlyn brushed Rebecca's cheek with a kiss.

Four weeks later Starlyn put every available driver freighting long days as he strained to stay up with their business. It seemed to Rebecca, from then things only grew worse. Her husband went on the road at dawn, hauling seven days a week, dropping into bed directly after supper. Sitting down to eat provided the most time their children enjoyed with him.

One evening on his way to bed, Starlyn said, "Growing prosperous may become more of a nuisance than a blessing. I must take some long hauls to relieve my drivers."

Dread swept over Rebecca. "It's been a while since driving kept you away overnight. Maybe your father can help."

"Father is already doing more driving." Stretching, he yawned. "No, we just need to see it through. I'll get caught up by February or March."

Days became weeks as the crops matured, turning some drivers back into field hands to work the harvest.

Each time Starlyn tended the tobacco crop at his father's, Ransom went. Rebecca took their girls along to help Thomas' servants prepare the midday meal for the field hands. On those days the family ate with Thomas and Felix.

* * *

Starlyn strolled into the common room where Rebecca mixed dough for bread. Kissing her he sat at the trestle table.

"I am almost through with this," Rebecca said.

She soon brought coffee along with a platter of molasses cookies, one of his favorites.

"The tobacco crop is still in the packhouse being graded before bundled into hands. We should finish before long." He took a cookie. "Soon as the crop is off to the warehouse I must do overnight hauls to relieve the drivers."

Rebecca looked up. "How many nights will you be gone?"

"Two, maybe even three." Starlyn wanted to stay home at night, but what was he to do?

A few days later, with the tobacco almost ready to go, Starlyn pulled three men out of the warehouse for driving.

The first week of October rolled in without much change in the weather. Starlyn blew a sigh of relief when the mild, fall weather continued. They made progress on the back-orders in the next two weeks.

* * *

November first.

The rain started early the evening before. Upon rising, it seemed to Starlyn like dawn disappeared into a full blown thunderstorm.

He pulled on clothes then hurried down to the common room where Rebecca and the servants prepared breakfast for the men. The two extra drivers from town were sure to enjoy something more to eat before they started out.

Rebecca set coffee in front of him. Starlyn motioned for her to sit down.

"There's a delivery going out today I don't want anyone hauling but me."

"Oh, when are you leaving?"

He studied the coffee mug. "With all the rain I should start early."

"Then you will return in a day or two?"

"No, it's more than a couple of days. I will return on the eighth, a week from today."

"I shall miss you every day, Star'n." Disappointment settled on her face.

"I should check the manifest, and look over the freight wagons before we eat." Starlyn rose. "We will get caught up soon. Then I shall stay home at night."

He went to the office to decide which driver took each run. Leaving the office Starlyn went to the freighting shed and helped drivers work on the wagons or horses.

Before long a servant came to announce breakfast was on the table. After a driver in front of him slipped, almost falling, Starlyn walked carefully up the path to the house. Once breakfast ended he went down to the shed to assign loads. Ruben, one of the men from down the road, hitched his wagon first.

Careful on the slick path, Starlyn hurried out to stop Ruben. "Since you're traveling past my father's house, tell him to hold off on deliveries until Friday."

"Anything else I should say?"

Starlyn pushed back wet hair. "Tell him the deliveries are not due until Monday."

"Yes, sir. I will make that my first stop." The driver

gripped the reins, tongue clicking to start the team forward.

Starlyn signaled the driver of a second large freight wagon to follow him. They headed for the tobacco shed, rain pouring off their hats. Stepping inside Starlyn motioned Ronald, a stout indentured lad, away from the men chinking the shed.

"Get clothes, a bedroll and put on a heavy coat. I don't know when the weather will get better or if we'll find accommodations for each night. We may have to sleep in the rain."

"Yes sir, right away." Starlyn thought he saw a flicker of excitement cross the young Scot's face.

He walked to the wagon, pulling out the lazy board for Ronald to sit on. Starlyn looked back at the house, feeling restless. Settling into the wheel horse's gait he was grateful to have six large Conestoga horses pulling the load as he led the way toward Petersburg. Already this year, it seemed like he had spent too many nights away from Rebecca and their family. The loneliness stung his heart.

CHAPTER TWENTY

Sunday, November 5

Reaching their destination Starlyn was thankful getting stuck in the mud only slowed them down. The rain went from a downpour to a drizzle. After they unloaded the wagons the three men headed to a freighter's inn for a hot meal.

"Let's stay here tonight. We'll have a good breakfast then get on the road before dawn." Neither man argued against that.

Starlyn paid for supper and sleeping accommodations. They brought in bedding, laying it down on the floor close to the fireplace. Shortly after they settled down, most of the other places had filled with freighters also seeking rest.

The next morning they started back home. That night they slept in the empty wagons. Traveling hard they arrived on the seventh, a day early. After they turned onto the road going to the freighting shed, Starlyn stopped the team, handing his wagon over to Ronald. He started for the house.

Inside, he hurried to the common room where Rebecca stirred a pot hanging from the trammel. "Umm, that smells so good."

She jumped back, with a hand at her throat. "You scared me. I didn't expect you home early with all that rain."

He removed the wooden spoon from Rebecca's hand. Pulling her into his arms, Starlyn inhaled the familiar smell of rosewater before kissing her.

"I sure missed you."

Color left her face. "Have you seen Jack?"

"No. I came straight home. You are so much prettier to look at than Jack."

"Starlyn, something's happened. We must talk."

Janey, Ransom and Rosie entered the room, faces solemn. They each hugged him then left.

"What's wrong with them?" A gnawing began in his stomach.

"I'll get you some coffee."

Starlyn took a seat. Rebecca placed the coffee in front of him and sat opposite.

"I would rather do anything but tell you what I must." Rebecca looked down.

"What is it?" Starlyn said, not sure he wanted to hear.

"Your father died the day you left."

Pain started so deep inside, it felt like he was being ripped apart.

"Starlyn, are you all right?"

He could not answer.

"Starlyn..."

Father dead? "No, I will never be all right."

She nodded, hands clasped together.

"I just don't understand how my father could be dead."

"It was from an accident."

"Then how...what happened?"

His wife looked away then into his eyes. "Your father had already left before the driver arrived to tell what you said."

"Who found him?"

"Felix tried to catch up, not wanting Thomas to make the drive alone. He said the wagon must have gotten stuck in some rocks traveling up a hill. When Thomas tried to dislodge the wagon it most likely slid, catching him under the wheels." Rebecca wiped her eyes.

"He is in the graveyard next to Mother?"

"Yes."

Starlyn rose and left the room, legs trembling.

* * *

Three days later, Starlyn rode to his father's house to retrieve some documents. The heavy door squeaked as it opened. He thought it a fitting sound as the empty house reminded him Father was gone.

He went up to the office, started a fire, and moved close to warm his hands. The door opened downstairs. Maybe a servant came to take care of chores.

"Starlyn."

"Jack, I'm up in Father's office," he called from the doorway.

Jack entered the room. "I don't ever remember the house being so quiet."

"This room doesn't feel the same without Father's presence. He never left the office in such disarray. It looks downright rifled." Starlyn scratched his head. "I will speak to Father's indentures. Try to figure out what happened."

"Well, there's no need to do that. I…I had started looking for the will, for the executor's name, when a servant arrived to call me away on business." Arms crossed, Jack continued, "I did not have time to straighten it up."

Starlyn placed a fist at his waist. "I'm the executor."

"How do you know? Father may have appointed me." Jack stared at him.

Going to their father's desk, Starlyn leaned down and pulled out the left bottom drawer. He pressed the spring Father had shown him, pulling out several documents. "This is how I know Father made me executor."

"Where did that space come from? As a child I played all around Father's desk but did not know it was there."

Starlyn shrugged. "It has been there since Father built the desk. I did not know either, until after the war when I resumed our tobacco business."

"I guess you are the administrator. What can I do to help?"

Starlyn's heart softened toward Jack.

"We must sort through Father's personal effects. Gather the important papers and correspondence, then pack up the office." He shifted position. "After the court appoints me executor I will file Father's will. Then sort out the papers to settle the estate."

They worked in silence for a while when Starlyn caught movement from the corner of his eye. Jack had turned away, placed a stack of papers in front of him then hunched over in a peculiar movement, one arm drawn toward his chest. Jack dropped the arm, turned back to face him, dragging a forefinger over each eye.

Sympathy rushed through Starlyn. "You alright, then?"

"Yes, I think so. I hope there's water in the common room. I need a drink."

"There should be. One of Father's servants I took on comes every day to maintain the house until we have cleaned it out."

Starlyn continued to work. After Jack returned they finished in the office, crating up the contents.

Jack stood on the porch. "Is there more for me to do? I must oversee a business arrangement during the week."

"No. I shall take care of the rest. Will you be over for

supper this Sabbath?"

Jack nodded. "Yes. Lydia and I intend to join you."

Clasping Jack's shoulder, Starlyn said, "Good. I will know more about Father's estate by then."

* * *

November 12th

Rebecca awoke early, dressed, then went directly to the cook-fireplace in the common room. She stooped down to scrape ashes off live coals before adding slivers of kindling, then blowing gently. Crisscrossing pieces of firewood over the kindling, she watched flames lick the sides before adding more wood.

She enjoyed this part of the morning. It took concentration to coax out a small, wispy flame, which seemed to free her thoughts. Had Thomas counseled Jack not to tell Starlyn about his attempts to court her years before? Rebecca's heart dipped at the thought of having to explain why she never told her husband.

She moved around the common room setting out foodstuffs for the servants to cook breakfast. The thought of cinnamon-dusted rice pudding at supper, along with Lydia's good company, brought contentment. They were friends.

After a hurried breakfast Rebecca changed for services, giving the children a look-over as Starlyn readied the carriage. The family arrived at church where Starlyn guided them to the Craighead pew. Jack and Lydia were already seated.

During the sermon Rebecca's thoughts turned to the death of Thomas, who had seemed to influence Jack more than anyone she knew. How would Jack respond to his brother's inheritance without their father to help him understand? Starlyn had said nothing about any problems, but to her it seemed Jack always resented not getting what he wanted.

A gentle shake brought Rebecca to the realization services had ended.

"I'm going out to pull the wagon up closer." Starlyn patted her arm.

"Can I say hello to Mrs. McClutcheon, Mother? I'll take Rance with me."

Rebecca was not sure who their lovely daughter wanted to speak with the most, Mrs. McClutcheon or her son, Fergie.

"Not today. We must go directly home." She took Janey's arm, guiding her toward the door. Rosie and Ransom followed. "I have so much to do before your aunt and uncle arrive."

* * *

Jack knocked on the door, Lydia beside him. Starlyn answered with a genuine smile on his face. He seemed so happy. It must be all that inheritance, along with everything else.

"Our door is always open to you, just come on in." Starlyn clapped him on the shoulder upon entry. "Rebecca's been working hard. She even made dessert."

He took Lydia's elbow, guided her through to the common room then to a seat at the table. Somehow the room looked bigger, the lamps dimmer, without Father's presence. How would he ever get used to Father being absent from the important affairs to come?

The room smelled of good food. After prayer, Starlyn took a thick piece of turkey off the platter then started it around the table. Soon, bowls and platters followed as the family filled their plates.

Jack ate in silence, only talking when spoken to.

Before long Rebecca served dishes of rice pudding. She had turned into a good cook, which did not surprise him.

"Rebecca, it's getting late," Starlyn said. "We will take our coffee in the office."

Jack rose and followed his brother. He took a chair close to the desk while Starlyn poked up the coals before adding more wood. Soon flames beat back the chill.

Rebecca entered with a tray containing mugs of coffee, as well as a plate of raisin cookies. Sipping the hot coffee, Jack stared at the orange-red flames licking up the sides of a log, wondering why Starlyn wanted him in the office. Only Starlyn inherited their father's possessions.

His brother shuffled a stack of parchments on his desk then separated them into two stacks, tapping a top leaf. "Well then, I inherited the land except for the five acres the house sits on, along with ownership of our freighting business and all the associated implements."

Jack shifted in the chair, neck muscles tightening, hands balling into fists over Starlyn's good fortune.

"I also received the cooling board along with everything in the house. That's the way Father wanted it. That's what he put in the will. I've written an exact copy of that for your records." Starlyn took parchments from a drawer, placing them on the desk corner. "After I am finished taking what I want from the house, you are welcome to everything else. Leave Felix what you don't want."

How generous, but then Starlyn could afford it, after just receiving everythi…

"Wait. What does Felix have to do with Father's will?"

Starlyn pulled a leaf from the stack, placed it on top, and smoothed out the parchment. "Here's proof that Father intended for Felix to buy the house. It's an accounting of small payments made the last two years. This also shows the amounts Father figured he owed Felix, starting the year Felix became a free man."

"Are you going to let that sale go through?" Jack said.

"Yes. I'm also letting him work for me to pay the balance."

Jack stood to leave, not trusting his reaction to this unexpected news about the will.

"Where are you going, Jack? Sit down while I finish reading the will." Starlyn smiled at him.

Jack took a seat. "Well, what else is important? It seems you covered everything."

"Not quite. There's the matter of your inheritance. Father left you five thousand in gold coin. Then there's the desk."

Jack's eyes flooded with moisture but he fought it back—far too old to cry in front of his brother. Father did not forget him. As a young child, some of the most contented times were spent playing in the office while Father worked. Now Jack owned the desk, a reminder of their father's love.

"We must head home before it gets too late. I'll make arrangements for the desk and other things sometime this coming week." Jack stood, clapping Starlyn on the shoulder as he walked toward the common room to collect his wife.

CHAPTER TWENTY-ONE

Tuesday, Second of March, 1798

Life continued for Rebecca's family after Thomas passed on. Starlyn's grief seemed to lessen, helped along by steady visits to the graveyard. Warmer weather meant flowers waited around the corner, their delightful blooms sure to come.

Starlyn had taken one of the best drivers, along with two other men, to undertake a long freighting trip to Hillsborough in North Carolina. Since arriving home the previous afternoon her husband seemed lost in thought. At breakfast Rebecca offered the meat platter twice before he took it, a sheepish smile on his face.

The day grew warm for late winter, sending them outside to enjoy the sunshine. The March air grew still, with hardly a breeze stirring the trees. It was then Starlyn spilled his thoughts.

"On the way to Hillsborough I stopped in Caswell County for a visit with Major Thomas Donaho, the officer I served under while in the Continental Army. The Major provided me with the documentation to apply for a bounty land warrant."

An overwhelming desire to be near Starlyn moved Rebecca closer, gently tugging at his shirt. "So then, you will get it?"

"Perhaps. Since I am not a resident of North Carolina I must take the papers to the state capital in Raleigh and apply for the grant. Then, wait to see if I get it. The Major seemed to think I would. I am glad he encouraged me to join the Continentals when the Rowan County militia disbanded."

"Starlyn, Jack stopped by while you were gone. Does he know about this?"

Starlyn placed a hand on her shoulder. "No. Don't you tell him either. I do not want Jack to know until after I get it."

"What are we going to do with it, Starlyn?" Rebecca gently swung from side to side, hands clutched in back and face tipped up toward him. "Where is this land?"

"It was in North Carolina, before that part became Tennessee. I earned that land grant, Rebecca. I do not want to see it wasted. Someone in our family must use it. Maybe Rance."

"Ransom? He's so…"

"Perhaps our son will start his adult life on the land I earned fighting for our country's freedom. Do not mention anything until it comes about."

"But wait, Starlyn. That is so far from us. We will never see Rance again! What ever will I do?"

"Our son shall become an exceptional man, Rebecca. You are going to be proud of him. Besides, I shall think of him as close to us. The new territory is also in the shadows of the Appalachians, like Virginia, only on the other side of the mountains."

Maybe her husband was right about this. She must not dwell on Ransom moving away. What a good opportunity using that land. Her mother's saying came back to Rebecca. "Do not worry about what might come. There will be time enough if that happens."

Springtime brought weather so perfect Rebecca

hoped it would never end. Then summer arrived. Hard work came with the heat of August as servants preserved or stored much of the food their family raised, or gathered for the coming winter. Starlyn's freighting business grew, as his drivers traveled great distances on Conestogas loaded with goods.

* * *

February, 1799

Winter turned bitter cold, unlike the previous year. Starlyn built up the cook-place fire then sat at the table, thoughts on their daughter who turned fourteen in June. Janey was beautiful to behold. Before long, he would look hard at the young men attracted to her.

Rebecca entered the common room, heavy skirt swaying gently as she crossed to sit down. "Do you want coffee or something to drink?"

"No. Just sit here next to me."

"You look like a man with something on his mind. What is it?"

His wife knew him better than he knew himself. "I'm thinking about that piece of land that borders our forest. It's for sale."

"I recall one of your wagons got stuck going over that land last spring." She swept a hand across the table, gathering crumbs. "So then, are you going to purchase it?"

"There is not enough time to fell the trees, much less pull out stumps. Then I must dig a drainage ditch. I will think on it, but one thing is sure. I cannot fall behind on my freighting."

* * *

Friday, August 23

Rebecca swung out the crane, stirred chunks of beef in the black pot hanging from a hook, added vegetables and returned the pot over the fire. She ran a sleeve across her sweaty forehead, wishing for a wet cloth.

Just then, Rosie hurried into the room clutching some folded material. "I learned how to use a chatelaine. Miss Margaret said I can make this into a dress for services, the week I stay at their house."

Rosie's face glowed with pride, when she held out the material for Rebecca.

Rebecca slid a hand over the cotton rubbed the material between fingers and thumb. "What a lovely blue. Now, you said something about staying with the Moores?"

"She says I must sew the material into a dress to demonstrate what I have learned."

"Stay there day and night, Rosie?"

"I think that's what Miss Margaret means."

Rosie's apprenticeship was now in its sixth month. Maggie Moore wants her to stay with them for the week? When did the woman want that? Uneasiness played around the fringes of Rebecca's mind as she remembered the Moores had no children.

* * *

Sunshine burned hot on Starlyn's face driving the last few miles. His mouth watered at the thought of potato chunks and carrots in Rebecca's turkey soup. Swallowing, his empty stomach growled, almost cleaving to his backbone.

Starlyn drove the team into the freighting shed as a breeze blew through, stirring the smell of leather. He climbed down, grateful for the saddle that kept most of the wheel horse's heat from him. Using a wide-brimmed hat to fan his face, he walked toward the house.

Rebecca smiled at him. The glow on her face made hurrying home worth every hard mile he traveled. Starlyn hurried to her, kissing her lips, stroking soft hair, inhaling the sweet scent. Finally he pushed away.

"How's supper coming? I am hungry as a bear."

"It won't be long. I'll pour coffee while you clean up."

The thought of good coffee sent Starlyn to the sideboard for soap and water. Finished, he sat at the table, took a sip from the coffee mug, savoring the taste.

"I almost forgot. I brought what you wanted from the apothecary." He took medicinal slips from a pocket.

"I'll just put them aside."

"Abb Moore asked about Rosie staying a week with them, after she completes the first year of apprentice. I told him that is alright with me. Is it with you?"

Rebecca looked down. "Oh, I thought Maggie wanted her to stay this summer."

"No, I don't think so. Isn't her first year in March of this coming year?"

"Yes, and of course it's alright with me."

* * *

Thursday, February 28, 1800

Time slipped away for Rebecca. December had brought snow with winter's blustery cold. Servants kept the house warm while she filled the air with the smells of good food.

Starlyn had arranged for a tutor to include Janey and Ransom in the scheduled sessions with four other families. The children studied from September to April, freeing them for the spring crops.

Maggie Moore had insisted Rosie continue on through June, despite Rebecca's objections.

"She will be home all day by July." Starlyn fixed a steady gaze on her. "Why does that matter?"

"It's just… well it seems like Rosie belongs here with the other two. It is lonely when she is gone."

Rebecca's answer seemed to satisfy Starlyn.

"Rosie's first year under Maggie ends on Monday," he said.

"That's Rosie's twelfth birthday."

"Yes, I know. The child will stay the week with the Moores then come home on Saturday."

"Then I'll pack some clothes in a satchel," Rebecca said.

She was so proud of all the girl had learned in her first year. The four year contract they had signed for Rosie, as an apprentice seamstress with Maggie, would end March third, 1803.

Rebecca cooked with Janey through the week. Something she especially enjoyed was teaching her daughter how to make good bread. She loved Janey's quiet, calm nature, so much like Starlyn.

The week ended and Rosie returned home, entering the common room with a blue garment draped over an arm. She carried something wrapped in beechnut colored material. Bringing the garment closer, Rosie said, "I sewed this from that material Miss Maggie gave me."

Rebecca grasped the hem of the dress, taking a critical look at the small, even slip stitches. "Oh, Rosie, it's lovely."

Janey entered the room. "Ooh, that's a pretty blue. May I look at it?"

Rosie handed her the dress, placed the package on the trestle table then folded back the material. "Miss Maggie gave me this."

Rebecca placed the pale blue wrap around Rosie's shoulders.

"It will look beautiful with your dress," Janey said.

"What else did you do?" Rebecca said.

"We cooked each meal together then I set the table." Rosie's eyes glistened. "I once found Miss Maggie crying over her children."

Heart clenched with pain, Rebecca remembered the Moores lost a daughter in 1787, then a son in 1793, the same year Felix brought Rosie to live with them. Margaret had almost died from the grief. The Moores remained childless.

Rosie shuffled her feet. "Miss Maggie asked if I wanted to stay with them another time."

"What did you say?" Rebecca looked down at the white knuckles of her laced fingers.

"I, uh, well I said they must speak with you."

* * *

Saturday, January third, 1801

Rebecca stayed busy during summer through the fall. She stored foods, gathered nuts and replenished their medicinal herbs.

Entering the apothecary she went directly to the counter. "Good morning, Abb. I'd like some of the Damask Lip Salve for the girls' chapped lips."

Abb bore down on her, eyes large and glistening. "I've run out of the salve. It should arrive on my next receipt from Richmond."

"When you get them, I will want two."

Abb cleared his throat. "I just received a supply of Doctor Church's Vermifuge Lozenges. Ransom may not need it now, but come spring..."

"Please send the lozenges along with the salve when Starlyn comes in next week."

"I'll have them ready. Maggie's here right now. I believe she desires a word with you."

Rebecca walked to the other end of the shop where Maggie unrolled a bolt of cloth. "Abb said you wish to speak with me."

"Yes. In March I'd like Rosie to stay with us for three weeks. During that time we'll travel to Richmond for the newest cloth prints, along with dry-goods from England." Maggie paused, and it seemed to Rebecca her face softened. "My brother will mind the apothecary for Abb." Maggie's lips stretched into an unaccustomed smile. "We will take Rosie to a play. They put them on in a large building, you know. We shall dine on a nice supper at the inn then stay overnight."

"I'll talk to Starlyn, but like the last time, I should think five days are enough…"

"But Rebecca, it takes time to travel as well as make the selections for my shop. That is also a part of learning for her apprenticeship." Maggie's mouth pinched up. "You wouldn't want Rosie to miss picking out the best materials, guided by my experience. One day, she will be a fine dressmaker."

Rebecca stiffened, unable to recall Maggie ever pressing so hard over a decision she had no authority to make. Usually mild natured, Maggie was well liked in Starlight.

"We will give this some thought, then make a decision. Good day, Maggie." Rebecca escaped toward the door, dreading the next encounter with Maggie.

CHAPTER TWENTY-TWO

Saturday, March the seventh, 1801

Before dawn, Starlyn entered the common room where Rebecca and a servant labored over breakfast. Yellow-red flames licked the bottom of the three-legged skillet as specks of ham fat sizzled in the fire.

After he sat down at the trestle table, Rebecca brought coffee. His wife ran a hand underneath her skirt before sitting next to him.

"Mister Shrewsbury wishes to speak with me." Starlyn drummed a forefinger.

The blue in Rebecca's eyes deepened. "How do you know that?"

"He sent word through one of my drivers." Touching her soft cheek, he said "I need to get over there soon. Francis Pickleheimer is also interested in that land."

"I must get food on the table for the children."

As she rose Starlyn gently touched an arm. "I appreciate the heat from the cook-place on these cold days, but how do you tolerate it during the summer?"

"I must cook so our family can eat."

The children entered interrupting thoughts about his wife's practical attitude. Ransom sat at the table while Janey and Rosie helped her.

* * *

Rebecca finally took a seat at the table. The faint smell of cinnamon from the rice pudding stirred hunger. Part way through eating she said, "This year, I don't think Rosie needs to stay with Maggie more than one week."

"What reason did Maggie give for wanting more time?" Starlyn said.

"She wishes to take Rosie on a purchasing trip to Richmond. Maggie said to teach the girl how to buy cloth, along with other items for the shop." Rebecca looked down. "I am inclined to refuse the request."

"But Miss Rebecca, I want to go," Rosie said. "How else will I ever learn how to run a dressmaker's shop? I will miss home but it's not for long."

Apprehension at the thought of Rosie being away so long draped Rebecca in dread. That clashed with the desire on Rosie's face.

"Well then, if it means that much, you should go."

Rosie's face brightened. "You'll not be sorry about this. I promise to learn everything Miss Margaret has to teach."

* * *

August the third, 1801

Rebecca awoke before sunup from a restless sleep. The bed felt lonely and far too big without her husband. He left two days earlier on a long freighting trip. She always had plenty of time to think whenever he was away. Donning a brown dress, she twisted her hair into a tight knot at the base of the neck. She found no joy in looking pretty without Starlyn there to see her.

He had once told her he fought so hard for their country because he was freedom's anchor. Their country was now free due to him and many others. She could not do without him. He was now her anchor.

She hurried to the staircase then down to the

common room where an indentured servant tended a roaring fire in the cook-place. Rebecca worked alongside Parthia preparing breakfast.

"Felix, along with the three drivers who work in the fields today, will eat breakfast at the porch table." Rebecca ran a hand down her apron. "They will also eat the midday meal with us."

"Yes, Miss Rebecca. I'll get to that table right away." Parthia glanced down. "Oh, Miss Janey said she is not hungry."

"Was that all?"

Parthia wiped her hand with a cloth. "Yes. Janey looked a bit out of sorts."

When Felix arrived Rebecca poured him coffee. "Breakfast is almost ready."

"I expect it to be a hard day." He took the mug.

Rebecca helped a servant set breakfast on the table, while Parthia took out bowls of food for the men.

After eating, Ransom lingered at the table, talking with Rosie. Rebecca cleared off the plates. They stopped when Janey entered the common room.

"Are you hungry?" Rebecca said.

"Mother, I don't feel well. I..." Janey bent down as a stream of vomit splattered the floor.

Rebecca rushed to pull hair away from her daughter's face.

"Get me a wet cloth and pour some water," Rebecca said to Rosie.

She wiped Janey's face. "Here, rinse your mouth. Spit it out."

Upstairs, Rebecca helped her change into a cotton shift and into bed, then felt her forehead. The heat scared her. Janey was burning up. She hurried down the stairs, where

Ransom waited at the bottom.

"What's wrong with her, Mother?"

"I don't know. Take a wagon for Doctor McKenna. Hurry!"

Rebecca took a bucket upstairs. Rosie sat near Janey's bed holding a cloth, with a pan of water on the table.

"Use this to catch the vomit." Rebecca set the bucket close to the bedstead.

"She needs to eat, Miss Rebecca." Rosie shifted in the chair.

"Make her some panada, Rosie. When she wakes up it will soothe her stomach." Rebecca dipped the cloth in water and wiped Janey's face.

"I cannot tell when the bread is boiled smooth enough, or how much sugar to stir in." Rosie looked down. "What if it makes Janey feel worse?"

"A servant will prepare it," Rebecca said. "You keep her brow cooled."

Downstairs, Rebecca paced the house waiting for the doctor. It seemed like a long time before Doctor McKenna arrived, carrying a worn black bag.

"When did this start?" the doctor said.

"I don't know, Hiram. Janey came down this morning and vomited." Rebecca searched his face. "She's burning up with fever."

"Let's take a look at her." Dr. McKenna followed her up to Janey's room.

"Rosie, get the doctor water and a clean towel."

"Yes, Miss Rebecca." Rosie left with the pan.

She gently shook Janey awake. "Doctor McKenna is here."

Hiram went to Janey's bedside. "Does it hurt

anywhere?"

"I'm sick at my stomach. My throat aches, too."

Rosie returned and the doctor washed his hands.

He felt Janey's brow then thumbed an eye open wide, before probing her neck directly below each side of the jawbone.

"Stick out your tongue." The doctor's eyebrows went up. "Hmm. Who have you been around lately?"

"I sat next to Liddy and Abigale Royce during services last week."

He patted Janey's shoulder. "That explains it."

"What do you mean?" Rebecca said.

"The girls are doing better, but their little sister just came down with it."

Rebecca glanced at her daughter. "It seems like Janey rocked little Polly when Abigale couldn't stop her crying."

The doctor nodded. "That is why Janey's sick. Keep the eating utensils separate. It may help."

Rebecca and the doctor went downstairs.

"Slow cook some slippery elm. Pare off the inner part from the bark then add honey to sweeten it. Give Janey a spoonful at a time. It will help her throat."

"Will she be ill for long?"

"Not too long, I suspect. Send for me if it grows worse." The doctor let himself out.

* * *

Tuesday, September first, 1801

Each day the heat left Rebecca exhausted. She was grateful when the weather began to cool, sleeping better at night. Janey recovered a few days after Doctor McKenna's visit. Thankfully, no one caught her illness.

After breakfast, Ransom teased Janey and Rosie. It looked like the girls might turn on him but, instead, they only left the room. Rebecca smiled clearing the table, wishing Starlyn was home to enjoy their back and forth.

"Mother," Janey called from the hallway.

"I'm almost through…"

Janey stepped into the room. "Mother, come quick. Father's home."

Rebecca smoothed her hair, clutched a patch of skirt and rushed toward the front room. Days had passed since Starlyn held her. Slowing to a dignified walk before reaching the door, she peered out, hungry for a glimpse of him.

Starlyn pointed toward the freighting shed as he spoke to a driver. A new Conestoga took the space next to him. The wagon's wheels, along with the running gear, gleamed bright red. The body was painted the bluest of blue. White canvas covered the length of the wagon top, extending over the bow on each end.

Rebecca blinked at the striking beauty of the wagon. The Conestoga's colors reflected the red, white, and blue of their country's new flag.

"Come give me a hand, Lad," Starlyn said. Ransom joined him as one of the field hands hurried over to help.

She lingered by the doorway while the men unloaded pieces of dark metal from the wagon. They deposited their loads in the common room close to the back door, opposite the cooking fireplace.

"Ransom, you two bring in the rest of the pieces," Starlyn said.

"Yes sir, Father." The worker followed Ransom out the door.

Starlyn turned to her. "After I picked up the Conestoga in Lancaster, I brought this stove from Bethlehem." He stooped down to stroke a piece of iron. "I purchased it from Mettle, who has moved back to Pennsylvania. The man does some of the best work around."

Her husband had talked about first meeting Mettle, a Moravian, who scared off a Tory out to kill Starlyn during the war. Mettle did this by simply being on the road that day.

Starlyn pulled her close. "Mrs. Craighead, I just couldn't come home without bringing you a surprise. I sure missed you"

She backed away as Rance, then the worker, returned with more pieces.

"This is the last of it, Father." Ransom placed the iron with the rest.

Giggling, Janey and Rosie came inside to stand next to her.

Starlyn put together the ten-plate, cast iron cook stove, using rods to connect the pieces before attaching the legs. Purchased from his old friend, the Moravian ironworker.

Humming, Rebecca wiped off the pretty stove while thinking about cooking on it. Even if, at Starlyn's insistence, a servant did the heavy cooking on unbearably hot days. Sleep would be sweeter tonight. Only in her husband's arms could she ever feel safe.

* * *

Starlyn took a mug of coffee to the office where he watched the sun's golden orb rise, before shuffling through parchments for freighting deliveries. Hot days continued into October. Toward the end of the month, when the weather had changed, Rebecca moved the cooking from the new stove back to the cook-fireplace.

Cold December mornings gave him an appreciation for the warmth the cook place scattered through the common room.

He had paid off the new land back in April, four

weeks after giving Mister Shrewsbury enough money to hold it. Starlyn wondered where to find the time to work that field. Perhaps he should hire someone to clear the land. This job might require all the coming spring, maybe part of summer. Starlyn would then put in the drainage ditches, and still manage the crops as well as the freighting. Over the winter he must draw up a plan. There were only a few months before spring arrived.

"Breakfast is ready." Rebecca came closer. "Are you hungry?"

He stood and pulled her into his arms. "I'm hungry for anything from you, even a smile."

Pink color bathed Rebecca's face before his lips brushed her forehead. "I'll just come with you. My stomach's hungry, too."

CHAPTER TWENTY-THREE

Wednesday, January first, 1802

After supper, Rebecca crisscrossed hardwood sticks inside a small oven built into the massive chimney of the cook fireplace. Lost in thought, she opened the flue, lit the fire and secured the cast iron door.

The year had ended with the family's recovery from a severe cough. Rebecca rubbed everyone's chest in bear grease. The rancid smell was almost gone, except for the last bundle of bed clothes needing a good scrub. Say what they might about the stink, bear grease, along with the right herbs, worked to cure the problem.

She waited for the oven bricks to heat, still thinking about their illness. The entire family rarely became ill at once. One servant stayed well enough to help during this hard time, until Rebecca grew strong enough to continue.

Happiness came with the family's recovery. Of all the illnesses Rebecca could not stop, she did know how to cure congestion. Meadowsweet's crushed leaves and flower tops helped with headaches, muscle pains, and fever.

The oven grew hot enough to bake. She closed the flue, scraped out the ashes then shoveled the bread loaves inside on a long handled peel. With the oven closed up so the heat could not escape, the bread would bake through the night, giving them crusty loaves at breakfast.

Starlyn entered the room, took a seat at the table and spread out a leaf of parchment. Rebecca poured him a mug of coffee then sat on the opposite bench.

"Something wrong?" she said.

"No, I just need to mark where ditches go on that wet land." Starlyn sharpened a pencil with his penknife. "Most of the land has good drainage, but a couple of acres in the lowest corner are almost swamp."

Parthia cleaned up after supper, leaving a saucer of macaroons on the table. Rebecca moved the cookies closer to Starlyn before refilling his mug. He worked a while, then pushed the parchment aside and reached for a cookie.

"This is good. You make them?"

She nodded. "Are you finished?"

"I have identified where to put in the drainage, but not who will clear the land."

Rebecca fought back a smile. "You have someone in mind?"

"Well, Felix still owes on Father's house. Clearing this land might just about pay me off."

Rebecca never tried to influence him in such matters. The man had a good business head, always knowing what to do.

"Then after you're through marking the ditches, shall we retire?"

"I am tired. It's been a long day."

* * *

Monday, February 15th

Starlyn pulled on a coat and stepped out on the back porch. The air blew cool and crisp, the porch showing no traces of moisture. Yesterday on their ride home from services it started to snow. He expected a heavy downfall but it soon thinned out to a few flakes. Were they still in for a big storm like last year? He must watch for bad weather, considering the amount of freighting on the roster.

As bowls and platters traveled around the trestle table, Starlyn said, "I will be gone most of the morning, maybe into early afternoon."

Rebecca took a slice of fried ham and handed Starlyn the charger. "Is there a problem?"

"No. Just business I must tend to."

He took two slices then passed the meat to Ransom. His family seemed quiet. Starlyn glanced at Ransom.

"Care to ride along with me today?"

He barely finished speaking when Ransom said, "Yes, Da. We can take care of manly things. I'm tired of being cooped up in this house with a bunch of ole hens."

"Hmm!" Janey stood, hand on hip. "Better watch what you say about us women, Ransom."

"If Janey does not get you, I will." Rosie shook a tight little fist.

"Let me get a coat, maybe gloves. I'll meet you at the barn." Ransom hurried off to the sound of the girls' laughter.

Starlyn smiled at Ransom's skirmish with the two young ladies of the house. He kissed Rebecca before heading to the barn. Ransom already had one horse ready. While he saddled the other one, Starlyn gave instructions to the workers.

Leading the horses outside, they mounted up as Starlyn took note of the unseasonably warm day. They could take the time to enjoy their ride. Ransom turned fifteen on the third of December. Starlyn wanted more time to guide the lad, take him on deliveries for experience in their freighting company before his boy became an adult.

They traveled in silence until Ransom said, "Where we going, Da?"

His son sat astride the saddle, back straight and

shoulders squared, like an experienced rider.

"I have some business to talk over with Felix."

Fifteen minutes later they reached their destination. Excitement stirred inside until he remembered Father no longer resided there. The house belonged to Felix now. Well, almost.

They arrived at the door as Felix swung it open. "Come in. Take a seat."

In the common room Starlyn looked around, feeling comfortable in this familiar home. Felix's square four-person table made the room look much bigger. Starlyn had moved his father's large trestle table to their house, refusing to leave it even for Felix.

"How much time do you have in the spring?" Starlyn said.

"Depends on what you want me to do."

An older woman brought mugs of coffee to Felix and Starlyn. "What shall I bring the lad?"

"Anything he wants," Felix said.

"I'll take some of that coffee, too," Ransom said.

Starlyn glanced at Felix. He still smiled at the tactics used, years ago, when Felix prepared him for Roger Woodson. Respect for the Irish servant Father indentured went beyond gratitude. In a way Felix stepped into the gaping hole left by Andrew's death. Their friendship bordered on trust formed throughout the years.

"I need someone to clear off ten acres, so I can drain it. The work you put in may satisfy the contract you made with Father."

"I must say, it's not every day a man gets the chance to pay off his house. Starlyn, I will do a good job. I pledge that."

"Well then, let me know when you intend to start. I cannot do the drainage until you finish most of the work. Until then, I'll be busy with other things." Starlyn glanced at Ransom, who drank his coffee as they talked. "I need it done by the end of summer. Do not break your horse's back pulling out stumps or rocks. Use my ox team."

"Then it is settled," Felix said. "Should be through somewhere around August."

Starlyn enjoyed another mug of coffee before they left for home. They stopped at the land Starlyn wanted Felix to clear out.

"Think he will be successful?" Ransom said.

"If anyone can get this ready, Felix can. He's a good man."

* * *

The first day of March brought cold rain with an overcast sky. Rebecca sighed, swept the front room then sighed again. Rosie, who turned fourteen years of age in two days, began a fourth year as apprentice to Maggie Moore. Her little Irish lass had learned so much about dressmaking under the woman's steady hand.

Rebecca trembled over the thought of the seamstress's growing love for this child who held such a tight grip on her heart. What if Maggie drove a wedge between…?

At the sound of a strong knock she set the broom aside and opened the door.

"Good morning, Rebecca." Felix said. "May I speak to Starlyn?"

She stepped back. "Come in. He is in the common room."

They found Starlyn at the trestle table working on a sketch.

"Have a seat, Felix." Rebecca said.

"What are you doing here today? Run out of work?" Starlyn's voice carried that comfortable tone that said 'I'm glad to see you'.

She brought coffee then sat next to Starlyn as the men talked.

"I start work on your land the fifteenth of the month."

"Sounds a little early. The weather could remain cold and wet the next two weeks," Starlyn said.

"Hard work heats up the body." Felix dipped his head. "Besides, rain won't hurt me."

She rose from the table as Starlyn picked up the sheet of parchment. Walking away, she heard a trace of Scottish brogue slip into her husband's voice as he spoke to Felix.

"Take a look at these plans for putting in the drainage."

After breakfast Rebecca and a servant hung the big pot on the trammel. They filled it with water to heat up before cutting up turkey. No time for daydreaming with chores still left after Felix's interruption. Then she must get back to the pot. Later, while the turkey cooled, Janey would take out the bones while Rebecca helped Rosie prepare vegetables for the soup.

The broom slowed as Rebecca relished the thought that spring lingered just around the corner. She ached for time outside with Starlyn and the children, working together or resting with cool drinks under a shade tree. The heavy, sweet smell of blooming lilacs would fill the air. Soon, she hoped.

* * *

Wednesday, March 31

"Father, will you take us to the apothecary?" Janey

said when Starlyn entered the common room.

"Umm," Starlyn grasped his chin. "Now, why do that?"

"We need ribbon." Janey clasped her hands.

His daughter looked beautiful when she smiled. "That's a long way to travel. Your mother surely must have ribbon."

"Miss Maggie gave me material," Rosie said. "I must sew up something to show what I have learned. We want to pick out ribbon to match that material."

"Material is expensive. Why am I not paying for it?"

Rosie dropped her gaze. "Because, well because Miss Maggie said it was my assignment as an apprentice."

"That's it then, Janey. Go tell your mother we're leaving, while I hitch up the wagon."

Starlyn helped the girls onto the seat, shaking out a blanket for their laps. Climbing up, he guided the animals forward. He heard words like "cuff" and "brown material" between giggles.

In town Starlyn waited while the girls went inside. A ray of sunshine brought hope of a more pleasant ride home. They appeared at the apothecary door with Maggie Moore trailing behind.

Starlyn stepped down to help them into the seat, as Maggie's sharp glance darted around to land on the wagon's contents.

After the girls settled under the blanket, Maggie handed Rosie a package wrapped in a scrap of cloth.

"Good day, Mr. Craighead."

"The best to you, Mrs. Moore."

He clicked his tongue, starting the animals forward.

The wagon slipped on the thawing road until the horses gained their footing. Two large rolls of rope, strong enough for ships, and other tools for Felix, helped weigh down the wagon.

A gust of wind swirled over the land, bringing a raw dirt smell that hinted of spring. The simple log shelter Felix built, after accepting the job, came into view. Oxen tethered at a stand of trees, Felix strode through the mucky acreage toward the shed where Starlyn pulled alongside.

"Come to see how I'm doing?" Felix tugged off gloves before walking over to Rosie.

Starlyn shook his head. "I brought that rope you will need, along with other things."

Felix ruffled Rosie's hair. "I see you brought me some help."

"Not today. I must start on my sewing." Rosie clutched the package closer when Felix reached for it.

Starlyn helped him move the rope and tools from the wagon into the lean-to, then climbed on the wagon.

"Well then, if there's no help guess I had better get back to work." Felix pulled on gloves and struck out toward the trees, stopping partway to throw up a hand.

"Let's go home," Starlyn said.

The sun shone golden on Felix's work, dimming the land's scars left from clearing. As they traveled along he thought about events Felix had been responsible for, such as bringing Rosie into their family. Felix bought Father's house, instead of it going to a stranger. Contentment filled Starlyn's heart at having such a friend.

* * *

Sunday, April 25th

"What's keeping Rosie from breakfast?" Rebecca placed Starlyn's mug in front of him.

"Mmm, I believe Miss Rosie stayed up part of the

night," Janey said.

"What is so important she does not sleep?" Rebecca said.

"It is not my place..." Janey stopped when Rosie entered.

Handing Starlyn a bundle wrapped in cloth, Rosie said, "This is for you."

He folded back the cloth. "This doesn't look like a dress to me. The material is too plain."

"No, sir. If I said the material was for you, then the jacket would be no surprise. I hope it fits."

"Place it on the serving table. I will try it on after we eat."

Rebecca started platters of food around the table. Occasionally her husband glanced over at Rosie's gift as they ate.

Laying the napkin next to the plate, Starlyn pushed back from the table and rose. Strolling to the package he removed the garment, shaking it out.

"Rosie, I do believe this is a new jacket."

The family gathered around as he stuck an arm through a sleeve, shrugging into it. "This fits like you measured for it. I see you paid close attention to Maggie's instructions. What a fine piece of work."

As their inherited daughter's face lit up with happiness, Rebecca stepped closer to admire the girl's sewing skills.

Starlyn gently tugged at the collar, before straightening the lapels. It seemed a perfect fit.

Just as quickly, he removed the jacket. "I will get dressed for services."

Rebecca urged the children to hurry, reminding them to dress in their best service clothes.

Once Rosie had asked what service clothes were. Brushing the soft hair from the girl's face Rebecca had said, "Your best clothes to wear in the Lord's presence."

They were gathered in the front room when Starlyn entered.

The new brown jacket outlined broad shoulders, continued down to the waist, the coattails ending just above the back of his knees. He closed the jacket at the waist with a large brass button. A trace of berry in the coat's color caught the occasional red strand in her husband's brown hair, resting just above the collar. Starlyn looked so handsome it brought a flutter to Rebecca's heart.

CHAPTER TWENTY-FOUR

Monday, May 3rd, 1802

Starlyn rose early and hurried to the barn. Animal scents mingled with the odor of loose, strewn hay, greeted him at the door. A pleasant smell he enjoyed even as a child. The soft lowing of hungry cows, their milk sacks bulging, filled the air.

As Starlyn worked, he remembered the final visit with General Daniel Morgan. Back in January a post came for Father. General Morgan had wanted Thomas to stop by if he freighted near Winchester.

The General must not have known of Father's death. A week later, after making a delivery near there, he went to the General's house.

"Welcome, Starlyn." General Morgan swung open the massive wooden door, looking past him.

Stepping over the threshold, Starlyn knew who the General searched for.

"I am alone. Father is not with me."

The General closed the door then shuffled slowly to a wingback chair, pointing toward a sofa. Starlyn remembered Daniel Morgan as a large man, with the ability to fast become a deadly foe. Time had changed that. Taking a seat he waited for the man to speak.

"Thomas is heavy on my mind. I want to see him again. I am sure my time grows close."

"General Morgan, my father passed away in a

freighting accident. If Father were alive, nothing would keep him away."

"I insist you call me Daniel. Thomas and your grandfather Cyrus always did. Now tell me, when did that happen?"

"Gen—I mean Daniel, Father joined the Lord the first day of November past."

"I did not hear about that." The General ran a hand over his face. "He was a God fearing man. I'm going to see Thomas again one day. Most likely soon."

Starlyn could still see the disappointment on the general's face.

The barn door opened.

"Da!" Ransom said. "What remains for us to do?"

* * *

Three days later

Ransom appeared at the door. "Felix is here to see you, Da."

"Soon as I finish with this bridle, I'll be up."

He looked for worn spots that might cause a fall if the leather separated. Satisfied with the condition, Starlyn saddled a horse then walked it to the house.

Felix joined him. "Star'n, just wanted you to know about the work."

Starlyn ran a hand over the horse's sleek, muscled shoulder. "I thought we might take a look at the land. I am beginning to feel good about it."

"Is there a certain use for the ground?" Felix said.

"Yes, I think so." Starlyn mounted and waited for Felix to settle in the saddle. "I am still working on it. I'll explain when we get there."

They crossed the boundary to the ten acres,

dismounting at the lean-to. He struck out toward a lone tree where the oxen were usually tethered. Felix kept pace, as they stepped around uneven, ruptured holes, left by stumps yanked from the earth.

He moved toward mounded rocks Felix first dug out when clearing the land. Toward the middle of the acreage, stumps smoldered.

"That is one massive trunk. I see you cut the deep roots to help the oxen pull it out," Starlyn said. "Did it take all day to pry from the earth?"

"Sure seemed like a full day to me." Felix shook his head.

Kicking a clod of dirt, he faced Felix. "I need this ready in time for seeding tobacco. I intend for Ransom to handle the crop. One day my son will own this land."

"Think you will get that low spot drained in time?"

"Don't know for sure, but I intend to try."

* * *

Thursday, July 8

The early afternoon sun shone bright when Rebecca stepped outside to sweep the porch, shading her eyes as Felix rode up.

"Good day, Rebecca. Starlyn home?"

"He's expected back at the freight shed soon."

"I'll wait down there." Felix started toward the shed.

Long ago her husband developed a friendship with the Irishman that lasted through the years. Their bond had grown strong, much like her friendship with Sarah.

She finished the porch. In the common room, Parthia mixed dough for the next day's bread. Rebecca stirred the contents in the kettle and tasted the broth.

"Parthia, prepare the vegetables for the pot after you finish. It is getting late."

"Yes, Miss Rebecca."

"Umm, that smells good," Starlyn said. "I'm so hungry."

Rebecca turned at the sound of her husband's voice, so strong and gentle. "It will be ready soon. I'll get you some coffee."

"I'll take it in the front room," Starlyn said.

Rebecca brought the coffee then sat on the sofa.

After a sip, Starlyn placed the mug on the side table. "Felix waited for me at the freighting shed with some news."

"He came here looking for you. Anything important?"

"Just that he is almost through with the land." He stood. "Is there time to go for a stroll?"

"Yes, I think so," Rebecca said.

They went out the back door, crossing the porch to the stairs. Below, they walked to chairs under a spreading oak. A breeze brushed Rebecca's forehead to tug at a curl.

"The air feels good."

She nodded. "I needed to cool off."

Sunshine filtered through the tree limbs catching strands of red in Starlyn's hair as he leaned forward. Head tilted to the right, blue eyes bore into hers. His lips drew back from evenly set teeth, as if to laugh. It was Rebecca's favorite smile. They sat awhile, quietly enjoying the shade and each other.

"I intend to stop at Rocky Mount court house next time I travel in that direction. Need to speak with the county clerk." Starlyn pushed hair back off his forehead. "I may use someone beside Morris Whitley to draw up a legal document with the terms we want. I will also take the land deed."

"I am glad you are getting this done," Rebecca said.

"Our son needs that land early, not years later," he said. "The lad will become a good businessman raising a profitable crop. Ransom also will learn the freighting business and our farm."

Lost in thoughts, they finally rose to answer Parthia's call for supper.

* * *

Monday, Second of August

Starlyn drove to the freight shed. Sliding off the wheel horse, he stepped around the Conestoga. The heat almost took his breath away.

Elijah came from the shed to help with the team.

"You'll drive the second wagon tomorrow, Lige. After we make the delivery you must go pick up another load bringing it back here."

Elijah nodded. "I'll rub the team down in the barn then give them fodder. Want me to go over the running gear?"

"Yes, each time you handle a team. When you're through, come to the house for supper."

Starlyn hurried toward the back porch. The desire to see his wife moved him forward at a brisk pace. Straight up the steps through the back door, he searched for Rebecca, who rolled out pie crust at the sideboard. A bowl of blackberries sat next to the sugar loaf and the wrought iron cutter.

Laying down the rolling pin, her hands fluttered over hair, then apron, before hurrying toward him, calling out, "Parthia, finish the pie."

"If you want to sit under the oak tree, I'll bring something cool to drink," Rebecca said.

Starlyn went out to wait, grateful for the shade. A bird high in the branches trilled a melody, as he thought about giving his son the land when the lad came of age. Why not have Felix manage the new plot? The man could guide Ransom through raising a profitable crop, having learned plenty growing tobacco for Father.

Rebecca set down a mug of water and offered a platter. "I made soft molasses cookies, the way you like."

Starlyn took a bite, savoring the flavor. "This is good."

"You looked so deep in thought," Rebecca said.

He reached for another cookie. "It seems like our freighting grows by the day. I wish Da had lived to see the profitable business he built."

"Starlyn, Thomas would be so proud."

Thoughts that Father could never participate in Ransom's climb to manhood brought regret. Starlyn swallowed hard.

"Rance should work the land, producing a crop before we tell him about our gift."

"You must do whatever you want," Rebecca said.

Starlyn declined the cookie platter. "Our family will grow stronger from this. After managing a crop year after year, our son will be ready for the freighting business and all the land he will own one day."

"Then Ransom will inherit all of our property?"

Starlyn nodded. "That is the Scot's way, my beautiful wife."

She smiled at him. "Nothing for Janey?"

"Yes, she will inherit. The land, the freighting business all go to Ransom. If Janey receives land it will go to a husband. Do we want that to happen?"

"No. The land must stay in our family."

CHAPTER TWENTY-FIVE

Tuesday, August 17

Starlyn lit the way toward the staircase with a candle lamp. Granda's clock struck five. Pausing at the top, the lamp's soft glow reflecting on the baluster, he followed the steps down. On the landing he ran a hand down the smooth maple of the clock case, while finalizing plans for the freighting trip that began just after breakfast.

Following the smell of ham to the common room, he thought about Uncle Isaac, who shipped the seven-foot longcase clock, after Granda moved from Baltimore County to live with them.

Not long after moving Rebecca and Janey into their new house, Father had brought Starlyn a small parchment roll that bequeathed the clock to him.

"Your Granda always set his clock," Father had said. "After he died I found the parchment at the base of the clock face the first time I opened the glass door to set the time."

"Why did you wait so long to give me the parchment and the clock?"

His father had simply said, "Up until you built the house you had nowhere to put it."

In the common room, Rebecca brought him coffee as Parthia and another servant rushed food to the table. The family ate in silence until Ransom slowed down and Janey pointed a finger at his food.

"You must finish eating what you take."

"Yes, Ransom, you cannot waste," Rosie said.

Ransom squared his shoulders. "Don't worry about how much I eat. None will go to waste. Maybe you should consider how much food to leave on the plate."

"What does that mean?" Rosie said.

Ransom gave that boyish smile Starlyn knew the girls loved. "Well, if Janey gets too plump she may have difficulty finding a husband. That goes for you too, Rosie."

"Better watch what you say Mister Ransom Craighead," Rosie said. "Else you'll find yourself in big trouble."

Janey rose, shaking out the dress clinging to a slim figure. "You think that you can get away with talking to us like that?"

The strained look on Ransom's face reached Starlyn. Maybe he could do something about that.

"Would you like to make today's freight trip with me? You may find the ladies more forgiving when we return."

"They don't act like ladies. I think they have a long way to go before…"

"Get your things and head for the freight shed— don't know how long I can hold them back." Starlyn glanced at Rebecca, whose hand covered her mouth.

Ransom hurried from the room, the girls grumbling behind him.

"Trip will be good for him." Starlyn rose from the table.

Merriment shone in his wife's damp eyes as she stood. "It's always good for our son to work with you."

He waited as she added food to the box for Ransom.

He lingered over a kiss, then picked up the food box.

"Star'n, take care. You must both come home to me."

He looked back going out the door, smiling at the thought that anything but death could keep him from her. Down at the freight shed Starlyn inspected the first six-horse team then carefully examined their shoes. Ransom hurried, breathing hard, clothes gripped tight.

"Whoa. Slow down there. You'll be worn out before we start."

Ransom sucked in air. "I just really want to go with you."

"Well then, help with the two other teams. We need to get started."

Moving to another wagon, Starlyn motioned Ransom toward the horse paired with the lead. They checked the leather straps and the gear, looking for weak spots.

"I'll drive the lead wagon from the left wheel horse. You can ride on the lazy board. Burl, the new man I hired, will drive the second wagon. I need to know how well he does on long hauls."

"Where are we delivering to?" Ransom said.

"The freight in our wagons goes to Mister Campbell, just outside of Charlotte Town."

"What about the third wagon?" Ransom smoothed out a leather strap.

The orderly way his son asked for information was not lost on Starlyn. "Albert Johns will turn off at Salisbury, headed to a store in Lincolnton. I let Albert choose the driver traveling with him."

They finished the final wagon as the three drivers approached with their belongings.

"Tie my horse to the back of our wagon." Starlyn waited until Ransom pulled out the lazy board before he mounted the left wheel horse and called softly, "Come on, we need to be somewhere."

The three wagons rolled toward the rise, Starlyn's Conestoga in the lead. As they crested the hill he looked back to see Rebecca on the porch, sweeping. Even in the distance the sight of her flooded his senses with deep happiness.

* * *

Rebecca carried a broom to the back porch, determined not to miss a spot. She straightened to watch the freighters as they disappeared from sight.

In the common room, she thought about Janey's dress. Using a needle with some beechnut dyed thread, Rebecca had made enough point lace to trim the neckline along with the bodice.

"Parthia, tonight we bake bread. Mix the dough and set it out to rise while I work on Janey's dress for the social. It's a little over four weeks away."

"Yes Mistress, soon as I finish chunking the stew meat." Parthia looked up. "Four weeks you say?"

"Yes, Saturday, the eighteenth of next month. September may be cooler."

Rebecca hurried to the sewing room, near the middle of the house. The shade from a big elm tree made sewing in August more pleasant.

Clipping the silver chatelaine to the leather belt circling her waist, she carefully unfolded the dress, basted together with single line stitches. Placing it on the smooth table Starlyn made for the sewing room, Rebecca sat on a stool and began to stitch up the dress.

The hemline of the narrow, straight length dress should brush the top of Janey's new shoes. Rebecca had not wasted a fiber of the expensive blue material cutting it out. The young men visiting family in Starlight were sure to take a look.

The dress Rebecca had worn to marry Starlyn required more cloth for the bunched out, full back contour. She had taken the dress apart to turn the ivory colored material into a Sabbath dress for Janey when she turned five. There was material left over.

She removed scissors from the case dangling off the chatelaine, and clipped loose threads from the material. Snipping a length of silk thread for the needle, her task began. She thought about Ransom as she worked.

Starlyn made long deliveries that sometimes kept him away at night. She was not used to Ransom being gone from home, especially for such a long time. Rebecca's thoughts turned to the social to be held at Alonzo and Ella Jane Sanford's house. Alonzo's grandparents came along after Starlyn's Great Aunt Elizabeth helped start the community.

Rebecca sewed the bodice, following the basting stitch. Rosie's dress needed looking over. When she grew older, Rebecca would make a pretty new...

"Mother, Parthia wants to know which vegetables to use." Janey stood in the doorway.

"Tell her I'm coming."

Rebecca stuck the needle crossway in the material, marking her place.

* * *

Saturday, August the twenty-first

As the sun rose, Starlyn remembered the previous night's red sky, indicating a clear day for travel. The five men stood in a grove of trees eating cold provisions from the food box. He thought about the good supper that waited for him, Ransom and Burl in Charlotte Town. After the men finished, Starlyn put Albert Johns' wagon at the head of the group for the drive to Salisbury.

Near the middle of town Albert turned right on the

road going west to Lincolnton. Four days later Albert and Johnathan would return to Salisbury, pick up a load, then travel with Starlyn and the others back to Starlight.

Starlyn slowed for Burl to catch up then continued through Salisbury on the Great Wagon Road for forty miles. They turned west toward Charlotte Town, with less than five miles to go.

"Da. Da!" Ransom called from the lazy board. "Burl's got a problem."

Stopping the team, Starlyn jumped down from the horse. Burl's right front wheel sat in a deep rut at a bad angle. One wrong move meant trouble.

He hurried over, calling "Don't move the wagon. You will break that axle."

"I regret this, Mr. Craighead." Burl looked into Starlyn's face, then down.

Starlyn understood.

"Then what happened, driver?"

"I did not notice the wagon drifting. Caught in the rut, I tried to drive out but the wagon veered off. I think that cracked the wheel," Burl said.

"Well then, what must you do to keep from breaking the new one?"

"I…I am not sure. Ain't ever done this before."

Starlyn rubbed his chin. "Get a spade, widen out the rut and drive the wagon back onto the road."

Burl dug hard for fifteen minutes, turning the rut into a straight trough, before Starlyn decided the wagon should roll through.

"Ransom, take off the brake then slowly start the horses pulling. Stop the team when I call out."

Several starts and stops later the wagon rested on

level ground.

"Burl, you need a new wheel. Rance, set the brake then unhitch the team."

Ransom worked, as Burl went after one of the wheels Starlyn insisted the freight wagons carry. Starlyn returned from the tool box with what they needed.

Placing the jack under the axle, Burl raised it then removed the linchpin to take off the busted wheel.

Satisfied his driver knew how to remove the wheel, Starlyn waited for him to finish. Burl rested the new wheel on the axle, dipped a cupped hand in the bear grease container to rub a heavy coating of thick yellowish tallow on the axle.

"Take the price of the wheel out of my pay," Burl said, as he worked to put on the new one.

"Maybe I will just consider that busted wheel part of your learning."

Until now only small problems troubled their trip. Starlyn bent down to check the linchpin, then straightened up, a hand on his lower back. The evening sun hung low on the horizon, the golden circle enveloped with red.

They were five days out on the haul. What he wanted was a fair night's sleep at Charlotte Town's tavern, stomach already growling at the thought of good food. The roughest freighters Starlyn knew frequented the tavern. Some slept with a mere blanket between them and the wood floor, so long as they got a good supper.

Only two miles out of town, with the sun sinking fast, Starlyn must hurry. "Ransom, untie my horse."

He went to the wagon, readied a lamp, grateful for the visibility the bright, whale oil light provided. Ransom returned with the horse and Burl.

"Lad, guide the wagon from the wheel horse." Starlyn tossed him the jerk line. "I'll signal with the light. When I shift the lamp in either direction, move the wagon closer to that side."

"How much do I angle over?"

Starlyn shifted the lamp, light reflecting off his son's creased face. "Move the wagon just a few feet. If I lower the lamp, stop."

Ransom nodded.

"Burl, drive behind Ransom. Do exactly what he does. There are spots along the road's edge with enough loose dirt to almost swallow a wagon wheel. We are stuck if that happens." Starlyn gave Burl the lamp. "Hand it up when I'm in the saddle."

Starlyn mounted, took the light and started the ride to Charlotte Town.

* * *

Ransom's shoulders rose, eyes trained on the lamp, trying to anticipate which side of the dark roadway to guide the wagon. It seemed as if they traveled for hours. Startled, he almost called out when he heard Burl's lead horse get close to the back of the wagon.

Slinging an arm outward, Ransom shifted atop the wheel horse, briefly finding some relief. He forgot the pain when Father completely lowered the lamp. Ransom slid off the wheel horse.

"Something wrong, Da?"

"We are coming up where Steel Creek crosses the road. I don't know the condition of the ground."

"I'll take care." Ransom stepped up on the wagon tongue, slung a leg over the wheel horse's back and settled into place. Reins in hand he urged the team forward.

They reached Steel Creek, where Ransom drove the team through the churned up dirt of the shallow creek with little effort. It looked like Father's lamp blurred into two lights. Squinting, Ransom realized the new light did not move. He was sore, tired, and hungry. Could that be Charlotte Town?

Soon more lights came into view. Lamp high, Father led the way toward freighters gathered around Conestogas, who stepped out to meet him.

"That you, Craighead? Where did you come from with just a lamp?"

"Yes, it's me, Arnold. Lost a wheel out a ways but decided to come on for the good company."

"Pick a spot for your wagons then join us. It's not often a man rides in by lamplight, much less two wagons following."

Men walked ahead to point out places for the wagons, smoking as they went.

Ransom positioned the wagon then climbed off the wheel horse. A man shoved a cigar into his hand, saying, "Any freighter traveling by lamplight deserves a free stogie."

"What's a free stogie?" Ransom said to his father as they unhooked the team of horses.

"Well then, they call them "stogies" because of the Conestoga freighters who smoke them when they travel. Free stogies only go to a driver who has earned it."

CHAPTER TWENTY-SIX

Wednesday, September 1st

Up before dawn, Rebecca hummed while fastening buttons at the waist, then up the front of the faded blue dress to the collar. After smoothing out the bedcovers she reached for a beechnut colored dress, trimmed in deep red, laying it across the bed.

In the common room, a servant set out food to prepare for the morning meal. Parthia, their longest indentured servant, did most of the cooking. Rebecca sliced fresh bread, thinking about how she had missed her husband and son. Back home for several days now, Starlyn worked on the freighting schedules, while assigning men to farming. He seemed pleased to have worked a full day on the new acres.

Rebecca wiped her hands as she spoke to Parthia. "Once the rice pudding is cooked, close the damper. Do not add wood to the cook stove. Today should be warm."

"I'll bank live coals for a fire to heat water later," Parthia said. "What about the back porch table for the men?"

"I'll send Janey and Rosie down."

Rebecca knocked on Janey's door. "Go help Parthia. Take Rosie with you. Your father will want to eat soon."

Not waiting for an answer, she hurried to change into the cream colored dress for her husband. Back in the common room, she put breakfast on the table before Starlyn and Ransom came in to clean up.

Rosie helped Parthia take food out to the men then returned to sit at the trestle table. Starlyn and Ransom joined the women.

During breakfast, Ransom said, "Da, are you working on the new field today?"

"Yes lad. I feel an urgency to get that done."

Ransom took two slices of ham off the platter. "Well then, I will work with you."

Starlyn tapped his chin. "I think you should help the women gather fruit for the winter. Maybe work with me another time."

"I do not want to do women's work. Let one of the hired men help them."

Rebecca wondered if her husband hid a smile resting his chin in a hand.

"No, I cannot spare anyone to help them. You must not let your mother lift heavy loads when you are there to help. Then there's Janey, maybe Rosie, to worry about."

"Sure hope they appreciate me giving up manly work to help a bunch of females," Ransom said.

Janey pointed a finger. "You're not old enough to call yourself a ma…"

"Leave it alone, Janey," Rebecca said. "I am thankful for your brother's help."

Red clinging to her cheeks, Janey said, "Yes Mother."

* * *

Friday, September third

Starlyn rose before dawn thinking about that wet field. He thought it would dry out during August's hot days, but the wet land stayed wet. At times it stunk when he worked on it.

Starlyn stopped digging to stretch out a muscle cramp. Directly overhead the sun shone bright. He had worked all morning, time forgotten.

"Da, dinner's on the table." Ransom motioned him to come before riding toward the house.

Starlyn caught a glimpse of Felix coming from the area he worked on, still dotted with remaining stumps. They met near the shed, where their horses grazed.

"The field will be cleared in a couple of days." Felix turned to mount.

"Wait. Come home with me. Rebecca makes plenty of food."

Felix nodded. "After I finish the stumps I can help you. I'm thinking next Wednesday is the last day."

"I'll need help. Two feet down, I found clay. That requires trenching. That stagnant water I'm stomping around in needs drained before I put in good dirt." Starlyn rubbed his chin. "You will be compensated for this. I did not include working with me when I determined your pay."

"Star'n, there's no need for this. You honored the sale of Thomas's house when you did not have to."

"I insist on paying you. Come. We need to eat before I starve." Starlyn mounted his horse.

* * *

Saturday, September fourth

Rebecca ate breakfast with Starlyn in their sleeping room before starting the day. After supper the previous evening Starlyn worked late again in his shop, coming to bed after she fell asleep. This morning she picked his clothing off the floor and swept up wood shavings, unsure why they were there. He had taken a large round of wood out there, staying late into the night. Perhaps he tended a sick animal.

Sewing the last bit of lace on Janey's new dress, she knotted the thread, satisfied with how it looked. The social was only two weeks away. The family enjoyed coming together with friends. Their daughter would catch the eyes of the young men, some coming from a distance to visit family for this yearly event.

A rustle from the sewing room door caught her attention. "Missus Craighead, are you too busy for a walk?"

Her heart beat faster studying his handsome face. Lips pulled to one corner in that boyish smile, his head tilted as if waiting for an answer.

"What a lovely way to enjoy our time together."

They walked down the hall to the back porch. Rebecca brushed a twig off the outside table before they started toward the steps. Sunshine warmed her face as they paused to gaze out over the land, filled with oak and maple. Starlyn took her hand when they descended the stairs.

"Let's go down for a drink," Starlyn said.

The man liked water directly from the spring better than a bucket. Once inside the spring house he dropped on both knees. Then he brought up water streaming from cupped hands for her. She enjoyed the sweet cool taste before dipping in fingers to fling at him.

Starlyn snapped his hands giving back some of the same.

"Better not do that if you want to sit at my supper table." Rebecca used a low tone.

He pulled her close then whispered, "I need your good food for nourishment, for strength. Do you want to turn me into a feeble old man?"

Laughter bound them together as Starlyn led her in a wide sweep toward the thick trees below the spring, where they strolled.

Her stomach tightened. "I'm hungry for a slice of the spice cake Janey baked earlier."

Clutching the shawl that covered her shoulders, she tucked each end into the bend of an arm, her gaze never leaving Starlyn's face.

"I shall have some, too. Only let us continue walking for a while longer."

* * *

Later at the house, Starlyn worked in the office assigning long distance loads to experienced drivers. After taking so much time to work the new acreage, he needed to catch up with their freighting business. He carefully entered drivers' names next to the short hauls on the roster with a thick, flat pencil.

He assigned one of the longer routes to Burl. The man had improved since the haul to Charlotte Town, when Ransom received a stogie.

Traveling back the following day when they stopped to eat, Burl had complained bitterly of busting that wheel until Ransom gave him the stogie. Burl protested at first, then stuck a twig to a coal and lit the stogie before scattering the fire.

Ransom had tied Starlyn's horse off the back of their Conestoga then crawled onto the lazy board. Starlyn looked back at Burl who seemed ready to travel. The man sat on his left wheel horse, reins in one hand, smoke curling off the stogie gripped in the other, face tilted upward. Starlyn struggled against a laugh as Burl proclaimed to the sky above.

"Driver deserves to smoke a stogie when he travels with freighting men."

A laugh told Starlyn his son would do well managing the men needed to run the business he would inherit. Everything that belonged to Starlyn would go to Ransom one day. Starlyn intended to spend his later years enjoying

Rebecca and their family.

Finished assigning routes, Starlyn went to find Rebecca.

He listened at the doorway but could not recall the name of the hymn she softly hummed while straightening up the sewing room. He waited until she turned toward the door to say, "When you are finished, I'd like to sit at the back porch table."

"I shall join you on the porch."

* * *

Rebecca set out two of Grandmother Craighead's saucers covered with wandering red roses, filling each with a slice of cake.

After serving Starlyn, something she found pleasurable, Rebecca sat at the table.

"How is the new field coming?"

"Hard work. I won't deny that. I am thankful for Felix's help." Starlyn took a bite. "Quite good. Must be your recipe."

"Yes, I taught her. In time, our daughter will make a fine cook."

They ate in silence until Starlyn said, "I want us to look at that land. We'll take the shay Father bought before I was born."

"I remember that carriage. It must be full of cobwebs." The thought of spiders troubled her.

"Not now. Burl took it out from the shed where it was stored and cleaned it up." Starlyn pushed his saucer away.

"Just let me get a shawl."

She returned and he guided her down the steps to the shay. He whipped the reigns starting the tall mare down the road. Occasionally a tree displayed leaves turning red or gold, providing a glimpse of autumn's beauty. The sun lay warm on her, a gentle breeze tugging at the shawl.

Starlyn pulled alongside the property, pointing to one end. "Felix worked hard to clear the trees. Ransom helped him burn the stumps."

He shifted to point in the other direction. "I will finish there, soon, and that wet part should drain. It will be ready for Ransom to work in the spring."

"He will enjoy that, Star'n."

"I rode over to Rocky Mount last week to sign the papers finalizing ownership of this acreage. Well, holding it in trust, that is, until Ransom turns of age."

Rebecca eyed the wetland. Cool air brought a faint stench that filled her nostrils. No wonder the man scraped his shoes before coming home then left them on the back porch.

"What is Morris Whitley's opinion of Ransom's trust?"

"I made the decision not to use him, buying the land through Mr. Shrewsbury's attorney." Starlyn turned toward her. "Nickolas Greer wrote out what we wanted and gave it to the clerk of the court, James Calloway, for recording.

"What did Jack think about not using your family attorney?"

"I did not seek my brother's counsel on this matter. I added Felix's name on the trust as an adviser to Ransom. His name comes off when Ransom assumes ownership."

"Do you think it best placing Felix on the trust?" Rebecca tightened her shawl.

"My father trusted him. I also trust him. Felix does not have a freighting business to run, like I do." Starlyn scrunched his chin. "He has more time to guide Ransom's use of the land."

"Then in December, on his birthday, do we tell

Ransom about the land held in trust?"

"Yes."

CHAPTER TWENTY-SEVEN

Monday, September sixth, 1802

Starlyn sat up, swinging his legs over the side of the bed, feet touching the floor. He stretched and took in enough air to almost burst his lungs. He had enjoyed the previous day's services. He only did the necessary work before gathering with the family. After supper he had sat on the porch with Rebecca until they retired for the evening.

Today, though, he must work that soggy field, something that surely tried his disposition. Pressing ahead on the land meant one day Ransom could work it and learn enough to make ownership worthwhile. Starlyn dressed, pulling on the old work boots, hungry for a good breakfast to take him through the day.

He hurried down the hall, passing a hand over Granda's clock while descending the stairs. In the common room Starlyn kissed his wife before taking a seat at the table.

"Breakfast will be ready soon." Rebecca handed him a pewter mug of coffee before sitting. "Parthia did a good job on your boots. It was thoughtful she set them by our door last night."

"Did you ask her to do that?"

"No, and I am not surprised a family in Starlight wants to employ her." Rebecca sighed. "When exactly does she leave us?"

"This Saturday, the eleventh, I will declare her

indenture completed to my satisfaction. I shall sign papers, furnish a set of new clothes as required, and provide Parthia, the freewoman, transport to Starlight.

"We have other capable servants," Rebecca said. "Still, I will miss her,

After the family ate, the children took care of chores while Starlyn had another mug of coffee. Placing the napkin on the table he stood and kissed her on the cheek.

"I must get started. Ransom needs time to dig out rocks. Then he will break up the big clods, for spring planting."

Rebecca rose, shaking out her dress. "That's six months away. Think he needs that much time?"

"Yes, if our son wants to raise a worthwhile crop on land that's never been planted."

Starlyn went to the freight shed and inspected the contents of the Conestoga assigned to Burl. The man had done a good job loading the freight. Now Starlyn expected better from this driver than a busted wheel.

He strode to the barn, saddled up, then headed for the wet acreage, mind already on the best area to place the furrows. Arriving, he struck out across the scarred land where Felix worked to pull a stump out using an ox. The acreage that once held an abundance of timber now contained only a small stand of trees.

"Need the animals today, Felix? I must put in a main trench."

"I will soon need both oxen to drag the timber where it goes. For now, take that one." Felix pointed toward the tied up animal. "Soon as I finish here, I'll bring this one."

Starlyn walked the ox to the wet land then studied where to put in the drainage furrows. He did not intend to leave land unused just for being soggy. After marking the first five furrows then harnessing the ox to a plow, the animal moved forward with some urging.

Swiping at his forehead with an arm, Starlyn struggled to keep the plow on course. It bit into the ground throwing wet earth up on each side of the blade. Encouraging the ox to pull, he worked through part of the morning.

Felix arrived and hitched both animals to a double wooden yoke, staying long enough to guide the team while Starlyn cut the first layer of trench.

The sun stood directly overhead. Starlyn stopped and almost went home to eat, but ignored the hunger to finish the trench. Felix needed those oxen tomorrow.

He deepened the cut, occasionally stopping to look around, but quickly returned to work. Back bent forward, forearms gripping the plow handles, Starlyn struggled through the trench behind the stout animals. His calf and thigh muscles strained as he held the line to move the oxen forward.

After each pass down the trench Starlyn turned the animals around to head back in the opposite direction. The mire reached his knees while struggling to keep the plow straight on the final pass. Rocking back the blade and guiding the animals away from the trench, his numb hands fumbled with the yoke as Felix walked up.

"Here, let me take the animals to cut in the last furrows."

Grateful for the Irishman's help, Starlyn reached for a shovel. Dirt flew while traveling the length of the cuts, removing the peaks of damp earth. Working until there was no energy left, he started the ride home.

* * *

Leaving Parthia to tend the contents of the big kettle,

Rebecca went to the back porch to wait for Starlyn. The sun cast rays on trees in the distance as it started its descent toward the west. The previous day Starlyn went directly to bed. Today at breakfast, he had filled his plate more than once as he ate and laughed with the children before leaving for the field.

A cool breeze reminded her to spread a heavier quilt on the bed. Far down by the freighting shed, her husband rode toward the barn. Happiness filled her when he arrived at the house.

"I made some progress today." Starlyn ran a hand across his middle. "Sure am hungry."

Struggling out of muddy boots, he carefully picked his way to the door. Rebecca followed, smiling at his tender-footed hop.

She helped Parthia set food on the table while Starlyn cleaned up. Janey sliced bread, setting the plate alongside a dish of mounded butter, while Rosie filled a pitcher with milk.

Starlyn entered in clean clothes, hair combed back. "Do I smell better now?"

"Considerably."

Later they sat on the porch with coffee and a slice of Rosie's apple-spice cake.

Starlyn pushed back his chair when they finished. "I am tired."

* * *

Starlyn struck out for the barn to saddle up. The black stallion snorted, head going up. He favored this tall animal over the others. Loosening the reins, he leaned forward, the breeze combing through his hair. After three more days of steady work, that field should be ready for Ransom.

Slowing the stallion to a walk, Starlyn cut across the

field, reaching the lower end of the land to examine the furrows. Last night's wind storm scattered debris that mixed with the mud, slowing drainage from the trenches. Reaching for a shovel, his work began.

He looked up when Felix arrived with the oxen.

"I finished early. Thought you could use the animals along with some help."

Starlyn heaved a sigh of relief. Maybe today would be shorter.

* * *

Saturday, September the eleventh.

Starlyn slept late. Three days had passed since putting in drainage ditches. He assigned drivers to freight shipments and oversaw crop storage for the winter.

Signing the papers concluding Parthia's indenture contract, he went to find Ransom.

"I am ready to take Parthia to her new home. Care to drive the wagon for me?"

"I'll hitch the horses right away," Ransom said.

Later at supper Rebecca said, "Something wrong? You barely touched the turkey soup." She leaned toward him. "I made it just the way you like."

"It's good. I just do not feel well. Going to bed."

"Yes, do that. You must feel better for next Saturday. It's the social."

Walking to the staircase at the front of the house, Starlyn wondered what could have him feeling so bad. Upstairs, removing his shoes, he fell into bed fully clothed, asleep by the time his head touched the pillow.

* * *

The next morning he awoke to an empty bed. Swinging legs over the side he sat up, blinking at the light coming through the draped windows. Standing, his knees gave way sitting him back down on the bed.

Rebecca entered with a tray, placing coffee and food on a small table. The smell of bacon almost emptied his stomach.

"Are you hungry?" She reached for the plate.

"I just want some coffee."

He took a sip, forced it down, then burped a sour smell before pushing the mug toward her. "I cannot attend services today."

"Still not feeling well?"

"I never felt worse. Send for Doctor McKenna."

Starlyn lay back, drifting to sleep. He awoke when Rebecca opened the sleeping room door and Doctor McKenna entered.

"What troubles you, Starlyn?'

"Hiram, I just do not feel well."

"What hurts?"

"My head. Pain around the eyes. The bitterest taste in my mouth."

Dr. McKenna listened to his complaints. "Starlyn, you are healthy. I want to see what comes tomorrow."

"You think that is best?" Starlyn said.

"Yes. I'll stop by in the morning."

* * *

Monday the 13th

Doctor McKenna swished the bucket of bile Starlyn had vomited overnight. He checked his tongue and found a yellow coating.

"Anything different about how you feel?"

"Muscle spasms make me tired. I want fresh air."

Hiram edged the vomit bucket closer to the bed, removing from his pocket a dark ivory container about the size of thumb. Taking out the small lancet the doctor felt for a vein in Starlyn's arm. A precise slit started the blood running off the patients arm into the container. Satisfied with the amount of bleeding, he sealed off the wound.

"Let's see how you feel tomorrow, Starlyn."

* * *

The next day

Hiram's gnawing fear that came when first tending Starlyn, continued. If he could not heal him soon, his friend might not last very long. Regardless, he must keep that thought to himself.

Rebecca seemed to have a foreboding of some kind. Reluctant to talk about his concern the previous day, he simply had instructed her to give Starlyn as much beef broth as he would eat.

Hand in a pocket, Hiram went to tend Starlyn but decided against another bleeding. How much good did purging, sweating or letting blood do a sick body, anyway? Especially bleeding, since the procedure had not helped the first time. Some physicians stood by all these methods, favoring one over another. Hiram preferred herbs, barks, or prepared medicines, having received good results from using them.

After tending Starlyn today, the doctor went to have that painful discussion.

"Is my father going to die?" Janey grabbed his arm. Ransom pulled her back.

"I am sorry, Doctor." Rebecca stood ramrod straight, her face pinched up. "Janey is so worried about him."

"I understand how this must affect all of you," he said.

"What's wrong with my husband, Doctor McKenna?

214

Will Starlyn get better?"

Rebecca's gaze raked over Hiram as if daring him to tell anything but the truth. As if he would do that. Brow wrinkled and lips pressed together, she looked up to meet his eyes.

"Rebecca, I'm doing everything possible to bring Starlyn through this. Right now it does not look good. Pray. You must all pray for the Good Lord's guidance."

* * *

Wednesday

"Rebecca, send Felix for Jack," Starlyn said.

"Felix is in bed, sick."

"What happened to him?"

"I do not know, only that Doctor McKenna is also tending him."

"Then send one of the men. I need to see Jack."

His wife must not suffer through this. Starlyn sat up in bed. Could Rebecca stand up under the strain if the outcome should be his death? Starlyn had determined that Jack must help construct a will and act as administrator. Starlyn trusted him to take care of Rebecca and their family.

When Jack arrived they set out the will the way Starlyn wanted. They needed one more witness signature. Morris Whitley, their family attorney, sent for Henry McClellan, who soon arrived.

Starlyn struggled to hold the writing quill. Jack stood beside his bed, watching. Starlyn's feelings reflected the mood of those around him. He must recover. The late afternoon light filtered in through the windows of the large sleeping room, mingling with the lamp light to create a peculiar glow.

"Whoo—whoo—whoo."

They grew quiet when the owl's call floated in on the evening air from the dense forest. All activity stopped. It interfered with Starlyn signing his name to the will. The elusive bird's forlorn call only added to the unhappy task at hand.

"That devil birds' gotta be wrong," someone said. "Starlyn ain't gonna die!"

Jack leaned over and took Starlyn's hand, guiding the quill into an "X", then stepped back. Starlyn was too weak to stop him. He had wanted his signature on the will, not an 'X'.

Sometimes this act of signing called forth the rumor a man could not write. Starlyn did not want this question raised, should he die. Few around were better educated than he. Still, it was done, he supposed.

After the witnesses signed his will they gathered around the bed to drink a brandy. Starlyn clung to the hope this get-together would prove unnecessary and one day they might laugh about it.

The men were hardly gone before severe muscle aches gripped him.

"Jack, pour me a dose of Hiram's paregoric elixir. I cannot stand this pain.

CHAPTER TWENTY-EIGHT

Autumn promised to be long and beautiful, such as Starlyn had not seen for several years.

"What did you work on prior to growing ill?" Dr. McKenna said.

"I put the men to harvesting crops then scheduled some freighting."

"I just cannot see that being a problem." The doctor scratched his chin. "Anything else?"

"Well, yes. I worked on breaking up a new field, with help from Felix."

"Felix, did you say?"

"He removed the trees. I worked on a portion so wet and stagnant I was forced to set up drainage. Felix also helped me put in a big trench."

The doctor said, "Why do this in the fall instead of waiting until early next year?"

"I wanted it dried up for Ransom to plant in the spring."

The doctor stood, a distant look on his face as he turned toward the door. Starlyn heard him speak to Rebecca in the hall before leaving.

No one knew how he had caught this illness. A flurry of speculation caused a few people in the community to get in an uproar. They started calling it 'a witching'. Shortly after surfacing some of that talk fell by the wayside. Most seemed to be forgotten but he suspected a few discussed it quietly with friends.

"Here's some broth and a slice of warm bread." Rebecca set down a tray. "What's troubling you?"

"I am still thinking about the gossip over my illness." These holdouts from the truth worked tirelessly to raise suspicion about others. "I was told that witchings had happened before in Starlight."

Rebecca dabbed at her eyes. "The thought that anyone in the community would see your illness as an act of darkness hurts me."

"We cannot change what they think," he said.

Rebecca nodded. "Our congregation is working against this. While these people speak of evil acts, we quietly pray against it. Their dangerous talk may soon die down."

Starlyn shifted in bed. "That will be none too soon for me."

"Doctor McKenna wants you to stop using the stairs for now. Is that alright with you?"

"Well then, I'll consider the doctor's wishes."

* * *

Jack's visits increased in the next few days, worrying that Starlyn could die. He recalled an incident in their youth when the Pritchett brothers caused him problems. The two came looking for a fight, always with both against him. Jack put great effort into avoiding them. That may have continued if not for Starlyn.

"We are brothers. If you have trouble, come tell me," Starlyn had said.

Then their cousin Andrew had taken most of Starlyn's time. They were always together. Jack was glad when Uncle Alexander moved Andrew and their family to North Carolina.

Starlyn survived the war and Jack decided no one must ever separate them again. He loved his brother with a passion. They would both continue on through life together until they were old men.

During one visit, Jack and Starlyn discussed the possibility of death.

"The thought of not being with Rebecca until our children are grown, troubles me. I never thought my life could end like this."

"You must not dwell on that," Jack said. "You are not going to die."

Starlyn looked down at his hands. "It breaks my heart to think they might be alone."

"If it comes to that, they would not be alone. I shall be there."

"Jack," Starlyn gripped his hand. "Promise me you'll take care of my family if I cannot."

"Do not worry, brother. I will do that."

Making him swear to do as Starlyn wanted was not an act either man was accustomed to. However, it seemed to bring his brother some comfort.

"Your family would not need much, except guidance on legal matters. I give you my word I will take care of them."

Relief filled Jack when Starlyn nodded. Both of them had been cautious handling their affairs. They learned this from their father, a prudent man.

* * *

September seventeenth

"Supper is almost ready. I wish to eat with you." Rebecca sat in the stuffed chair. "Have you thought about not using the stairs for now?"

"Being on the first floor will help if I choose to sit

outside." He smiled, eyes lighting up. "Ransom must assist me down to the common room where I'll have supper."

"Janey will help Rosie get Parthia's old room ready." Rebecca stood. "We're having beef chunks in broth, with vegetables."

The sunlight at her back, she left their room, knowing he would soon recover.

Later, when they ate, he took several bites of the beef then leaned back, gazing at her.

"Tomorrow is the social. You could take the children." He spooned up broth.

"I am not sure, Starlyn. It just does not feel right…"

He slumped forward, head sideways, words garbled by the liquid.

"Father, don't try to talk." Ransom lifted his head while Rebecca used a napkin to wipe his mouth. "What should we do, Mother?"

Rebecca laid a hand on Starlyn's forehead. "We must get him into bed."

Janey and Ransom helped him down the hall, as Rosie ran ahead. When they got there Rosie had the covers turned down, with a pail set close to the head of the bed.

Rebecca spread another quilt over him. Starlyn soon fell asleep.

* * *

Saturday, September 18

Rebecca poured Starlyn coffee when he came to breakfast. He seemed to feel better. They ate until Starlyn spoke up.

"Jack and Lydia are attending the social. The children could accompany them."

"I don't know," Rebecca said.

"Father, will you and Mother attend?" Ransom said.

"No. I don't believe we will go."

Her husband's gaze rested on each child before meeting her eyes.

"There is no reason the children cannot attend with their uncle Jack," Rebecca said.

"Then it's settled," Starlyn nodded. "They are stopping here first."

Later, Rebecca brought out Janie's new gown. She had mended Rosie's best dress. It looked almost new. When they went to change, she brought out Ransom's clothes. A dark blue frock-coat with lapel and black pantaloons hung over the crook of her arm.

"I did not expect to dress in such handsome clothes." Ransom gave her a kiss on the cheek. "Mother, you found the time to sew me such a fine frock?"

"Yes, Son. The girls are not the only important ones in the family. You are, too." She handed him the clothes then took a pair of black Hessians from behind a table. Those boots should fit. "Hurry. Uncle Jack will soon be here."

She went to sit with Starlyn in the office. "They will enjoy the social."

"Yes, I know. I just do not feel well enough to attend this time."

They sat together until Janey called out for them from the common room. Rebecca's heart lurched at the beauty of their daughter in the narrow, straight length gown brushing the top of her shoes. The blue material was worth everything Starlyn paid for it.

Rosie slowly turned around in a dark green dress, a gold corded belt with tassels at her waist. She was a sight, their little Irish beauty.

"Ooooh," Rosie said when Ransom entered the

room.

Janey said, "He almost looks like a man."

Rosie giggled. "Like a handsome man."

"Sister, your gown is sure to attract a suitor," Ransom said.

As he turned to Rebecca, the waist pleats in the back of the dark blue frock coat gave an excellent swish to his garment. She had fitted the frock over the shoulders and chest, drawing it back from the waist where it fell close to his knees. A row of rounded-out brass buttons ran down one side, the appearance of button holes stitched on the opposite side. No doubt Ransom would fit in with other young men. She sewed the black pantaloons to fit close through the hips and upper thigh area, following the style. Their son was a dashing lad, from the ruffled lace at his wrists to the tips of the black knee boots.

After the children left for the social they talked until Starlyn stood up. He almost fell.

"I will help you to bed," Rebecca said.

"No, I'm too heavy for you. Burl's at the freight shed getting loads ready for delivery."

"I'll send Dorcas. She's here doing the wash," Rebecca said.

"Try to keep her on," Starlyn said. "She could be some help."

"At her age, I don't know, but she has offered to stay for room and board."

"Poor soul needs some place to live. Keep her if you—hurry, send for Burl."

Before long, Burl arrived. He helped Starlyn from the chair, walking him down the hall to the sleeping room. He also helped Rebecca get Starlyn into bed.

After Starlyn fell asleep she went to the common room where Burl waited. She served him coffee with a slice of apple cake.

"Will Starlyn be alright? He doesn't seem well enough to look over deliveries," Burl said.

"You may have to wait on that."

"I am going to send out word that you need help." Burl rubbed his chin. "Right now I must get those wagons loaded."

Rebecca walked him to the door. She did need help with Starlyn at night.

* * *

Sunday

It was barely daylight when Jack came by to see Starlyn. Rebecca let him in, and he stopped to talk.

"Some men will stop by to sit with Starlyn. I intend to help some, too."

"Such a relief to hear that." The last few nights, she had tossed around before finally getting to sleep.

"I'll let myself out when I am ready to leave," he said.

They were not attending Sabbath services today. Rebecca went to the common room to build up the cook fire, something a servant did unless she got there first. Janey and Rosie started breakfast while she went to see Starlyn.

There was hardly anything in the bucket.

"You feeling bad? Should I send for the doctor?"

"No. I am better today." A smile crossed his face.

She gave him a kiss. "I'll bring some breakfast when it's ready."

Back in the common room Rebecca said, "Jancy, take your father a mug of coffee. He's feeling better."

Rebecca worked with Rosie getting breakfast on the table, then tasted Janey's stewed apples. They were good.

Once in the bowl the apples only needed a dusting of cinnamon.

A knock sent her to the front door. It was Moses Bryant.

"Come in. Care for a mug of coffee?"

"No. I came to offer Ransom, Janey and Rosie a ride to services." Moses followed her to the common room.

"As one of our circuit riders, don't you usually replace other pastors in the pulpit? Are you visiting Malcolm's church today?" She sliced some bread.

"Malcolm left for Tennessee two days ago. Reverend Ewing, a fellow minister, requested his attendance at several revivals. One in Kentucky."

"Oh, I did not know Malcolm had gone."

"Yes, and for a while. I am standing in the pulpit until he returns."

Rebecca laid the knife on the sideboard. "Moses, your offer is very kind, and I know Starlyn appreciates your friendship. I believe the children will stay home with me today."

"Is Starlyn awake?" Moses blinked. "I want to visit with him."

"Rosie, will you show Moses the way? Tell Janie to come help."

Later in the day, Rebecca went to sit with Starlyn. When it grew late, Janey came in to light the candle lamp. Rebecca rose to leave, kissing her sleeping husband on the forehead. He felt warm. Back in the common room Ransom entered with Burl. Not long after that, Abb and Maggie Moore came in.

"Abb and me are sitting with Starlyn tonight," Burl said.

"I came to make the coffee," Maggie said. "Even put together some food. You do not need to worry about any of that."

Rebecca patted Maggie's arm. "Thank you for coming. I am just so tired."

"Go on to bed. I will take care of things." Maggie's hand gently urged Rebecca toward the door.

She climbed the stairs, the baluster smooth as satin under her hand. Undressing, she pulled on a cotton shift then slid under the covers. Too exhausted for tears, sleep came quick.

In the early hours before dawn something woke her. Still groggy, swinging feet over the side of the bed, she struggled into clothing and inched her way toward the door. Stepping into the hallway, grateful for the light, Rebecca started toward the stairs.

She entered the common room as Burl set down a coffee mug.

"Is everything all right with Starlyn?" she said.

"Seems to be. I am just going in to take my turn." Burl stood.

"Why don't you have more coffee? I'll sit with Starlyn."

"I'll get it," Maggie said.

Rebecca passed Abb in the hall. Her step quickened on the way to Starlyn's room.

Uncertainty flooded her thoughts, the night so still, as she grasped the cold knob and pushed open the door.

CHAPTER TWENTY-NINE

Starlyn awoke with chest pain. Bile crept up his throat when he tried to sit up and spit. He could not move. In a corner, dim lamplight flickered off a large armoire, casting shadows along the walls. He drifted in and out of sleep, confusing the shadows with people. Did Father call for him?

A gut-wrenching thought of losing Rebecca brought him part way up, pushing bitter gall into his mouth. How long before Burl or Abb returned? He would ask for his wife.

Did Roger already take her away?

The door opened. Rebecca entered the room and came to his side. God had answered his unspoken prayer.

He took her hand, feeling skin so soft it felt like his fingers might sink on through. "I love you. Concerned about our family..."

"Do not worry. You shall take care of us."

He clung to her words as his legs drew up. His body writhed as if he had tumbled down a hillside. Perspiration blurred his vision. Did Granda just hurry away? Wait...he was off fighting the British when Granda died. He scrabbled at the covers trying to reach out to stop him, to say "Good bye". He loved Granda.

He turned toward her touch. "Promise me you will not go with Roger—that you will say 'no'."

* * *

What was her husband talking about? Years ago

Starlyn and Roger agreed that the loser of their fight must stay out of her life. Did he speak of that?

"I promise you Starlyn. Roger never enters my thoughts."

"I am thirsty."

She filled a goblet then steadied his shoulders while he sipped. Water trickled out of his mouth, pooling in the hollow of his throat. She grasped the hem of her skirt, wiped his neck then pulled a chair close to the bed.

He did things she could not understand. His fingers scratched at the quilt and he mumbled toward the corner of the room. The thought he might die entered Rebecca's mind. She drove that thought away.

"I love you Starlyn. Save your strength to get well. To be free of this bed."

"Do not leave me," he said.

He found her hand and she drew strength from his touch.

Voice trembling, face turned toward the lamp, Starlyn said, "Let me talk to you."

Rebecca scoured the corner looking for what he spoke of.

* * *

The shadows melted away, as bright light draped the room. In the distance members of his family came into view. "Andrew, where have you been? I missed you. Where is Granda?"

"I am here, Starlyn, waiting. Look. Granda is coming."

Starlyn turned toward Rebecca. He could not leave her. "Hold my hand. I must not go."

Her grasp tightened. "The only place for you to go is breakfast, when you feel better."

A man strode down the white graveled road that ended at the foot of Starlyn's bed. Was that the big man from the battlefield who did not die?

"Who are you?" Starlyn said.

"I have been sent for you."

"What do you want?"

"I am here to take you home."

"What about Rebecca?"

The light grew and the road widened as he searched its path going up the hill. People smiled at him as they called greetings. They were his family. The ones standing to the side smiled too, and waved. He had never seen grass so green or flowers as pretty as these.

He looked at Rebecca. She was his family. It grew dim in the room. She asked him what he was talking about. He had trouble understanding why. Starlyn wanted to go with the big man, but Rebecca's grip on his hand was strong.

"You are going home," the man said. "She will be along when her time comes."

Tears filled his eyes, as his body groaned to be in the beautiful light that spilled over from the man. It dimmed as the man stepped away.

As the man reached out, he looked down at his wife who grew distant. "I will see you when it is time."

Starlyn took his hand. They started up the road where Granda waited along with their family in a field of blue flowers.

In the distance, beyond Granda, a man shrouded in white with a golden light in his face smiled and Starlyn's heart leapt with joy.

* * *

Rebecca tried not to cry as Starlyn squeezed her hand.

228

Then his grip loosened. She hung on as he thrashed around on the bed. What had he meant by, "What about Rebecca?" Or when he said, "I shall see you when it is time?"

She thought maybe he had not spoken to her, but who could he be talking to?

He rolled toward the edge of the bed. Raising an arm, he clawed toward the air and groaned before dropping back. She used both hands to enfold his.

* * *

Starlyn looked back at Rebecca again. She and the children would need to manage without him. Jack had promised to take care of them and that brought comfort.

"I will always love you."

As his body strained, he broke free of the bonds that held him to the world.

* * *

"Tomorrow I will fix that turkey soup you like. It will give you strength."

Rebecca pulled the covers up around his shoulders. The night air was cool.

She sat beside him, unwilling to turn loose of his hand. As long as she could feel some warmth she would not acknowledge he was leaving. He sighed, his breath sounding like seeds rattling in a dried gourd.

Grey dawn cast shadows over her husband's body. When his fingers grew cold, Rebecca turned loose. Loneliness engulfed her as she struggled to stand.

She must hurry now. Time was short. Rebecca started toward the door.

CHAPTER THIRTY

Monday, September 20

Today Starlyn's body lay on the cooling board, covered from the waist to the knees, waiting to be readied for the casket before the cold death set in.

"You wished to speak with me, Rebecca?" Doctor McKenna said.

Rebecca dug deep in a pocket and handed the doctor two silver coins. "I would like these to replace the coppers Burl put on his eyes. I just do not feel right about doing it."

"This can be troubling for a wife." The doctor removed the copper off the eyes and rested a silver coin on top of each eyelid.

"I will wait with the men until you need us," the doctor said.

Elizabeth, Starlyn's aunt, came to stand beside Rebecca. Janey entered with Fergus' mother, Matilda McClutcheon, who had offered to help them clean the body.

Rebecca sighed, grateful for the help. "Matilda, when you lose someone, we'll be there during your hard time."

Elizabeth patted her back. "We must get started."

Rebecca recalled their last visit to Aunt Elizabeth, and the gift they took home. It seemed longer ago that Starlyn's aunt presented them with the beautiful quilt, but it had just been three months earlier.

Every woman in their community envied Elizabeth

Craighead Shepard's sewing skills, with the stitching perfect, the weight substantial. It was no small thing to receive a bed covering from her. The soft, bright colors made her work desirable. She arranged the blocks in an original pattern, showing little evidence of stitching.

Their quilt had the Craighead family mark sewn on the bottom, as did all she made for the family.

"Aunt Elizabeth, I want to place your quilt in the coffin." Rebecca held out the quilt. The look on her face caused Rebecca to wonder if this woman already knew the question before being asked.

"No, I think you should keep it for the children."

"I trust your judgment, Aunt Elizabeth."

Rebecca had saved the first quilt she pieced together as a new bride. She thought it important that his body lay on something familiar. Before they put him in the coffin, she would spread her quilt over the boards.

As women, a death in the family was something they could expect. Just as surely as a lively new soul came kicking and screaming into life—they would suffer the death of a loved one passing out of their world into the next.

Janey stood beside her, eyes turned away from the cooling board. Sorrow now lay over the room so thick it could almost be felt.

"Mother, what do you want me to do?"

Janey needed to help get her father's body ready, even if that work troubled her. Their daughter should take her rightful place, no matter...

"Maybe Janey can bring what we need and keep the pan filled," Matilda said.

Rebecca agreed. "Such a relief not to worry who will take care of the water."

Janey left the room with the pan.

231

Matilda moved closer. "I did not intend to meddle in your affairs."

"No. You are right about this, Matilda. She needs to learn and can still get experience another time. I'll see to that."

Janey stayed busy providing supplies until Rebecca said, "Please get clothes to dress your father for the coffin."

She soon returned. "Will this do, Mother?"

Rebecca nodded when Janey held up what she chose.

"Yes. Let me fix it." Rebecca split the white shirt up the back. "It will go on easier."

They dressed him, but Rebecca insisted her daughter help with the shirt then comb his hair.

"I need the camphor oil along with a dry cloth," Aunt Elizabeth said.

Janey returned, handing Elizabeth what she asked for.

"After I apply oil, my work is finished."

Janey said, "Why do you use the camphor?"

"It will slow down the discoloration."

Elizabeth soaked the cloth with camphor and wiped his face, adjusted the coins on his eyes then said, "Goodbye". She did this as their family matriarch, an aged and grand woman bidding a final farewell. Wracked with grief, she hovered over him mourning their loss. Bending her stately head, she kissed him on the forehead.

"I'll be seeing you again, lad, when the heather blooms for me."

Elizabeth raised herself up as a ray of sunshine came through the window. The light caught the gemstone-lined combs placed in the twist of silver hair piled atop her head. It produced a brilliant sparkle of colors that glinted off the walls, like flecks of light cascading through a stained glass window.

* * *

Doctor Hiram McKenna accompanied the men to
Starlyn's body. He had not intended to be there but Jack
wanted him in the room. Felix, Starlyn's friend, also helped.
Abb Moore, the man chosen to lead the work, seemed to
study the situation. The doctor knew Abb, the town
apothecary, to be well experienced in such matters.

Hiram pulled out his watch. "We should start. Time is
running out."

Abb strapped a wide piece of cloth up under the chin.
The doctor pressed a hand beneath the cloth, closing the
mouth until Abb tied a secure knot on top of the head. Felix
folded both arms across the chest. At Abb's insistence they
tied the knees together, along with the upper ankles. Working
as one, the three strapped the body to the cooling board. If
their work held, this body would fit the coffin after the cold
death set in.

Felix checked the coins on his friend's eyelids and
carefully adjusted them.

Doctor McKenna was glad that he did, remembering
when one of the coins on old Jeb Dickson's eyes slipped
before the funeral. They had him laid out but no one noticed
one eye glared around the coin.

"He's looking at me," a child screamed as he ran
through the house. They had caught the boy, finally settling
him down long enough to get through the funeral.

"When will the coffin be ready?" the doctor said, as
the men gathered around the wash pan to clean their hands.

"Burl and me took last night's watch," Abb said.
"Soon as we knew Starlyn passed on, Burl left to build the
coffin."

"The cold death should have his body ready by that

time," Felix said.

* * *

The early morning was pleasant like fall should be. Ransom gripped the railing with both hands and sucked in a mouthful of air. Grey squirrels gathered food down by the trees. The tranquility found on the back porch might help him with what was to come.

"Ransom, Mother sent me to get you. Hurry, she's waiting."

He looked back at Janey, who stood in the doorway.

"What does she want?"

"You must watch for Burl. Let her know when he arrives."

"Tell Mother I know what I am supposed to do."

Before long, Burl drove the wagon in, along with another man. Ransom helped unload his father's coffin then went ahead to tell Mother.

* * *

"Abb, Burl is here." Rebecca straightened up the room as they brought in the wooden container built for her husband's body. She spread the quilt over the bottom, smoothing it out.

After Abb removed the straps, the arms and legs stayed in place. They moved the body from the cooling board, placed it on the quilt then closed up the coffin. The doctor left and the other two waited to move it where Rebecca wanted.

"Be careful taking it through the door," she said.

The men angled the coffin to the front room that opened to the right off the large entryway. The curved staircase, which ended close to Starlyn's office, lay directly across from the front room door. The following morning

234

there would be visitation. Later in the day they would put him in the ground. Following the burial, family would gather at the house with neighbors, to break bread and remember Starlyn.

* * *

While the children slept, Rebecca began her Widow's Night. It was time to say goodbye to her husband in a fashion that had been a part of her family for generations. She knew what to do, just as her mother, grandmother and the women before them had known. This night belonged to Rebecca. She spent it with Starlyn. Widow's Night began by clipping a length of his hair to add with the silver coins removed before burial. These objects of mourning, destined for remembrance, must be placed in a carved box Starlyn had once given to her.

She drew her memories of their love, their life, on his coffin using different colored paints. The big house that witnessed so much laughter through the years now remained silent. The thick wooden planks of the front room floor gleamed richly from years of polish and wear. Lamps cast light on the room, chasing the darkness back into the corners from where it came, draping the coffin in a soft glow.

She included the Lord in her night of grief. The words that brought comfort in worship service thundered around the room tonight. She sang the hymns that drenched her soul in peace, claiming them for her own.

A woman possessed by grief like no other, she poured her heart into completing this labor of love. She completely broke down, crying out.

"Lord, be merciful to me, your faithful servant."

The night wore on. Tears coursed down her face as she hurried from paints to coffin in a race to beat the dawn. She swiped at the wetness using the backs of her hands and arms. Grief progressed to deep sobs as the task moved forward.

* * *

When her mother died, Janey would become the new keeper of their death traditions. Unable to sleep, she crept partway down the staircase where she could see through the doorway. The wall mirror Father brought home for Mother so long ago reflected the pain on the face of the woman he loved so well. Her mother's dark hair, shining under the room's soft light, had partially broken free of restraints to tumble down.

A creak from the downstairs floor sent Janey back up, where she huddled under the covers, grieving her mother's loss. She too cried for the man they loved so much.

She had been there through her father's illness, then his deathwatch. Old enough to be included in his burial preparation, she would be there when they put him in the ground. Janey would have seen death from illness and bed, to coffin, to the grave.

"Lord, please help Mother—and me." Janey pulled the covers over her head, escaping into sleep.

* * *

Rebecca brought her night to a close. She used up her last energy painting a final memory of their life together, their children's names, on the side of the coffin. First she printed Janey, then Ransom in large bold letters using red paint. She turned away, but came back to place Rosie's name after Ransom's.

Drained of emotion, Rebecca aimed for the staircase that lead upstairs. Once reaching the handrail, she could pull herself up to bed. Partway through the room, though, unable to go farther, Rebecca gave in to the inviting sight of the sofa. She lay down and went to sleep.

Lurching awake, a gnawing pain gripped the pit of her stomach. Something was wrong. She turned her face toward the back of the sofa. Then Rebecca remembered they would bury Starlyn today. She looked toward his coffin. There were four names, all in red. She sat up straight, rubbed her eyes then slipped back into sleep.

Later she awoke, confused, blinking in the predawn light. She had slept little during her Widow's Night. Propping herself on an elbow, she rubbed bleary eyes, crusty from dried tears and lack of sleep.

Last night she thought there were four names, Janey, Ransom, Rosie and another name that seemed familiar. She strained to recall, but like wisps of vapor rising from the ground, to be burned off by the morning sun, she almost remembered. Then the name was gone.

She perched on the edge of the sofa, eyes closed. It was a strange thing, those names. Right now, though, she must find strength to get through the day, for her and for the children.

The door opened. "Mother, are you going…I mean will you be…" Janey sat next to her. "I'm so worried about you."

"I am all right." Rebecca pulled her daughter close, rubbing her back.

She sang as she gently rocked her. "Thence He arose, ascending high, and showed our feet the way…"

Thoughts of the suffering her children must go through clouded her mind.

CHAPTER THIRTY-ONE

Wednesday, September 22

Jack stepped across the front room entryway to wait in Starlyn's office for the funeral to begin. He sat at his brother's impressive desk, fingers drumming, but soon stood to pace the room. The hair close to his collar swirled, tickling his neck, jaw dropping open in deep thought as his step quickened.

After their father passed on the fall of 1797 Starlyn inherited the family estate. Jack had not expected anything of significance, but Father willed him $5000 in gold coin. That, along with his desk and whatever mementos Starlyn did not want. It surprised him to get Father's desk, even more than the gold, but he received no land. Starlyn received all the land.

As second born, he was not entitled to anything Father owned, unless left to him.

Jack squinted, determined not to lose composure. After Starlyn had read their father's will, the unhappiness pressed in, despite what he received. With the thought he had not known such unhappiness since his father's death, Jack returned to Starlyn's desk to brood darkly over the past.

One hundred and twenty acres of timberland lay between the house they grew up in and the acreage Starlyn purchased. The family home sat on five of Father's one hundred and twenty acres. Thomas willed that land to Starlyn, which Jack understood. He did not understand why Father sold the family home on five acres to Felix, instead of leaving it to him.

Jack recalled going through their father's papers and personal effects with Starlyn when he came across a surprise. Trembling at the realization of what he held, Jack had turned away long enough to entertain a thought. 'Slip it in a pocket—just slip it in a pocket'.

That had seemed a good thing to Jack. That was also the first time he noticed the strange little feeling deep in his stomach.

* * *

"Virginia's a fine place to live in the fall of the year." Ransom heard his father almost as clearly as if he stood next to him. Standing on the broad planks of the back porch, staring down at their timberland, he thought about the good days now gone.

"Ransom Andrew Craighead, where are you?" Mother's voice startled him back to the present.

Not now, Mother. He needed more time.

Time to grow accustomed to being fatherless. And, time to become the man of the house. Swallowing hard, Ransom realized there must first be time to become a man. Something he must yet learn how to do.

He must still sit for academic lessons from Mother, like before Father's death. Glancing over a shoulder at the thick woods, recalling thoughts about their previous life, Ransom called, "I am coming, Mother."

He passed the table covered with food. Someone brought fried chicken with biscuits the size of a man's fist. Spotting a favorite, blackberry dumplings, he inhaled the aroma before moving on.

On any other day, Ransom may have drooled over

such mouthwatering fare. Today, he took no pleasure in knowing all that food was there for the eating.

Mother already laid out his shirt, jacket and trousers for the funeral.

* * *

"Mother, where is Preacher Bryant?" Ransom said.

"You will find him in your father's office."

Ransom crossed the entryway from the front room that went into the office.

Did her son interrupt Moses for something important, or did he need a man to talk to?

She stood by Starlyn's coffin as family or friends came to greet her. Her heart tightened in pain as several older women from their community paid their respects. Some hugged her or spoke encouraging words before moving aside.

Returning to the front room, Ransom had walked with a lengthy stride. His manly swagger was something only recently discovered, she suspected. Did the set of his shoulders speak of a new, unfamiliar sense of purpose? He stopped at Starlyn's coffin and Rebecca's gaze lingered on him.

The top would be nailed on the coffin before Moses said his final words. The preacher exited Starlyn's office, only to pace the wide entrance floor. His hand sent frizzy blond hair streaming away from his neck. Around the man's head, hair bounced off the back of his long bony neck as he increased his pace.

She must get the girls' attention. Moses was almost ready.

"Janey, Rosie, draw everyone closer," she said in a low voice. The girls did this with an appearance of proper order.

* * *

Preacher Moses Bryant waited in painful suspense, anxious to start the funeral. Today they must put a good man in the ground before his time. Moses cleared his throat and began to speak. Like a good hunting dog turned loose, he got on the scent of Starlyn's respectable life.

Around the room women broke down in tears. Men placed arms around loved ones as if to ward off the pain.

Determined to give his friend a proper burial, Moses stayed up half the night putting words to a eulogy that did right for a man who had always done right by him. Now, only the Lord knew of occasions when Starlyn gave Moses the benefit of the doubt.

"Starlyn Craighead was a decent man. A good friend to many in our community." Moses' voice grew keen in his ears. "At Cowpens, Starlyn held his cousin Andrew while he died. That could have been Starlyn, but the Good Lord had a purpose for not taking him yet."

Moses rubbed at his forehead, lower lip dropping as his tongue searched for that familiar chipped tooth. A welled-up tear almost defied his effort not to cry.

"Shortly after Cowpens, Starlyn received the Lord. He married Rebecca and they brought Janey and Ransom into the world. They took in little Rosie. Starlyn lived life the way the Good Lord said we should, in accordance with the principles in our Bible."

Pain welled up in Moses' heart from the grief in the congregation. He put voice to the truth about Starlyn's exceptional life. Skirts rustled, feet shifting as people cried out in pain from the loss of this family member, a neighbor, a friend.

"Go ahead, dear friends. Say goodbye to that God-fearing man. No doubt we shall see him when we pass over to the other side."

* * *

The closing words of the sermon rang out as the funeral march began. Men gripped the carrying staves as they toted Starlyn's wooden coffin out the front door. The haunting sound of hymns rolled out in front of the procession and into a clear sky. Almost bowed from the weight, they trudged up the path. Ransom carried the left front and his Uncle Jack carried the right.

The freshly dug grave waited on the hill, alongside his grandparents' graves. The pall bearers set the coffin down, next to the hole soon to fulfill its only purpose. Preacher Bryant asked the Lord to receive Starlyn Peter Craighead, as the pallbearers lowered the coffin into the ground.

A solemn group stood on the hill the early afternoon of September 22, in 1802. Ransom dropped the first clump of earth on his father's coffin then moved aside. Soon the air filled with the lonely sound of dirt hitting wood.

* * *

Rebecca's harsh cries escaped, filling the air. "Lord, help me. I don't think I can make it through this day."

As her plea flowed to Heaven, the pain became unbearable. Rebecca's world would never be right again. Others rushed to comfort a woman who could not be comforted. Rebecca joined in as the group's sorrow and pain poured forth in hymns that always brought peace.

"Hark! From the tombs a doleful sound;
My ears, attend the cry;
Ye living men, come view the ground
Where you must shortly lie."

The wind picked up, swirling leaves around Rebecca's feet. Heavy skirts moved under the strain of long dark fabric as women swayed in wide circles, keeping pace with the songs that accompanied Starlyn home.

* * *

Hiram McKenna hurried from the home Starlyn worked hard to build, for the only woman, it seemed, he ever loved. He left behind food and friends, stomach empty except for a growing knot. A dignified physician, and knowledgeable about the misfortunes of life, today he reached deep to keep some composure.

"Easy, Boy." He stroked the stallion's muzzle before mounting up for the ride home.

On the way, Hiram reverted to something that brought relief in his younger years. Loosening the reins, he slapped the horse's rump and the muscular stallion ran as if to catch the wind. Hiram leaned forward, enjoying the air blowing past his face before engaging the deep feelings surrounding Starlyn's death.

The horse settled into a fast gait, as the steady rap of hooves on the ground kept rhythm with the blood pounding in his temples. Cool air lifted the hair off his neck as the horse ran in the dim light filtering through the trees.

Usually a reserved person, today Hiram shook a fist at the sky in indignation. Face drawn up in agony, eyes focused on the blue above, he demanded, "What did I do wrong?"

Receiving no satisfaction, he vehemently declared of God, "Why—just tell me why I could not save this one?"

The horse slowed down, but the doctor continued to look for the one thing that may have saved this good man entrusted to his care. It was something that bothered him since Starlyn first took ill.

A sudden cloudburst sent Hiram riding along, miserable in the downpour. Passing a hand over the front of his face, he groaned. He had learned medicine from Dr.

Joseph Alexander twenty years earlier in South Carolina. One medical condition Joseph instructed his students on was a 'bilious fever'. He recalled Joseph's explanation for this instruction.

"While I studied medicine in Pennsylvania, a fever epidemic broke out in Delaware. They called it a bilious disorder. Many died." Dr. Joseph had slipped a hand in his pocket. "I made a decision to include the treatment learned during that epidemic in my training of all doctors."

Hiram wondered if Starlyn's strange illness had anything to do with this disorder. His symptoms sounded suspiciously like what the doctor said. He now suspected that could be what killed his friend.

He took his horse to the barn, rubbed him down and put out grain before going inside. The hired woman had been in to straighten the house. She left supper on the cook stove, table set, but Hiram could not find an appetite. He climbed upstairs, peeled off his clothes then fell into bed. The emotions in Hiram's heart struggled with his thoughts, as tears dampened the pillow he lay on.

* * *

After the activity from the funeral, it grew quiet around the Craighead place. Their community went about the necessary business of living. Meanwhile, Rebecca and the family huddled together in their misery. For the first time she fully understood they were alone, except for Jack. Without Starlyn to steer their path, to comfort them when life seemed unbearable, it almost became impossible to move forward.

Rebecca and her children must now take care of their property. Ransom was not accustomed to making those decisions. Nor was he familiar with being the man in their household. They had no one to do this but him.

She had to contend with Starlyn's will. They all wanted an answer to the question, "What would come from the will?"

And then there was Uncle Jack.

What about Uncle Jack?

* * *

Wednesday, September 29

Rebecca awoke early. Dressing, she went downstairs to prepare breakfast. Pushing away thoughts of Starlyn, while moving around the kitchen, she wondered why this day seemed more difficult than the last.

Later in the afternoon, that changed. It started when a stranger showed up at her door to make a delivery.

"You have the wrong place," she said. "We are not expecting anything."

"No, Ma'am," he replied "It belongs here." The man looked again at a document he held.

"You must be wrong."

She moved back when he stepped closer to point out Starlyn's name. She started to close the door when Jack rode up.

"I'll take care of this, Rebecca," he called.

Grateful Jack arrived, she turned to the man. "You can bring whatever it is to the back. I'll meet you there."

* * *

Jack slid off the horse and swiftly took the stairs to the front porch. The man whirled around to face him, an unclear look crossing his face.

"I'm Clayton Baxter," the man said, followed by a sharp nod. He swaggered away toward his wagon.

"Rebecca should consider herself fortunate I arrived in time," Jack said under his breath.

The man drove his wagon around back of the house

as Jack followed.

The deliveryman knocked and Rebecca opened the door.

"My name's Clayton Baxter. I deliver for Washington Iron Works. This is what Mr. Craighead sent with his order."

He handed Rebecca two blocks of wood. One had the Craighead mark carved into it, the other the form of a bird with one wing extended.

"I don't understand what this is," Rebecca said.

"Mr. Craighead, your husband I imagine, provided these blocks for the foundry, with the words and dates he wanted placed on a fireback."

"Yes he did. He is deceased. I am his brother, Jack Craighead. You can direct this information to me."

Clayton ignored Jack. "Mrs. Craighead, those blocks were pushed into the sand to create a mold in which molten iron was poured, to form the fireback."

Ransom came away from the barn, stopping to look.

"Hey, will a big strong feller like you give me a hand?" Clayton said.

"My young nephew has other things to take care of," Jack said. "I'll help you."

After Ransom backed off from the fireback, Jack helped Clayton pack it into the house.

The two men attached the fireback tabs to each side support to keep it from tipping forward, while Ransom cleaned out the fireplace. It took all three to push the fireback against the rear of the cavernous opening.

The excitement mounted in Rebecca and Janey.

Jack's eyelids tightened with suspicion as he probed for the truth about this traveler who seemed so intent on pleasing Rebecca. A warning took root. This man would be trouble.

It was timing that put Jack at the wheelwright's to place an order shortly after the ironmonger delivered Big George's iron shipment. The ironmonger had asked George for directions to Starlyn Craighead's home to make a delivery.

"A man just here wanted to know how to get to Starlyn's. I wondered about that with Starlyn dead a week, Jack. I don't know what..."

Jack had not let George finish his comment, but mounted his horse in one smooth stride then gave the animal his head all the way to Starlyn's place. Fortunately he heard about this. He did not need a stranger hanging around Rebecca.

CHAPTER THIRTY-TWO

"There is what?" Rebecca turned from the stove, wiped her hands then straightened out the apron.

"Umm, that smells mighty good, Rebecca."

The aroma of four freshly baked loaves rose from the nearby table. Rebecca stared in disbelief at his words. She pulled out a chair for Fletcher.

"Here, sit down."

Rebecca shook her head at the power of food over a man's thoughts. Placing a loaf on the cutting board, she sliced off crusty slabs.

"Janey, get Fletch the butter and jam."

"This enough bread, Fletcher?"

"I think so." He took the plate.

Rebecca patted her hair and swept a hand beneath her skirt before sitting.

"Now, what did you say?"

"Starlyn's will has a 'no appraisal' clause."

"Starlyn went over the will with me the day it was written," she said. "I do not recall that. I am sure I would remember."

"After I talked with Matilda, she thought you should know about the clause."

"That just cannot be true, Fletch. Starlyn would have told me."

Fletcher shrugged. "Matilda wanted you to know,

that's all."

"But how will Jack know the value of our possessions, Fletcher?"

"I do not know. Only that I heard Jack says Starlyn did not want an appraisal on his estate."

Rebecca pushed hair from her face and stared at a spot toward the wall. She remembered the day Jack helped her husband draw up the will. Starlyn had gone over every detail with her. Knowing this, she began to reason with Fletch.

"Just you ask Jack about that appraisal in his brother's will. He'll tell you Starlyn wanted it there."

"Rebecca, several men have tried to talk to him, only Jack's never home. He is over at Morris Whitley's just about every time someone stops to see him."

Rebecca heard him, but paid no attention. She had already made up her mind to speak with Jack. He would take care of everything. He promised Starlyn that he would stand by her and the children. Still, she should hurry to straighten out the matter.

Fletcher wiped his hands and rose from the table. Rebecca wrapped a loaf of bread in some cloth for him to take home to Matilda.

Ransom had eaten in silence, listening to their conversation. After Rebecca thanked Fletcher for coming, Ransom walked him to the door.

"I need the carriage, Rance. Hitch up Sampson and Delilah." She had always wondered why Starlyn named the horses that.

Reminding Janey to stir the stew, she picked up a well-worn shawl before going to the barn, where Ransom helped her into the carriage.

She gathered the reins, clicking her tongue softly. The

two horses started forward then increased their pace when she snapped the reins and clicked again. Rebecca settled into the seat, the thoughts in her mind moving as briskly as the horses taking her to see Jack.

Her instincts said something was not right. A tremble started as she drew closer to her brother-in-law's house.

She gathered her skirts then climbed down to tie up the team. An unfamiliar weight pulled at her heels as she started up the path, hesitating at the steps that led to the wide front porch. She remembered when those stairs seemed shorter, with Lydia's smiling face shining like a beacon guiding her into a safe harbor.

"Don't be so slow," Lydia would call, twirling around, her skirt hem brushing the porch.

On warm days the two sat there enjoying the breeze. They sipped something cool while talking about new fashions or their love for their husbands. Occasionally they spoke about how each seemed to fit so well into the Craighead family.

She had giggled at the look on Lydia's face when she first tasted a lemon. Lydia had sliced off the end, sucking hard, only to pucker up and exclaim, "Ooh, that's sour."

The Craighead family's freighting business took her father-in-law, Thomas, to the Virginia coast. He had brought back the rare treat from a Spanish trading ship. The two had enjoyed the sweet, cool lemonade, shamelessly emptying the pitcher.

The good times they shared, just a short time ago, seemed distant now. Sadness welled up as memories overwhelmed her. She pushed it all aside and crossed the porch, knocking on the door.

"Oh, Rebecca. What are you doing here? " Lydia said.

"I wish to speak with Jack."

"He is not here." Lydia dropped her head.

Her sister-in-law had never been good at hiding her feelings. Something was wrong. Lydia did not invite her in.

"Please tell me that Jack intends to do what he promised Starlyn."

"I do not know." Lydia rubbed her hands together, looking down. "Jack said if anyone questions how he handles his brother's estate, they can demand the magistrate determine who's right."

Did apprehension cross Lydia's face? Rebecca turned, hurried across the porch and down the stairs.

* * *

Defeat seemed obvious from Rebecca's bowed shoulders as she left. When she dragged herself up in the buggy, Lydia wanted to stop her—tell her she was sorry. Even ask her forgiveness, but she could not. The brief glimpse into Rebecca's turmoil made things worse for Lydia.

She should talk to Jack. It was not like him to have difficulty with his brother's family.

Lydia bided her time before broaching the question of Starlyn's estate. She looked for the perfect opportunity. When she finally spoke, the look on Jack's face was prideful and stormy.

"Someone like Clayton will not get his hands on Starlyn's money. I think that's why he is over there so much. She may not hold out for long."

"Are you sure about that?" Lydia said in a humble voice. She had to be careful here. Pushing would get her nowhere with Jack.

"I hear that Clayton hangs around like he belongs there." Jack looked away. "Someone said I should enforce that 'do not appraise' clause on the property, with Clayton running after Rebecca. I searched for other legal means to stop him, but I am satisfied with this."

She waited, but he did not tell her that person's name.

"But you know that is their inheritance, even her right as his wife. Jack, it seems to some people you are trying to keep the money from them."

The room grew still. Lydia's breath caught in her throat. When Jack reared back with a snort of anger, fear shot up her spine. She had gone too far this time.

"Do not question me about something that is none of your concern, Lydia Craighead. Do you understand me?"

That was enough for Lydia. She dropped her head and nodded. She must not take sides against her husband, no matter how wrong. Rebecca would have to figure this out for herself. Nothing was worth arguing with Jack.

* * *

Lydia's words pricked Jack's conscience as he stormed out of her presence. In the office, he reached for a decanter to pour a drink. The amber liquid filled a short crystal glass. He thought about Clayton and his own motives. Why work so hard to devalue his brother's estate? Jack did not find an acceptable answer, at least not one he chose to accept.

He had suggested his brother make the change two days after they drew up the will, just before his death. Changing his will was out of character for Starlyn, but he had agreed. Jack did not know why he wanted Starlyn to make this addition. He just did. The three men who witnessed the will also witnessed the 'no-appraisal' addendum. The Craighead family knew the first two men, who signed without remark. McClellan, the third man that Whitley provided to witness, did the same.

Jack mulled it over again. It did not seem that Rebecca would fall for the likes of Clayton Baxter. She was still in love with Starlyn. Jack had liked her from the first time they met. He even envisioned marrying Rebecca if only she had accepted him. But she did not.

Jack again asked himself why he was laying a scheme to claim most of Starlyn's estate. Unwilling to fully address this question, he assured himself that it was for the good of the family.

Then he made a promise to his dead brother. He would keep the money belonging to Rebecca and the children separate. They would get every cent of it when Clayton got out of their lives. He would see to that.

Yes, Jack vowed. Nothing would stop him from doing what was right—when it was over with, that is.

At that moment, in his heart, Jack fully believed this was true.

CHAPTER THIRTY-THREE

Saturday, October Second

Rain beat against the windows in Rebecca's sleeping room. Thoughts of the upcoming court struggle had begun to wear on her. Despite her resistance, the memory of Starlyn's illness crowded in to fill her thoughts. He had fought so hard to live, but the struggle did not change anything. In the end, she still had to bury him.

"Lord, I don't know how much more I can go through."

Adding wood to the fire, she sat down with the hairbrush when her daughter entered. Janey set down a tray before hurrying to her side.

"Mother, what's wrong?"

"It's a gloomy evening, Janey. That's all."

"Do not worry. We love you. Rosie made the sugar cookies. I steeped the tea, and Rance came in from the barn filling the wood boxes."

Janey took the cookie plate to the table. She handed Rebecca a pressed handkerchief, the corners embroidered with roses, then handed her the tea cup.

"Take a sip. I made the tea just the way you like." Janey pushed back a wisp of hair. "I only used one rounded teaspoon of the dried chamomile flowers from the tea chest, like you said. I strained the tea into your favorite cup, mindful of how much sugar I used."

Rebecca handed Janey the ivory-handled brush. She sipped the tea as her daughter finished brushing.

"This tea is so good."

Janey tied Rebecca's hair at the nape of the neck with a white ribbon. She smiled when her daughter kissed her on the cheek before leaving with the tray.

She poked up the fire before settling under a quilt in her rocking chair. She pushed off the floor with an arched foot, setting a slow rhythm back and forth. She thought back to the delivery the previous week with a smile, her heart lifting at the memory.

The unexpected surprise had been Rebecca's only true happiness since Starlyn's death. It seemed like her husband had visited her one last time. Their names and wedding date were centered in the top middle of the fireback. Directly beneath it was the Craighead mark. Up in the corner a dove took flight, the left wing extended up and the other out, as if circling to land.

She recalled the nights Starlyn stayed late in his shop. He must have worked on these carvings, intending the fireback as a surprise. Secretly he had made arrangements for the fireback's delivery. Clayton gave her the paper with Starlyn's instructions confirming this.

* * *

Rebecca leaned over the porch railing gazing at the harvested fields. She worried about what they would do the following spring when their family must take care of planting. She could see the big wagons through the open side of the shed as she thought about Starlyn's successful freight business. Could a woman, two girls and a growing boy manage to run all this? Restless for answers, Rebecca went back inside to sit at the trestle table.

Morris Whitley had petitioned the court to place

Starlyn's will on the calendar. He wanted the will accepted and Jack appointed executor, as Starlyn had requested.

Court always met on the first Monday of each month. The fourteen-day waiting period ended Monday, October 4, which made the court date two days from today. She had conserved the cash Starlyn had on hand before his death. Money, once plentiful, was now scarce.

Rebecca went to Starlyn's office, sifted through the bills on his desk, then placed them in a stack. She could not put it off any longer. They might already be in trouble. Dare she ask Jack for help?

Desperate to know the immediate truth, Rebecca pulled down Starlyn's accounts ledger and took it back to the common room for inspection. She hunched over the table checking the figures through tired eyes, when her daughter entered the room.

"What's wrong, Mother?"

Rebecca patted her hair into place. Her apron lay in her lap, wadded up in frustration.

"It's nothing to worry about, Janey. I'm only looking over our debts."

"I'm not a child, Mother. I'm almost sixteen years old. You can talk to me like you did Father."

Rebecca reached out and took her hand.

"You mustn't be concerned. This will all work out."

"All right, Mother, but should you need me…"

Rebecca nodded, observing the troubled look on Janey's face before she turned, picked up candlesticks and left the room.

Starlyn's business ledger lay open in front of her. It would not be easy to keep problems from Janey, now that she had caught her in distress. She would not have the children worrying about the state of their affairs, though. She must not let that happen. Worry was not good for their young minds, the burden too heavy. They had the money, only tied up in court.

She looked over the pages again. The money she expected to be available could not be touched yet. Rebecca's heart sank. They would not have funds until the final resolution of Starlyn's will. The family must do without, like years before when paying off their land.

The extra supplies Starlyn insisted be on hand were dwindling. Ransom had replaced two wheels on one of their larger freight wagons before hauling the last freight contract. Ransom drove one wagon while Burl, who came back to help, drove the other. Starlyn had previously received partial payment for that job. The balance went to the estate.

* * *

Early the next morning, Rebecca sat at the table with Rance discussing the two wheels— much like she used to sit with Starlyn.

"Let's take 'em to Big George," Ransom said. "He's always taken care of us."

"Yes, let's do that directly."

Ransom's face was downcast, his shoulders slumped. Could he be wrestling with the thought there was no extra money? After Rance loaded, they started toward town.

"You're so quiet. What's wrong, Son?"

"I have been thinking. If I knew how to fix the wheels we would not spend money for them."

The sincerity reflected in his young face moved her to say, "Your father would be so proud of you."

Ransom squared his shoulders, wearing a look of pride. They arrived at the wagon shop in Starlight and he rolled the wheels inside.

"Ain't s'posed to do no more work without payment first," George Watson told Rebecca, looking at a spot somewhere above her forehead.

"You will receive payment as soon as our affairs…" Rebecca began, but George already shook his head.

"Unh, unh. I just can't do it."

He stood there, sleeves rolled past his elbows, huge forearms crossed on his chest, with massive hands tucked into his armpits. Carroty red hair on his arms matched a thatch of hair on his head, separated into clumps.

She felt sympathy for George. How awful it must have been for him to twist and turn in front of her, not wanting to refuse them help. After they left, Rebecca felt out of sorts. Fear overcame her. Would they get help from the other establishments without any cash?

* * *

Rebecca moved the empty flour bowl toward the back of the table. Later, while she prepared biscuits for the bake kettle, Janey or Rosie would boil the potatoes. Early that morning, Rance had shot a young turkey and gutted it for her.

"Rosie, start the water boiling. Make sure we have plenty." Rebecca gave her hands a quick wipe.

"But, Miss Rebecca, it ain't my turn. It is Janey's, cause I did it last. Don't ya member?"

"Never mind who helped last. We're cleaning this turkey, so heat the water."

"I'm startin' it fast as a can." She looked back at Rebecca, her large brown eyes distressed.

Rebecca set the turkey in a large pot on the sideboard, holding back a smile as Rosie grumbled her way through the task.

Rosie poured hot water over the turkey, then belched.

"The smell of boiling feathers makes me sick—it stinks so bad."

With nose wrinkled up, her hands flew as she plucked feathers before yanking her fingers away from the heat.

Rebecca poured water, while Rosie complained bitterly. She pushed back wisps of hair from her face with a forearm, mindful to keep her fingers away.

"Pluck fast Rosie. The feathers will cool, tightening up the quills. Then we'll have to do it again." Rebecca had a burst of energy directed toward the largest quills, too difficult for Rosie.

While they worked, Rebecca thought about Rance's hunting skills. He regularly put meat on their table. She worried about the gunpowder keg, though. It was the last one and emptying out fast.

She was waiting for delivery of their food and other supplies. Lee's Mercantile usually brought their orders on time. If they took much longer, she would send Rance to inquire about the problem.

Rosie was learning to take flour along with other ingredients from the dry barrels. Salted meats and wet foods came from the wet ones. She knew to replace the lids securely, keeping the food clean and free of vermin. Rebecca thought about this as she watched Rosie eye the bowl. The last time Rebecca went for ingredients more barrels were empty than full.

"I'll get the flour, Miss Rebecca," Rosie said. She grabbed the deep wooden bowl from off the table then ran for the pantry door.

"Quick, Janey, go help her," Rebecca called over her shoulder.

* * *

Janey hurried into the pantry as Rosie pulled the flour

barrel back, resting it against the stool's top step.

"Don't do that, Rosie. Let me help."

"Leave me alone 'cause I can get it."

Janey held her breath, rooted where she stood.

Rosie climbed the stool and bent over, reaching into the barrel with a large dipper. She grunted, stretched to push down deeper then lost her balance. She pitched forward into the barrel. It rolled away from the stool, crashing to the floor.

Janey hurried to help her. She arrived in time to pull an addled Rosie out of the barrel, flour covering her head and shoulders.

"Rosieee!" Janey wailed.

Rosie blinked away flour from her eyelashes, leaving two round holes as she ran past toward the common room.

* * *

Rebecca had just singed off the turkey hairs with a flaming stick of kindling when she heard footsteps. She pitched the stick in the cook fireplace and turned as Rosie headed toward her, squalling at the top of her lungs.

"What happened?" Rebecca said.

"I didn't mean ta knock it down. I just wanted ta get flour!"

"Stop crying. It will be all right. Now, go clean up." Rebecca took Rosie's shoulders to gently turn her toward the door.

Rebecca and Janey went to inspect the flour barrel. Together they pulled it upright. The flour level had been too low for much to spill out.

"I tried to stop her, Mother, but she's so hard-headed."

"I know she can be stubborn," Rebecca said. "I guess we should be thankful she did not go for molasses."

The two broke down laughing. They looked at each other and laughed harder, clutched their stomachs, skirts dancing outward. Fresh tears of mirth ran down their faces until, wiping her eyes, Rebecca came to her senses.

"Enough of this. We have work to do."

Janey poked up the cook-place, swept the hearth and added wood.

Rebecca placed the spit in the turkey then into the copper roasting oven, a reflective box on legs with one side open to the fire. She set the drip pan in the bottom, cranked the spit handle to be sure it rotated and closed the top. Then she went to comfort Rosie.

"It's alright now, child. Go crank the turkey until I get there to help."

CHAPTER THIRTY-FOUR

The friends Rebecca's family acquired before Starlyn's death had thinned out. She wondered what now caused the cool reception from women in their community.

One afternoon, Beulah Mae Richards came to visit. They sat in the dining room, sipping tea and eating Janey's special peach jam teacakes. Rebecca was proud of Janey, only a few days from her sixteenth birthday and acting like a young lady. Janey's choice of dainty pink roses on light blue plates against the white tablecloth finished the setting.

"There have been quite a few days of good weather, considering the time of year," Beulah Mae said.

"Yes, indeed," Rebecca smiled, thinking Beulah Mae charitable. She could only remember a few days of mild weather.

"Oh my, what a tall young man Ransom is growing into. Will you look at the size of his arms? So handsome, too." Beulah Mae fluttered her eyelashes when Rance passed through the room.

"What a lovely compliment. Yes, he's growing up right in front of me."

It grew quiet in the room. They nibbled on tea-cakes until Beulah May spoke again.

"I was over at Ella Jane Sanford's house the other day. She's planning this winter's dinner party, you know." While she talked, Beulah Mae used the palm of a hand to push salt-and-pepper colored hair up toward the stingy little bun perched tightly on the back of her head. A few little sprigs of loose hair waved when she shifted position.

"Oh, yes. I guess it's that time of the year again." Rebecca sighed. "Where has time gone?"

A perfectly round spot of rouge, brushed high on each cheek, grew brighter as their guest plunged deeper into her story.

"Well," Beulah May tucked her chin on a shoulder and looked up at Rebecca through sparse lashes, "your name was mentioned."

"Oh?" Rebecca had been there to help plan last year's party.

"I was scandalized when I overheard Ella Jane tell her new friend, Martha—" The rest of her comment rolled out in one quick breath. "— 'A certain perfect widow won't be attending dinner this year.'"

"Oh, Mother…" Janey said.

"I'll just have another one of Janey's lovely little cakes." Beulah May looked up when Rebecca stood to hurry from the room, skirt gathered in her hands.

Beulah's remark almost caused her to miss the banister. She went upstairs and lay down on her bed. Ella Jane's painful remark indicated they were not her friends. Not any more.

Did they fear Rebecca turning their husbands' heads in her direction? It would not be the first time a married man had left his wife and children for someone else. Women stayed with an abusive man or a heavy drinker, because having no husband could be worse.

Rebecca felt the sting of being rejected by a friend. She knew Beulah Mae did not mean to hurt her. The lady just did not know any better.

She opened the door when she heard Janey's voice below.

"I know Mother would want you to take these tea-cakes home to enjoy," Janey said before the front door closed.

Did her problems have anything to do with Clayton Baxter? This was not the first time she worried about his intrusion into their lives. There were no problems to speak of before he came along. Now it seemed she had plenty.

Clayton appeared out of nowhere after Starlyn passed on, to make that fireback delivery. Rebecca tried to discourage him from visiting the house. He always found a reason to help Ransom with this or that, it seemed, before finally leaving.

Rebecca felt sure some in the community wondered about Clayton being around, with Starlyn gone. She was sure others whispered behind her back. There was the day when she walked into Abb's Apothecary for salve and a bit of lace.

"...and can you believe he's always out there? A nice looking man like him is only there for..."

"Shh! She's behind you—just walked in." Ella Jane Sanford nudged a woman beside her.

Old Abb shook his head as the two women left. Rebecca fished payment from her reticule, blinking back tears as she paid and collected her purchases.

Some women considered Clayton Baxter handsome. Rebecca did not. He was not the kind of man Starlyn had been. Rebecca's instincts told her to be wary of him. There was something about him that almost made her recoil in his presence.

Understanding the truth about certain matters was something she had come to trust, just as she trusted the Lord.

Rebecca found herself depending on this knowledge about things not readily apparent to some.

* * *

Jack stared out his office window into the late afternoon light, watching autumn leaves drift to the ground. The struggle to get past the pain of losing Starlyn, and the community's reaction to how he handled his brother's estate, gripped him. He was doing the right thing. Starlyn would have agreed.

Irritated by the gnawing in the pit of his stomach, Jack made a fist. He would be happy when all their noses were out of his business.

Before Starlyn's death, their family had been a big part of each other's lives. Now the distance between them had grown. Shoulders slumped, he caught a reflection of himself in the window. There was no need to see the creases between his brows to know they had deepened. Pain cast shadows over his heart, blinding him to the waning day.

Rebecca no longer welcomed him into their home. He rejected the thought that it could be his fault. When he discovered Clayton hanging around Rebecca's place, it bothered him that Ransom remarked, "I like talking to Mr. Baxter."

Starlyn was gone. Now it was his responsibility to protect Rebecca's and the children's inheritance from the likes of Clayton Baxter. Jack paced the floor, not deviating from his path around the perimeter of the room. That leech might suck them dry if he did not stop this. They would be thankful he stepped in. As administrator of the estate, he had notified the businesses in town not to deliver unpaid goods or services to the Craighead household without consulting him.

Jack remembered when Clayton showed up at Rebecca's door. He had a bad feeling about him from the beginning. He knew Starlyn had placed an order for a fireback from the foundry near Rocky Mount. With him dying, Jack had forgotten that it was scheduled for delivery.

He was supposed to be the man in their lives now, protecting them. Clayton was little better than a peddler. Only in town a few days, the man had Ransom admiring him. This heightened Jack's anger. He must corral Rebecca and the children quickly or Clayton would become entwined in their lives. No matter what, Jack determined he would find a way to stop him.

* * *

Monday, October 4th

The day lodged in Rebecca's mind had finally arrived. The family gathered early at the table for a cold breakfast of corn apple muffins and rice pudding. They ended the silent meal.

"Rosie, if you want to go there's still time to bank the fires, while I close up the house. We can get to the courthouse on time."

"I'll stay behind, Miss Rebecca. There's work ta be done here. Later, I'll have supper waiting."

"All right, Rosie. If you wish."

She looked into Autumn Rose O'Reilly's golden brown eyes and smiled. Without a mother or any family in America, Rosie was like her third child.

Rebecca slipped into her coat. Picking up three quilts, she went to the door where Janey waited. Ransom pulled the carriage in front of the house. Sampson and Delilah, their two-horse team of matching bay roan Brabant's, turned their heads to look as she stepped onto the porch.

"Mother, I'll take that." Ransom pitched two quilts on the back seat. "Here, take my hand."

He helped her into the carriage and reached around for Janey.

A thunderstorm struck as they traveled to town. The countryside glistened in the wet morning, plastered-down leaves along the roadside reflecting the rain. Only the squeaking springs interrupted the silence when the carriage hit a bump.

"I'm going to freeze, Mother," Janey said, as rain sprayed in.

Shivering, Rebecca pulled a cover up to Janey's neck and tucked it around. She looked to see Ransom had a quilt bunched around his lap and knees before settling into hers. Any fears over the conflict with Uncle Jack went unspoken.

As the courthouse came into view, she could not recall feeling so differently. Years earlier, their family participated in the town's growth. The courthouse had been a friendly place. Today she just needed to get through what would come.

"Here now comes the Commonwealth of Virginia, County of Franklin, hearing the matter of the estate of Starlyn Craighead, deceased."

Rebecca had not slept much the night before, recalling kinder memories of the children's uncle Jack. Today, she remembered his determination to control every part of their lives. She struggled to stay alert, to understand all the important information.

On first arriving at the courthouse and going to the gallery, Rebecca thought about what brought their family to this unsettled state of affairs. Distrust had peaked over the 'no appraisal' clause in Starlyn's will, as dread grew. Lydia's suspicious actions added confusion, but Rebecca refused to believe Jack would actually hurt them. It did not seem possible. She grew alert when Janey tapped her arm.

"…and verify the signatures of the witnesses."

Rebecca leaned forward as the court called up the three men.

"Are you the first witness to Starlyn Craighead's will?"

"Yes, sir," the witness said.

"Did you place your name on the document?"

The man nodded.

The magistrate hunched forward, brows pulled together, eyes fixed on the witness. Through pinched lips he said, "You will speak up in this courtroom. Do you swear that it was Starlyn Craighead who signed the will?"

"Yes, sir, it was him. I used to work for his father, Master Thomas." He clutched his hat with both hands.

The following two witnesses gave like answers. The men's testimony, as witnesses to her husband's signature, proved the validity of the will. The court accepted Starlyn's final request that there be no bond and no appraisal for his estate.

Rebecca sat there numb, confused. Jack would not be required to appraise the estate? During the next appearance, the court would formally accept his executor's report of burial expenses, debts, and any related obligations. The magistrate continued on, but Rebecca was not present. She wandered the halls of her memory searching for answers to explain how this happened.

"Place this matter on the calendar for next term," the magistrate abruptly instructed the court clerk.

Rebecca cleared her head when Janey shook her arm.

They started for home, Rebecca's thoughts on the day's events. "I must immediately pen a letter to the magistrate asking for a review of the will."

"Why, Mother? What do you want them to review?"

"I will ask the court to take another look at the clause requesting the estate not be appraised."

Her father-in-law, Thomas, had not written his will this way, making her suspicious of how the clause got inserted in Starlyn's will. Her husband had mentioned nothing about this to her.

Rebecca tried to get Jack's attention before court, but he stared past her. She tugged his sleeve when he went by, but he kept going.

Her chance to object had been during court. Grief from Starlyn's death and confusion over Jack's actions had kept her silent. Her next opportunity to get this action changed would only come if the judge agreed to her request.

* * *

It's almost over.

Jack pushed papers around on his desk. Since their court appearance he was sure Morris Whitley had everything in order. He would see Rebecca and the children received a nominal fee from the estate. After Clayton was gone, he would give Rebecca the remainder of Starlyn's estate. In a day or two he would speak with Morris about this.

"Come in, Morris," Lydia said. "Would you care for something to drink?"

"If it's not too much trouble. Then I would like to speak with Jack."

He had not expected his attorney today.

Jack moved away from the desk inherited from his father, to a large corner window looking out toward a grove of trees on the side of the house. The other corner window looked past Lydia's garden to a hollow containing the barn, shops, and a good-sized smokehouse. It was well known Jack's ability for success in business had made them quite the envy of several prosperous families.

The Craigheads were an educated family. Starlyn's pursuit of Rebecca Thompson, and his marriage to her, seemed unusual. Her family had not enjoyed the social standing of Starlyn's, but that changed somewhat after they were married.

Starlyn's strong desire to marry her had surprised their father, but Thomas had stood behind his eldest son's decision. He thought highly of Rebecca. When Thomas made a decision about someone that was final. No one questioned their father's judgment. Jack recalled that he, too, had liked Rebecca at least as well.

He turned from the window when Lydia opened the door to tell him Morris waited in the front room.

"Send him in. We'll need some time without interruption."

Morris strolled into the room, legs taking long steps and chin held high.

"Rebecca petitioned the court for a further review of the will. I did not anticipate that. I am starting to question our legal position."

"Can she cause problems?"

Morris cleared his throat. "I just don't know about this, Jack. I know Starlyn went along with the non-appraisal clause, but it was not to deprive his family of their rightful inheritance. Some around town say this is your intention. They think it's deliberate."

Jack realized he could be in trouble. Whatever else happened, she must not win in court. He had to stop her. Should the magistrate find for Rebecca he would lose control of the will and his brother's family. Jack clamped his jaw. Only Clayton Baxter would benefit from this. He would not be beaten by a man no one ever heard of before. He was a stranger who only wanted to steal away Rebecca and his brother's money.

Jack decided to do what he must to win. He missed what Morris was saying.

"What was that?"

Morris looked at Jack with a question in his eyes before starting over.

"I belong to a group looking for new members. It's of the Masonic Order. Called the Grand Lodge of Virginia. I belong to the lodge out of Staunton."

"The Masonic Order?"

"Yes," Morris said. "Some of us in the Staunton lodge are looking to open one closer to Starlight. That is, if enough exemplary members can be found to carry it. They want community members in good standing who can contribute to the betterment of the lodge."

Morris tilted his head to meet Jack's eyes. "You could be a candidate for admission. Another member and I will recommend you. Along with a request for consideration, you would become a new brother in the lodge. After that we can take care of any court problem. There's a meeting later this month to consider new members. Will you attend it with me?" He crossed his arms, looking directly at Jack.

"How can this help get around Rebecca's protests over how I'm handling Starlyn's estate?"

Morris sucked in his upper lip, lids dropping part way over his eyes, looking much like someone had lowered the curtains. Jack thought he heard a hint of promise in his words as the tone of Morris' voice dropped.

"The men in our group help their brothers with problems." Morris added in a matter of fact tone, "They expect the same in return from every member."

He went on. "Judge Breckenridge is one of my lodge brothers. He will be the magistrate who decides Starlyn's estate. There are others, too, who are in the position to say 'yea' or 'nay' to a person's needs. All according to the special trust one brother may want to embrace in another."

Morris hesitated, "Um—from personally knowing his brother's exemplary character, that is."

Jack was still considering this information when Morris pressed him. "Will you be attending?"

"I'll think about this, Morris, and give you an answer."

He needed time to study the proposal. Jack suspected that if his father were alive he would advise him not to join. Someone had approached Father, too, years ago, about joining the Brotherhood of Freemasons. He turned them down.

His father wasn't there to advise him, though, and Jack needed a guarantee the court would decide for him. This was so important Jack decided to do whatever he must to guarantee the outcome.

He would even join this unfamiliar organization, if it would help him win.

CHAPTER THIRTY-FIVE

October fifth

Tomson 'Polecat' Searcy had started his trip to Lee's Mercantile in Starlight, Virginia several days previous. His partner, Robert Clover, accompanied him to the destination for their final delivery.

Polecat knew being raised in Boston, and surrounded by servants, had not helped Robert any. With his father's wealth reflected in his social manner, he had run away to become a man of the new frontier. On occasion, Robert slipped back into the refined speech of his genteel education. Regardless of that, he was someone Polecat had come to trust during dangerous times.

"What all do you think we will find in that town?" Robert pushed back shaggy hair riding his horse alongside Polecat's wheel horse.

"Don't know—can't recall ever passing thru, Bobby." Polecat resisted a smile, as Robert's eyebrows rose being called the name his Irish mother used.

Robert sighed. "Well, I'm lonesome as can be, starved for something good to eat, like a stuffed leg of veal, potato cakes and raised bread." He hesitated then continued. "I did not know how terrible my cooking was until I had to eat it regularly. Not that long ago I would have given a month's earnings to get my hands on a buttered apple pie dusted with plenty of cinnamon."

"I met a man once, who owned a freighting business

somewhere around Starlight," Polecat said. "Seems like they called him Craighead. I ate supper with him at the inn where I laid over. He said he intended to stay home with his wife once he had enough drivers to make his long hauls."

"Now that you mention it," Robert said, "there is a freighting family there, originally started in Baltimore Town, I believe. Quite prosperous, too."

As the heavy wagon rolled along, Polecat thought about his time working with Robert. The two had long-hunted the past few years, including the previous spring. It seemed neither had enjoyed it, since the wilderness had become overpopulated. The profits from earlier years made their recent earnings look small. The two combined their money to purchase a large Conestoga wagon and team. They signed on as shipping agents, driving long distance freight. They drove for eighteen months. Their financial holdings grew considerably before the urge overcame them to move on from freighting. Starlight was their final stop.

Arching his back, Polecat shifted position on the wheel horse, then gripped the reins of the lead horse pulling the Conestoga. He looked west, toward the Blue Ridge Mountains and the Appalachians beyond. His eyes dimmed recalling life in the wilderness.

He had enjoyed the wind swirling through the trees. The sound comforted his restless soul. At the distant howl of wolves he threw another tree branch on the fire then pulled his rifle close before burrowing into his blanket. At early morning light birds flitted through the forest shattering the silence.

Polecat preferred camping near a stream. The sound of running water soothed him at night. There were people in the forest besides him and Robert. He was conscious of the limited contact they had with anyone, even small bands of natives that called this wild land their own. A lurch cleared his mind. Good company might be a welcome change for them both.

Rising before dawn Polecat took care of the team, while Robert laid out a bit of salt pork they cooked the night before, some hard biscuits, and wooden mugs of hot coffee. They were on the move at daybreak. They would be in Starlight by early afternoon if things went right.

Polecat glanced at Robert before drifting back to a memory of the wilderness seven years earlier, during one of their long hunts. That morning, at the crack of dawn, he had reached down to cover Robert's mouth while shaking him awake. Robert stiffened when Polecat whispered, "Quiet— we are not alone."

He pointed at the horses then toward the river. Robert gathered up the animals, and like darkness fleeing before the dawn, disappeared in that direction.

Polecat had heard the forest grow silent during the night. He knew someone was there. They were beyond the Appalachians, in territory where Polecat had not spent much time. Instinct sounded a warning in his gut. He had not slept, only waited out the night to warn Robert.

Rubbing out signs of their presence he had started after Robert when the back of his neck prickled. He scrunched down close to a cottonwood overrun with shrubs and briars. The hope that Robert made it to the river filled his mind before realizing shadows streaked through the morning's grey light.

Tree limbs draped with thick green-black moss gave the forest a dim, haunting look. Fractured sunlight filtering through the trees did little to light up the area. A man ran into view. His brown skin had a red cast. Below his breechclout, buckskin leggings encased muscular legs with moccasins reaching up his ankles. His shirt fit over powerful arms with a soft colored blanket draped over one shoulder. It almost covered a pouch at his side. Polecat stiffened as the man, a hawk feather in his hair, stopped in midstride. Raising a bow, an arrow pulled taut, he pivoted toward Polecat's position.

This man's instincts were also good.

A shrill birdcall split the silence as the man teetered in his direction, before lowering the bow to run straight ahead. Quicker than Polecat expected the man was out of sight. He joined Robert and they had continued on.

Polecat looked around. They were now close to Starlight. They must deliver the shipment to the mercantile, first thing. He was anxious for this to be over.

He glanced toward Robert. "We will be there shortly."

Before long, they would mingle with proper folk again. With that, Polecat gave thought to finding the things they needed to ease back into Virginia society. He must ask around for the best man to repair his worn saddle. He also wanted to replace his old clothing with something more acceptable.

The sign hanging above the door said "Blue Horse Tavern". The two men finished a much-needed scrub-down in a back room and came out smooth-faced, looking respectable. They chose seats at a back table. Polecat's stomach growled from the smell of good food that lingered in the air.

They dined on spoon meat with dumplings and salt bread, accompanied by wild sweet onions. A heaping slab of apple pie finished off the meal. Polecat wiped greasy fingers on a napkin, not his trousers. They were now in civilized territory.

"I shall meet up with you here, Robert. Don't let anyone out there get the best of you, or your money."

With that, Polecat left Robert Clover to the business of running down that fancy pair of horses and buggy he described, night after lonely night around their little campfires. On those treks they made through unknown territory, both men wondered if they would make it out alive. After they went into freighting, Robert had earned the money for what he wanted.

* * *

Tomson William Searcy was his given name. Early in life someone started calling him 'Polecat'. After a crafty man might get the best of him, they did not know he was around again, until he struck to right their wrong. Then, quick as ever, his tall stealthy figure was gone.

He was a reasonable man, even quite likeable until someone caused him undeserved trouble. The problem with crossing him was no one knew the rules like Polecat. By the time a man realized his mistake, it was too late. A decent man, he expected others to be the same.

The Commonwealth of Virginia seemed a tame place to Polecat. He had traveled the Ohio and Mississippi rivers all the way to New Orleans. He came from North Carolina to work his way toward the new state of Tennessee and places beyond. He wondered just how much Virginia living he could enjoy before the desire to wander overtook him again.

He ambled out the door of the Blue Horse as a familiar voice in the background, near the horses, caught his ear. Turning, Polecat recognized an old acquaintance. Clayton Baxter stood talking to a man. Polecat walked over and leveled a degree of scrutiny at Clayton that would rattle a reasonable man.

"You're a mighty long way from home, Baxter!"

* * *

Clayton jumped as though someone cracked a whip over him. He whirled around to say, "Polecat! What are you doing here?"

"Just going to ask you the same," Polecat said.

Gaining control over his outward manner, Clayton searched his memory for the last time their paths had crossed running freight. He stifled a sigh of relief, recalling no bad feelings between them. Someone once likened Polecat to the elusive wampus cat—a half human creature said to track down and destroy unsuspecting backwoods folk.

Clayton's next stop was the Craighead place. It could be beneficial to take Polecat along. Somehow, being in his presence made a man appear manlier. Clayton had watched more than one man brag, then look to Polecat for approval.

He wanted to raise his stature in Rebecca's eyes. Polecat could be the person to help him do that. Clayton did not deserve a woman like Rebecca, but still, if he kept everyone away, maybe he could get close to her for a while. His plans never included anything more than that.

"Say, Polecat, I'm headed out to the Craighead place. How'd you like to come along?"

"The Craighead place? Well I have to be somewhere later, but—say Baxter, you're not taking me where there's going to be trouble?"

"No, Polecat, no. I wouldn't do something like that. Not to you."

Relief filled Clayton when Polecat grunted, and mounted to ride along with him.

* * *

Rebecca did not feel well. The sunny day brought on

a headache, sending her scurrying to a dim room and the bed. The headache deepened as thoughts flowed in from yesterday's court date. Knees drawn close, she buried her face in the cool feather pillow.

Her grief had become difficult to hide from her family. Still, Rebecca just could not tell them how bad it had become. Not now—they already had so much to worry about.

How would the magistrate rule on the next decision? She did not know if she had the courage to stand in that courtroom again and face Jack. There would be hard decisions to make if her family did not prevail. Now was not a good time to burden the children with more worry.

She was almost asleep when men's voices drifted in from down the hall. Someone was at the front door. It was dark out, who could that be? She got up and patted her hair into place. Leaving the room, she moved toward the front of the house, arriving in time to hear Clayton introduce her son to a new man.

Ransom turned toward her as she entered the room. "Mr. Polecat Searcy, this is my mother, Mrs. Rebecca Craighead."

A twitch began up near the man's eye. His face flushed upward, disappearing into the roots of his hair.

"My proper name's Tomson, Ma'am, Tomson William Searcy." He brushed a hand over the twitch on his face, as if it bothered him.

Rebecca appreciated the tall stranger's sense of respect. He was not a handsome man, not in the manner or traditional fashion of the day. Neither was he of the class she had grown accustomed to associating with in her marital station in life. No, this man was not well mannered, nor dressed. He most certainly was not a dandy.

He handled himself with such confidence it put him near to being imposing. His hazel eyes seemed to flicker green at first glance. High cheekbones flanked a slightly crooked nose. Those facial features and body build were something that no amount of fine clothing could add to. Rebecca cautioned herself to be careful her first impression did not grow.

Clayton started speaking about something he and Polecat had once done. When she did not give him full attention, he started the story over. Right now, his bragging did not seem to end.

Rebecca wanted to get away, to run a damp, cool cloth over her face. Then, perhaps, she could lie back down for a while. She would be satisfied if only long enough to start feeling better.

"Gentlemen, I was resting when you arrived—if I may be excused?" Amid their apologies she gathered her skirt and left the room.

Rebecca paced the floor before finally lying down. She could still hear their voices, picking out Tomson's low baritone over Clayton's. She grew drowsy as her thoughts turned to Clayton. Why had he brought Tomson out to her house? It did not seem like the two men were cut from the same cloth.

Then, that little warning bell inside her head said, "Beware", just before she dropped into sleep.

CHAPTER THIRTY-SIX

"Today I will speak with Morris," Jack reminded himself. He took the long way into town, riding slowly. Pine trees in the crisp fall air had been a favorite smell when he and Starlyn were boys.

"Suppose I'll be accompanying you to the meeting this evening," Jack said when Morris let him in.

"I'm real pleased to hear that, Jack." Lips pursed, Morris's eyelids narrowed before his hand shot out to clasp Jack's shoulder in a strong grasp.

"Come sit down," Morris purred smoothly, as he indicated a chair on one side of a carved maple desk. The sunlight through the window enriched the glow of the furniture.

Jack took a seat. "I'm hesitant about this meeting, though."

Morris cleared his throat, fingernails softly tapping the desk. "Jack, you must be thinking about your future. Now is the time you should secure it."

Rising, Morris poured them whiskey in crystal glasses. They went on to discuss the news about town.

* * *

After Jack left, Morris strode to the fireplace, setting his glass on the mantle before continuing to the window. Jack hurried down the street to his horse, casting a darting glance over his shoulder before saddling up. Morris continued to stand there, arms crossed over his chest, pleased to know

Jack would be accompanying him tonight.

The Craigheads were an old, respected family in the community. Jack's initiation would be good for the Masonic order and the new lodge.

Jack would be the first from his family to enter their organization. Once one joined, it seemed easier to get the next family member into their group. He had witnessed it happening before. It could be a struggle to convince the first man from a substantial family to join them. Then resistance lessened, and another kinsman became interested.

Almost as if they were supposed to become part of it. It was just plain difficult to figure out, and odd to think of it that way. Almost like the first man in a family to join somehow changed the destiny of the others.

* * *

"Where are you going?" Lydia sucked in her top lip.

"A meeting with Morris," Jack said.

"Another one? You've been there once already. Must you meet him again, so late in the day?"

"I have to arrange something for the next court session. I'll be back later." The door slammed behind him.

Lydia sank into an armchair, clutching her handkerchief. She had felt unsettled all morning. With him gone, her apprehension continued to grow. Lydia had felt worse after Jack shot her that 'don't-question-me' look on his way out the door.

* * *

The sound of birds grew loud, no doubt searching for a place to roost among the trees Jack passed. He had time to think as he rode toward the old oak tree where he would meet Morris. He had just about enough of Lydia's interference in his affairs. What if it was late in the day? That was his business, not hers. He flicked the reins across the flank of his horse and it broke into a run.

Morris was waiting for him at the junction by the tree. His horse fell into line next to Jack's, but then Morris turned east.

"Why aren't we going toward Staunton?" Jack said.

"We're gathering at John Garrard's house tonight for the meeting." Morris squared his shoulders.

"I see," Jack said. Meeting Morris here put them on the road toward the Garrard place. John was the local clerk for the circuit court.

"Our lodge is proposing new candidates for membership tonight, like you. Discussions will take longer so it's fitting we meet closer to home." Morris' hand rested on the saddle horn. "Everyone is hoping we set up a lodge in our area."

Jack had begun to grow weary of the ride when a large barn came into sight. They rode past it through an open field. An impressive home sat at the base of a rugged hill. The house commanded a wide view of the woods surrounding it.

"This house is much too big for John." Morris dismounted. "His Polly has passed on to her Maker, with the children having families of their own." Morris hesitated briefly. "His place offers plenty of space and privacy for just such meetings."

Morris rapped three times. The massive walnut door swung open to the sound of his insistent fist. John ushered them inside. Jack noticed that the house was dimly lit and filled with men. A heavy cloud of tobacco smoke hung over the room, stinging his eyes. Lightly interlaced with the smoke was the musty odor of a house with closed-up rooms.

Morris introduced him around. Jack recognized some of the group. The house contained prominent men from the area, including a legislator and a constable. Before long, the group grew quiet when someone proposed opening the discussion for new candidates. Morris stepped forward, indicating Jack should follow him. Henry McClellan, the last man to have witnessed his brother's will, stood on his other side, becoming the second sponsor requesting his admission. Jack soon became an aspiring Mason.

"Jack, this is Representative Hibbits." Morris introduced him to a rotund little man dressed in an important-looking black suit with shiny patches on the sleeves. His thin, kinky brown hair was offset with surprisingly thick mutton-chop sideburns that almost closed the circle on his short, thick neck.

"Yes, of course, it's our representative, Marshall Hibbits. How are you doing, sir, after such an impressive election?" Jack reached out a hand.

"Well,—exceptionally well." The man smiled. Jack managed to hang onto the sweaty hand pumping his, a little overcome by his new social status. Then, without warning, two men came up from behind and, bracing him on each side, herded him down the hallway toward a distant room. Someone slipped a blindfold over his eyes after they pushed him through the doorway.

"Wait just a min—" Jack reared back in panic. The urge to run was strong as he took a swing at someone.

"Settle down," a voice grated in his ear, "You don't have to make it that hard."

He stumbled around in the room and felt what could have been a knee pushing his back as a heavy, oppressive cover was yanked down over his head. Then something landed around his shoulders. His stomach turned over when they tugged on his neck leading him around like a blind animal. He could not tell where he was going.

He was pulled down. Someone slid an object under his hand.

"Lay your hand on the book," a voice said. "Repeat everything, just like I say."

He started swearing to something that caused the sweat to pop out on his forehead. Before he could completely grasp the meaning of one oath, it changed to something new. In the end, the only thing he could remember was the feeling he had quite possibly traded away his soul. The next thing he remembered was the hood being pulled off, with pinpoints of light swirling around his head.

Later, Jack stood with the other new members. He swore an oath of allegiance to the Masonic Brotherhood. They were to hold other members' families in high regard. Congratulations abounded for each of them as glasses were passed around. Jack could not place the contents of the smooth liquor, although he knew it was strong when his head grew light and his thinking dull.

He noticed that the ties between the various members appeared as strong as any he ever witnessed. He was vigorously slapped on the back and called "brother" while words of encouragement from others accompanied the whacks.

On the ride home, Jack listened as Morris instructed him on the responsibilities of belonging to the brotherhood.

"I know it's difficult the first night, Jack. You'll learn more about the rules in meetings to come."

They reined their horses to a stop at the crossroads. Silvery shards of moonlight shone on the fields around them, reflecting off their horses' bridles. The light did not reach Morris' face. His horse let out a low whinny that echoed over the still night.

"Remember, Jack," Morris' voice dropped to a husky whisper, "this is a private organization, with rights and responsibilities. You are to tell no one what happened tonight. Not even Lydia. If you have questions, talk to me." He nudged his horse and the animal trotted off in the moonlight.

Jack sat there, watching Morris' figure disappear from view before he started forward. He was not thinking clearly, but he knew one thing—when he joined the Brotherhood, the direction of his life had been changed. He did not know if he could ever go back. Still, he thought with a certain fierce pride, he could get out of this if he wanted.

He urged his horse on, blinking to clear his vision. Soon the house came into view. He found his way into the sleeping room and quietly began undressing for bed. Lydia's face was to the wall when he crawled in next to her. His last thought before sleep was gratitude he had not awakened her.

* * *

Lydia had slept fitfully. The sound of Jack arriving home roused her. She slowed her breathing, trying not to move or make any noise. When Jack finally began to snore she was ready for sleep. Not, though, before wondering why such dread overcame her when he slid into bed. So much so that briefly it caused her difficulty breathing. A last thought crossed her mind before sleep took over.

What has he done now?

* * *

Jack noticed a higher level of acceptance from some men in the community. Socially comfortable in most settings, his family had already enjoyed a greater level of prosperity. He was not only a charming man, but higher levels of society in this part of Virginia now sought out his company.

The rising sun shot over the tops of the trees into the kitchen, where Jack sat at breakfast. He hurried to finish the sliced mutton and egg pie Lydia had set before him. He still had time for another slice of warm bread before meeting with Morris. Finishing, Jack rode into town. He did not want to be late. Dismounting he entered Morris' office.

"Well, Jack," Morris said as he lit a cigar, "this legal action is a done deed. It's mainly because of your acceptance into the Brotherhood." A smile twitched around the corners of Morris' mouth then spread across his face.

Jack accepted a dark, crudely made cigar reminding him of stogies smoked when hauling for his father. He settled into an oval back chair and lit it, drawing deeply.

He should put some distance between himself and the good Brotherhood. But not right away. He must first win that court decision. Morris studied him with a curious look in his eyes.

"Alright then, I am practically guaranteed to win this decision. It is just a matter of the court receiving the information the estate's accounts are satisfied, something you will file. Then I can divide the inheritance according to its value. Will this end it?"

"Without a doubt." Morris touched his chin. "Providing everything goes as it should. I feel it will."

The two men parted with a quick handshake

* * *

Long after Jack returned home, working in his office, Morris' words continued to stir in his mind. Leaving the building he had looked back toward Morris' window. Morris appeared to stare back, face becoming a brooding mask— something Jack had seen before. Sometimes, the gold in Morris' brown eyes glinted like that of a predator. Jack thought he heard someone whisper, "We finally have a

Craighead in our lodge."

The vision of Morris was so troubling he swiftly covered the distance to his horse.

Jack stood, sweeping the contents of his desk to the floor, compelled by a feeling of strain in his stomach. Needing to break free of the dark thoughts assaulting his senses, he fled to the window.

Sunshine spilled through the glass as birds looked for bugs near the flowerbed Lydia vigorously readied for winter. Her folded shawl lay on a three-legged work stool she used when gardening. She stopped to remove her bonnet, tilting her face toward the sky, the sunlight picking out a few strands of gold in her chestnut colored hair. The birds sang louder. The sun shone brighter. Jack realized he was smiling. The sides of his cheeks tightened as his heart beat with happiness. Just as quickly, it passed. He abruptly turned away, going back to his desk. That uncomfortable feeling settled deeper into the pit of his stomach.

The feeling was something Jack wasn't used to, although it came more frequently now. Had his mother been alive she would have helped him identify what was wrong. But Sophrona Craighead was not alive, and Jack continued his struggle.

Then it happened. Jack recognized the emotion warring inside him. It was similar to several years ago, when he found the old land note Father held on Starlyn's property. It was prime land. All the family had wondered how Starlyn talked that German, John Guttener, into selling it to him at that price.

Starlyn and Rebecca had a strong desire to possess the land, strong enough to go into debt. Thomas had insisted on one condition for the loan. There would be a beneficiary to the note. Starlyn agreed to the terms, and Jack's name was added, should Thomas die.

Starlyn repaid the loan, but Thomas must not have returned the note. Jack was not sure why, but remembered finding the note after his father's death. It was purely a matter of opportunity that day. They were going through their father's papers when he came across it. Trembling at the realization of what he held, Jack turned away from Starlyn long enough to entertain a strange urge.

Slip it in your pocket—quickly. Slip it in your pocket.

Jack had done exactly that.

He had anticipated an inquisitive look from Starlyn after turning away. He faced his brother, dragged a hand across his cheek then dropped it to wipe his fingers on his breeches. Starlyn gave a shake of his head as if he understood, and the two continued.

That had seemed a good thing to Jack. There would be no record left of the debt being satisfied. He now held that power in his hands. Even though he almost forgot it, Jack realized that was the first time he had that strange feeling deep inside.

CHAPTER THIRTY-SEVEN

"Hrnnnh."

Fletcher McClutcheon drew his fiddle bow across the strings. The screech brought children running from different directions. He warmed up with "The Ramblin' Labourer". Matilda hurried in, skirt swaying. Little Susanna's bare feet slapped the floor as fast as her fat little legs could pump. The children danced as Fletcher admired their efforts to wear out the floorboards. Even Matilda joined in. He smiled with delight as he twirled and fiddled for his family.

Much as he loved music, he could not hold back thoughts of playing at tonight's community social. He hoped if Rebecca came she would do more than sit, looking miserable. It had been too long since their family had seen her familiar smile or heard her laughter. Before Starlyn's death, he and Matilda had enjoyed being a part of the Craighead family's social life.

Lately they had included her three children in these occasions. He knew Rebecca appreciated their efforts. It kept her children from being left out of Starlight's festivities because their father had died. She accompanied the children to one or two events but did not participate.

Things had changed in the Craighead household since Starlyn's death. Their friends had dwindled, and the house, once filled with so much life, appeared now just a place to live. It seemed to Fletcher laughter no longer resided at the home Starlyn had built on Craighead Lane, outside Starlight.

Maybe tonight's social would be different. He hoped she would attend.

* * *

Saturday, October 16th

Ransom helped Polecat replace the tongue on a smaller freight wagon in their shed, a long three-sided structure with an open front. He was lonely enough to appreciate Polecat's companionship as well as his knowledge about wagons. He could not help thinking about tonight's social. He observed the big man, and his heart softened. Just then Mother appeared.

"Rance, it's time to clean up."

"We'd welcome your company at the social tonight," Ransom blurted out, remembering how his father showed appreciation for a man's help. It grew quiet as Polecat shifted his weight from foot to foot. Ransom cringed at the look on his mother's face.

"Yes—yes, you're welcome to join us, Tomson," Rebecca said.

He should have discussed it with her before asking Polecat to join them.

"Then it's agreed. We'll all go together." Ransom took off toward the house, making it difficult for Polecat to decline his invitation.

* * *

Rebecca calmed her breathing, dampness clinging to the palms of her hands. She had wavered in her customary strictness with Ransom. That was just not like her. Perhaps it was the respectful way Tomson treated Ransom that caused her to let her guard down and not stop this invitation.

Rebecca was not concerned about what the community might think, not yet reaching a conclusion about

Tomson. She was uncomfortable in his presence, not knowing him well or for very long. He had been mannerly toward her from their first meeting.

Tomson had a reputation for settling scores in the world of men. That Rebecca did not understand most of this world of men was of little concern to her. Almost everyone called him "Polecat", even the children at times. She preferred "Tomson". His shyness and the respectful way he treated her seemed more like having a brother around the place. Rebecca gathered her thoughts, putting her attention on the children.

They arrived at the social in the company of Tomson Searcy. The moon lit up the night in a silvery glow, as the music spilled outside. Ransom helped her and the girls out of the wagon while Tomson tied up his horse.

Inside she observed a few men going toward the back door.

"They aren't going out there to sip cider," Ransom said to Tomson.

When things got out of hand at these gatherings, the worst that happened was an occasional fistfight or two which usually signaled the evening was drawing to a close. The incident made for lively discussion traveling about town the next day. At times, from all the additions, the true story was hardly recognized.

Rebecca had smoothed out the folds of her heavy skirt and sat down when she noticed Clayton Baxter. He appeared to be having a fine time. She remembered from their first meeting how socially charming he could be. The one thing Rebecca knew for sure, she did not feel any need for his company. Not now—not ever.

Clayton made his way around the dance floor several

times before appearing to notice her presence over his partner's shoulder.

"No—don't bother me tonight," she mumbled under her breath, realizing how complicated her life had become with him around. Would she ever be free of him? His frequent visits to their home vied for her family's time. Rebecca had not encouraged him but manners, thus far, had kept her from vigorously offending him. She might do that if this continued much longer.

"Rebecca." He stood boldly in front of her, seeming certain of himself. His sky blue eyes, suddenly dark and smoldering, caused her to feel she needed a good cleansing.

"Would you care to waltz?" He reached out and grasped her shoulder.

Startled, Rebecca jerked away. No man had ever touched her in such a way. Not even Starlyn, who had been the only one allowed to touch her. She regained her composure with difficulty. What was wrong with his mind? Did he not remember she was a recent widow?

"No—no thank you, Clayton." She folded her hands in her lap before looking down. Maybe he would leave her alone.

He strolled to the punch bowl where he dipped a cup of cider and brought it to her. His intense scrutiny appeared to be appraising her as he held out the cup, a slight smile on his face.

Rebecca shook her head at the offer, wishing he would leave. He finally drifted toward a group of people. Perhaps one of those women would be more sociable.

She took a deep breath. A feeling in the pit of her stomach said trouble was coming. No, it could not be. She was just bothered being around him. There had never been serious problems at any social before. Surely there would not be this evening, either.

Rebecca's shoulders slumped as fatigue plagued her. Mostly from sitting ramrod straight in the chair, muscles tensed to protect herself from Clayton's advances. Earlier, she had asked Fletch and Matilda if they could take her children home. She looked around the room for an escort. She refused to ask Rance, Janey or Rosie to leave. Tonight they were happy, laughing with friends. Not finding anyone available, she would make the trip by herself. No need to worry. The children would go with the McClutcheons and Tomson had his horse.

Early in their marriage Starlyn had taught her how to drive a carriage. She became very good at this under his guiding hand. He also instructed her on how to handle a large wagon and team. He had been unlike some men, who would never have allowed their wives to drive, considering it too vulgar.

Standing up, Rebecca looked around. She paid attention to the movements of everyone in the room, much like a hunter tracking an animal. This was learned growing up from watching her mother scrutinize their family's daily affairs. She slipped toward the door when Clayton was deep into the evening's events. Tomson was caught up in a conversation, seeming to miss her departure as well.

She took the few steps to the door. Then she was gone into the night.

* * *

Clayton made his way around the dance floor a few times. There were always women eager for his attention. No matter who, or how pretty, no woman captured his desire like Rebecca. Clayton had noticed that she was gone. He had lurked on the outskirts of her life long enough to suspect she might leave early.

He drifted out the back door and looked up at the turbulent sky before untying his chestnut stallion. The horse snorted softly as he slid a foot into the stirrup then flung his leg across its back. Moonlight glinted off the edge of the metal stirrup he captured with his foot. Taking the reins in a gloved hand, he slapped the stallion's rump with the other. Soon he was not far behind her. If things went well tonight, he decided, Rebecca could find she liked him much better than she thought.

All he needed was a chance. He lay low over the saddle letting the horse find its way.

* * *

Drifting clouds dimmed the half moon, casting dark shadows on the road. The deep woods threatened to pull Rebecca in as she drove the horses past.

"Whoo-whoo." A great horned owl flew past, shattering the quiet and her few remaining nerves with a gloomy prediction of a bad night for its forest victims.

"Git'up, Sampson. Come on, Delilah." Rebecca vigorously snapped the reins. The moon broke free of clouds, shining down as she bent forward adding extra force to her outstretched arms, snapping the reins again. Rebecca ignored the premonition that had plagued her at the social and, with great relief, turned down the tree-lined lane to home.

She drove the wagon into the shed then hurried out. The smell of sweet evening air slowed her as she tried to capture the silence of the night that seemed so great, like just before a storm. She shook off the feeling. Looking around, she hurried toward the house, rough material of her shawl pulled tight and skirt swinging.

No one was there but Parthia, who had returned to help her wash clothes and stay the night. Her former servant must have retired for the evening, with the house so quiet and dark. After a long day, no doubt she slept the sleep of a hard working woman.

Rebecca was grateful for the bit of moonlight peeking from behind the clouds. It lit the pathway for her uncertain feet going up the wooden steps, though the house itself lay in deep shadows. She gripped the handle of the big oak door and pushed with all her strength, but once again that nagging feeling said something was just not right.

She looked back over her shoulder into the night, where a ray of moonlight lit up the face of Clayton Baxter.

CHAPTER THIRTY-EIGHT

Rebecca rushed inside, thrusting a shoulder against the heavy wooden door. If she could only get the bolt turned, she would be safe.

Clayton rammed into the door. It swung out of her grasp, slamming against the wall.

Rebecca backed away, hands out to ward him off. She stumbled, falling against a table as she attempted to flee.

He moved quickly, pinning her back to the staircase as he found her lips. She could not breathe.

She slid sideways trying to get away, but he grabbed her hair and spun her around. He dropped his weight on her, pushing her to the floor and stretched out on top, his strength too much. His left hand captured both of hers, pressing them against her chest. His right hand edged her skirt up around her waist.

"No! Clayton—Stop—!" She jerked from side to side. He pressed her flat against the floor, briefly forcing his lips against hers, muffling her cry.

"Don't fight so hard, Rebecca—you know I'm the best for you."

Rebecca stopped listening, sure she was going to be sick. She had to fight him or...

She screamed and clawed at him. Then she felt the coarseness of his breeches against her skin, gagging at the odor of sweat mingled with shaving ointment. Then he was there, and his weight flattened her out. The stiff texture of the

Persian carpet pressed into her backside and legs as everything in her rejected the act.

She screamed until his hand covered her mouth. Wrenching her face away she tried to scream again, but he found her face. Bile rose up in her throat as she desperately prayed for the horror to end.

The front door swung open as shards of glinting moonlight streamed in.

Clayton was picked up and sent headlong across the floor, crashing into a wall. He grunted, pain in his voice as he stumbled to his feet and straightened his clothes.

Confused from Clayton's assault and the sudden stop, Rebecca could only think to get out of the way so she would not be hurt. She crawled across the hallway when a crash in the darkness sent her scurrying toward the front room entrance.

"Get outta here, Polecat! You're not needed!"

Tomson!

Relief flooded Rebecca's mind. She put a fist in her mouth to keep from calling his name. Her shoulders heaved from the tears.

"If she wanted you here, Clayton, why did you have to sneak out after her? Or hide your horse in the woods like you did?" Tomson's voice lowered, sounding like he needed to clear it. "Why did you have to force yourself on her?"

"Better get back, Polecat. I am gonna hurt you." Clayton made a lunge.

Tomson stepped aside and booted Clayton when he went by. "You are going to get what you've got coming. I'm just getting started."

* * *

Fear touched Clayton's heart as he scrambled off the

floor. He swung at Polecat, who weaved, causing Clayton to almost lose his balance. Then Polecat was upon him. Clayton put all his weight behind a right cross from the shoulder.

Polecat grunted.

The realization he could not beat the man grew in Clayton's gut. His arm movements shifted in the moonlight as he swooped toward the floor, reached into his boot, and pulled out his best helper. It had seen him through rough times before. The handle, made of thick dark hickory molded to Clayton's hand, carried a rich sheen that extended along the blade's edge. It was sharpened so keenly a person could almost be cut by looking at it. Silently he squeezed its comforting grip.

He hesitated. If he used the knife he was in trouble. Wherever he went, he would be watching over his shoulder for Polecat Searcy. This would continue until he or Polecat was dead. That was, unless he killed Polecat now.

Clayton lunged for Polecat, but only slashed the air. A fist rattled the side of his head. He could not see Polecat in the shadows, away from the moonlight. His heavy breathing echoed in the entrance way and he could not control it.

"Alright, Polecat, I am through. Let me out of here."

"You used me Baxter, to get to Rebecca, bringing me out here like you did that first night. Shouldn't have done that or what you did tonight. Now I am mad."

A whirlwind of blows stung Clayton like he just fell into a hornet's nest, almost knocking him down. He shook his head to clear it and slashed out with his helper.

Polecat grunted as the knife found its mark. "I'll get you, Clayton—I will find you no matter where you go!"

The desperate act bought Clayton the time he needed to run.

He heard Polecat coming off the porch after him.

The sound sent fear scurrying up his back, speeding up the departure to reach his horse.

"I'll kill you, Clayton, when I catch you! I will kill you without mercy!"

Clayton cleared the saddle, digging in his spurs.

* * *

Rebecca fumbled around in an attempt to quickly straighten her clothing. She could not see well with the fire burning low. Pain filled her arms, circling around her back.

Heavy steps moved toward the door. She shuddered with dread. Then Tomson called her name, as he reached to pull her out of the corner. She struggled to get away as the memory of Clayton clouded her mind, but Tomson hung onto her.

Rebecca's fear of being hurt caused her to shake. Humiliation pushed at her. "Turn me loose! Don't touch me."

He let go, lit a lamp from the fire then turned toward the hallway. "Do you want me to wake Parthia?"

"Do not disturb her."

More than ever, her feelings toward him seemed like that of a family member. Her hands were damp and sticky.

"Tomson, what's wrong?"

Blood seeped through his shirt where a bloody gash showed in the fabric.

"We have to take care of this. Quick, remove your shirt."

She examined the wound running up and down his rib cage. It was a bloody cut, but not deep. Rebecca hurried to get the things she needed to dress his wound.

"Tomson, this will not take long. Tell me if I hurt you."

She ignored his smile as she worked, rinsing out the cloth in the pan. She tore strips off the linen and dabbed ointment on a compress before holding it on the wound. "Put your finger on this."

She leaned toward his chest to pass the bandage around his back then tied it.

Rebecca got busy cleaning the floor. She did not want the children to see any traces of the blood. The three would be home soon.

Tomson must be gone.

* * *

Polecat gently traced his bandage. He felt awkward when he tried to ask what had happened. Each time he approached her about it, she found something else to clean, face distressed.

This was enough for tonight. "Don't say anything about what happened here." He started for the door and turned back. "Not to anyone."

Now, if only Clayton did not tell it until Polecat found him. After that he would not be able to. Polecat intended to kill him. More for what Clayton had done to Rebecca, than for the sneaky gash Clayton had given him.

* * *

Rebecca could not stand to have Clayton's scent on her a minute longer. Working quickly she pulled the tin tub into the kitchen. While she heated up enough water to take a lukewarm bath, she combed fingers through her hair, pulling out strands. She wondered if there would be any skin left when she finally felt clean enough to stop scrubbing.

In an odd way, the pain from the scrubbing cleared her mind long enough to think again. Troubled that it might be her fault, she combed her memory for any sign she had encouraged Clayton. A thought flickered briefly. If she had paid more attention to God's teachings in the first place, she would have run him off, not worried about bad manners or hurting his feelings. If Rebecca had it to do over, she never would have allowed him to enter her house.

She dried off quickly and hung the cloth on a wooden drying rack in the wash room, where she returned the tub. She just could not be in an emotional state when Ransom, Janey and Rosie came home—especially Janey. She would know something was wrong. Her daughter was too close to her not to sense something had happened. She tried to push it all out of her mind.

Attesting to the benefits of hard work, Parthia had slept through the night. That was something that Rebecca now hoped she could do.

* * *

…Tomson…

He heard the pleasing sound of her voice float through his head as he stood at the edge of the Staunton River, watching it flow by. He was a day's ride from Starlight and night was coming on. Rebecca seemed to prefer Tomson. She always called him by his given name. He did not care so much what she called him, only that she continued to talk to him. It felt more family-like when she called him Tomson instead of Polecat, as most others did. Tomson was the name his mother, Gracie, had always used. He missed her.

Polecat's last memory of his mother was dim. He stood at her bed one night when he was very young, while she asked him something that seemed important, but he could not remember what. Too many years had passed. A small draft of air caused the light from the lamp to flare up when he had answered her. She laid her Bible down and pulled him close in a hug, tears in her eyes. He did not understand why she had burst out crying after the lamplight flickered.

Over the years he wondered what he had done to cause the tears. He remembered answering her question from a strong feeling inside, but could not remember what she asked or his answer. It had been too long ago. She died a few nights later. Now all he could do was hope he would one day remember. Never a man to grieve over the past, Polecat pushed the painful memory of his mother's death back down. It had hardly troubled him since meeting Rebecca.

He tried to talk plainly to her, just as he would to anyone else. This made the relationship manageable for him, even keeping it somewhat distant in his mind. They needed to talk, but he had been unable to get anywhere with her. He wondered what Rebecca would do if people found out about Clayton. There would just not be any explaining this, at least not for the way it truly happened.

He could almost hear them. Everyone knew Clayton had been spending time around the Craighead place. He had begun to hint there could be a wedding for him and Rebecca sometime in the future. Some did not believe it. Some did. Some just plain did not know. But, Clayton forcing himself on her? Now, some would just laugh at that.

He had not found Clayton this time, but he would not stop looking. One day...

CHAPTER THIRTY-NINE

November first, 1802

Men milled around outside the courthouse in the early morning drizzle, some caught up in heated debate. Rebecca and the children walked toward a group of men blocking their way when she observed George, the wheelwright, shake his fist at a local merchant.

"It had better turn out different than what they say Jack Craighead's going ta do," he said.

"She don't deserve a penny," the merchant retorted, "way she ran after that ironmonger Clayton."

"Pipe down or she'll hear ya," someone whispered.

Big George's fist uncurled when Rebecca and her children approached the men. He reached over, clamped down on the merchant's shoulders with both hands, lifting him off the ground, feet dangling. Then he set him to the side so they could pass through.

She avoided looking at the man George lifted up, keeping her eyes on the ground. Ransom firmly gripped her elbow, steering her through as she pulled Janey closer. Heat crept up her face as she hoped the children were too distracted to notice the merchant's comment about Clayton.

Rebecca's steps slowed. Eighteen years earlier the honorable Wayne Allen Grey presided over court at the Wildcat's Lair, a local ordinary that provided food and a bed. He had called a town meeting and almost everyone showed up.

"I've been informed there's going to be a new county split off Bedford County, although it hasn't been made public yet" the Judge said.

"That's useful knowledge, but why's it important to Starlight, Judge Grey?" Thomas Craighead stepped forward. Two probing flashes of blue looked over steel-rimmed spectacles at the Judge.

Judge Grey matched the stare, but held his tongue.

"My second question, Sir. What's the purpose of this meeting?" Thomas continued.

Starlyn moved up to his right side and Jack his left, and when Thomas sat down, his sons stepped back.

"Well, Thomas, the new county will be south of the Staunton River, the dividing line between it and Bedford county. Your town could become the county seat, easy as any other this side of the river."

Rebecca sat at the table making notes for Thomas, Lydia next to her.

"What's your interest in this, Judge Grey? You planning on living here?" someone asked.

"That could be, if a certain widow accepts my proposal—she's already declared she's not moving," the judge replied.

The laughter died and he continued. "It's my opinion the town's chances of being selected would be greatly increased if you had a courthouse to accommodate the county seat's business."

"It needs seating for the women," a man suggested.

Judge Grey listened. The town indicated their willingness to work for the chance of being the county seat, and he called for another meeting to discuss plans.

Despite their efforts, the town lost the hard run race

to Rocky Mount, which became the county seat of Franklin, the new county. They didn't complete the elaborate plans to beautify the courthouse's exterior, satisfied with the looks of the building they had put up. A circuit judge still rode to Starlight to hold court the first Monday of the month and on special occasions.

When court wasn't in session it served as a place of auctions. In addition, the second floor held two rooms, one for special meetings and the other for the musical students of Miss Mabel, the traveling music teacher.

On auction days, the auctioneer started outside on a twenty-foot square platform next to an open space that held the bigger objects. Buyers moved into the courthouse to pay for their things and the auctioneer finished up inside with the smaller items. Rebecca and Starlyn had attended some auctions where begrudged buyers bid down to the half cent over this or that.

Now, for the first time, this monument to a hopeful community frightened Rebecca of what was going to transpire. Today, the courthouse didn't reflect the excitement it had in 1784 when master craftsmen built a beautiful, rectangular brick building. No, today the building whispered of suspicion and fear over what waited inside for her family.

Rebecca started up the steps to the courthouse, still surprised the judge had granted her request for another look at the will. She looked at the wood-trimmed brick building with new eyes. Inside, past the side window, a steep staircase ran up the wall to the second floor.

Further back in the room, a railing with a swinging gate separated the gallery from the lower court where the magistrate presided. A row of empty benches in the lower court waited for jurors.

Today Rebecca hoped to challenge the 'do not appraise' clause in her husband's will. The question of whether his property had been clear of debt, something not satisfied during the last appearance, was not a concern. She knew there were no liens on the property. They owned it free and clear.

Deeper in the gallery and closer to the railing, she looked around. This session would not be any friendlier than the last, she suspected, despite her desire to peacefully straighten out their family's affairs.

Jack was there along with his attorney, Morris Whitley, who looked commanding. She glanced at Jack as he moved through the gallery talking to men she did not recognize as being among his or Starlyn's friends. As he flitted around, Rebecca thought he must have said something witty when a man boomed in laughter, "Morris warned us about you!"

Jack darted a glance in her direction. The look on his face troubled her.

She could not deny that Morris, Jack's attorney, was good at what he did. Evidently most of the town had turned out to see what that might be. The courtroom brimmed over in anticipation, holding the promise of an exciting day. Envy was etched on the observers' faces as Morris strolled toward a small bench to one side of the magistrate, a few wisps of hair floating freely from his head. He seemed in high spirits for someone who still had his work to do.

The Court of Franklin County came to order. The clerk identified the men who had witnessed Starlyn's will the previous session. The court called them to testify they had witnessed, and then signed the 'no appraisal' addition to the will. Morris sternly questioned each one. If a witness did not immediately answer, Magistrate Breckenridge ordered them to do so.

After a brief pause proceedings resumed. Rebecca felt her stomach dip. Something was wrong. Morris's confident stride bode no good as he approached the magistrate.

"John Craighead has engaged me to represent him on another matter concerning his brother Starlyn's estate." He softly coughed into a fist. "It has greatly distressed John to find there is an outstanding note on the Craighead estate for a substantial amount."

"Hmm," the magistrate murmured, "and do you have the note in question?"

With head high, nose quivering, Morris approached the bar and struck a pose. His left leg straight from hip to the floor, right leg bent at the knee, displaying a muscular physique encased in close fitting, expensive pantaloons. Silk stockings extended from under the pantaloons, over the calves. Silver buckled black pumps encased his feet, the right foot extending toward the wood trim of the bar.

"My! What a handsome figure he strikes," a woman blurted out.

"Crash!"

The gavel bounced back as Magistrate Breckenridge brought it down again. "There will be no interruptions in my courtroom today."

In one sweeping motion, Morris retrieved a paper from his pocket. Smoothing it out, he placed it on the bar for inspection. The courtroom gasped in what Rebecca thought must be appreciation for his dramatic presentation. The court clerk walked the parchment to the judge, who sat further back in a high seat on a raised platform.

Grunting, he looked over the parchment then said, "Bring the Widow Craighead forward."

The clerk motioned to Rebecca. She pushed open the small gate, pulled her skirt to one side, and went down the steps to the lower floor. The straight fabric of her black mourning dress floated around her shoes as she shuffled toward the bar, clutching a cape close around her shoulders. She hoped the peak of her black bonnet hid the strain in her face as she clamped her jaw, wondering what Morris could have.

She had previously sought out Sarah and her husband, Reverend West, for guidance.

"Why should I trust Jack or Morris, Malcolm?"

"It may seem like you have not a friend in the world," Malcolm had said, "but you do."

Trembling, she had fought back tears. Sarah held her until the anguish ended. She finally went home, clutching Malcolm's words of comfort.

As she approached the magistrate, her shoe caught on a rough patch of the floor. She stumbled then caught herself. Her mind churned. The only note they ever owed was the money borrowed to buy their land. They paid back that note before it was due. It had been completely satisfied. What could this be?

Rage shot through her as she suspected what Morris had submitted to the court. Thomas had not returned the land note to Starlyn the day they paid it off. The family came together for supper after services, when her mother-in-law unexpectedly grew ill. Sophrona, then Thomas passed on. Starlyn concluded Thomas found the note and destroyed it, not being left in his papers. Had they been wrong?

Wagging a finger in his face, she declared, "If that is our land note it was paid more than eight years ago, Jack Craighead!"

"No. According to that note the loan was never

repaid," Jack said.

The courtroom grew deathly silent.

"Don't call my father a common thief, and you better leave my mother alone," Ransom shouted. The gate flew open and the sound of his feet hitting the steps echoed through the courthouse.

"Stay out of this, Laddie," Jack said.

"I'm gonna fist-whip ya, Uncle Jack, like my father woulda done if he'd lived!"

Ransom balled up his fists, assuming a position. Hands gyrating in front of his face, he lunged in Jack's direction, landing a blow.

The courtroom erupted as the crowd took sides.

"Whup that boy good," one man said.

Someone else yelled, "Leave him alone. He's just a lad."

A fistfight broke out in the gallery when a man ridiculed another's wife for saying, "He shouldn't be grabbing the boy like that."

"Turn 'em loose," others said.

Jack held Ransom back by both shoulders and shook him while the boy swung wildly at a belly he could not reach. The noise escalated. The crowd grew rougher.

The state of the courtroom brought the magistrate to his feet. "I'd have refused to hold court today had I known it would be this contentious."

His frizzled, gray-streaked black hair broke loose from the cord at the nape of his neck, hair springing out from one side of his head. As he bore down on the courtroom with bulbous brown eyes glistening with rage, the gavel crashed again and again.

Flecks of spittle flew from his mouth as he shouted,

"Not another peep! I'll have the lot of you jailed!"

The excitement subsided. When the confusion cleared enough for the court to resume, the magistrate ordered, "Please review this note, Mrs. Craighead. Now tell the court, is this or is this not your husband Starlyn's signature?"

"That's not possible!" Rebecca exclaimed. "You cannot expect us to pay for a note that's already been paid!"

"You must answer the question now, Mrs. Craighead."

It looked to Rebecca like the magistrate's eyes were going to pop out of his head.

"Yes, that is what Starlyn signed when he borrowed the money for our land."

Morris cleared his throat.

Rebecca leveled a finger at Jack, "But wait—wait! We paid this note. Jack you know that is true."

"That's enough, Mrs. Craighead. Take a seat!"

Rebecca's breath caught in her throat, face growing hot at the magistrate's harsh command. She hurried to a jury bench, the closest place to sit.

His large body tucked further back into his seat, lower lip swallowing the upper, the magistrate looked down at the court, leveling a defiant glare at the crowd.

"I'll review the new information presented today and render a decision on the 'non-appraisal' clause. My decision will become a part of the court record." The Judge shifted his gaze in Morris' direction.

His gavel coming down brought the session to an end. The courtroom cleared out, except for a few who stayed around to discuss the day's events.

Rebecca started for home with her family, first thinking about Starlyn, then his brother. Her chest heaved as she fought back tears of defeat. Why did Jack not handle

Starlyn's estate the proper way?"

The wagon rocked, jostling Janey up against her. Rebecca leaned forward, "Don't push the animals so hard, Ransom."

"I hate him!" Ransom shouted over his shoulder. "I'm gonna kill him if I get the chance."

She sat there too numb to move as he cracked the whip.

"Ransom, it's not your fault. We all trusted him." She wondered if this boy, who was too big to be a child but not yet a man, could hear her. He whipped the reigns again and again, head thrown back as he screamed in pain.

She hung on to Janey until the horses finally slowed to a walk. They continued home in silence. Later, gathered around the table for Rosie's food, almost too tired to eat, Rebecca repeated a saying her mother used to describe a bad deed.

"Just you mark my words and remember them well. What goes over the old devil's back, always comes up under his belly." She looked off in the distance. "What he's doing to us will be long remembered, unless he makes it right."

Janey sniffled and Rosie reached out to take her hand.

Ransom said, "What does that mean, Mother?"

"Somewhere in time, what Jack has done to our family, will come back to haunt him. It may take a while, but still it will come."

"Why is that, Miss Rebecca?" Rosie said.

"Not many get away from the ole' devil, once they do his bidding."

"Will it always be this way for Uncle Jack?" Janey said.

"Yes. He will always reap what he sows, good or bad.

That is the way of the Lord."

    "Mother, will Uncle Jack ever find salvation?"

    "I don't know, Janey. I hope so."

CHAPTER FORTY

December, 1802

After the previous court date, Rebecca had time to think about the events that happened since Starlyn's death. How she missed him.

She struggled over Jack's actions in the courtroom. He was a different person than before Starlyn passed away. She would not have thought he could be so dishonest as to claim that a satisfied note was still unpaid. What had come over him? Even considering the way he had always been, this was just too much of a change.

The cough she developed after losing her husband had cleared up. She still did not feel well but could not understand why. Some of her clothes fit more snugly than they had before, and it was no wonder, the way Janey and Rosie baked such good things. She ate every crumb they offered.

What if this was not just a bout of illness coming on? Things would be considerably different for her if she were going through the change of life. Deep inside, Rebecca suspected this might be the problem. The menstrual flux she went through each month was not regular.

As a small child, Rebecca was in the room when her mother had muttered to her grandmother, "It's the curse that's on me."

As if that explained why Mother complained so

much.

Rebecca's grandmother also called those days she had gone through "the curse". She had told Rebecca, finger wagging, that when Rebecca became a woman it would be there to visit her, too.

She then had some sleepless nights trying to understand what her grandmother meant. Did a visitor come to the door that would not leave? Soon after that the troubling thought gave way to more immediate concerns.

Now she knew why it was not coming anymore.

She must find out how to avoid that dreaded mustache that accompanied the change. If anyone knew the secret, it would have been her mother. It took close inspection to see the one she had grown, but her mother had passed on. Rebecca could glean no answers from her.

Starlyn's great Aunt Elizabeth would know the answers. Perhaps it was time for Rebecca to visit.

* * *

"Starlyn, I miss you," she whispered, as the Shepard house came into view. Her heart beat faster when she tied up the horse and walked the pathway toward the door.

She had always admired the broad span of colored stones that made up the rock path. Jonathan Thomas Shepard, Starlyn's great uncle, had scoured the riverbeds for the beautiful rocks, back when he built the Shepard place. Starlyn said Jonathan used every skill he possessed, along with many of his neighbors', to make a comfortable home for his new bride and future mother of his children.

The second floor contained the sleep room. Although Elizabeth was of great age she had refused to move downstairs after Jonathan's death. She made the slow climb upstairs each night, most likely wanting to end her day in the log bed he had made for them. She remembered what

Elizabeth had said when she and Starlyn encouraged his aunt to change her sleeping to downstairs.

"We brought six babies into this world, four of them boys, then never had the joy of raising any one of 'em beyond their fourth birthday." Elizabeth's eyes clouded over as she spoke about the graveyard out back that held six little burial stones.

"But Aunt Elizabeth..." Rebecca had started before Starlyn nudged her with his shoe.

Elizabeth continued. "In our life together all we ever had was each other after I disappointed him so and..." She stopped and pressed a delicately embroidered handkerchief up against the lashes of each eye before continuing. "My Jonathan's gone now. All that is left of our life together is the bed I lay my head on at night. No, it helps me remember when I was loved."

"But Aunt Elizabeth, you know he..." Rebecca said before Starlyn interrupted her.

"You should sleep where you feel best, Aunt Elizabeth. Do not let anyone change your mind." Starlyn had lovingly gazed at his aunt, giving her one of his boyishly handsome smiles.

Rebecca had just reached the porch railing when Elizabeth swung open the door. She was a small woman whose once chestnut-brown hair was silvery white and heaped on top of her head. Starlyn's aunt wore the ivory combs Uncle Jonathan had brought home from Staunton years before. The sunlight touched strands of her hair, turning them into silver threads as she reached to pull Rebecca into a hug. Elizabeth ushered her into the house where Liza, the serving woman, prepared the table.

"Come sit down, Rebecca."

Elizabeth grasped her elbow, guiding her into the front room where they took a seat on the sofa.

While they discussed the children, Rebecca watched Liza across the room. The servant moved her ample body quickly around the table, setting down what must be apple cake and other foods.

They moved to the large table, where Elizabeth presided, her eyes following Liza's movements.

"Do you or the children need anything?"

Rebecca shook her head. Then she blurted out what was on her mind.

"It—uh, the change is upon me. I don't know what to do. What is good for it?"

"Oh, my dear girl. How long has this been going on?" Elizabeth said.

Eyes on Rebecca, Elizabeth said, "Liza, there's work to be done in another room."

Liza immediately hurried out of the room.

"Well, let's see now. I noticed it last month.

"Hmmm," Elizabeth murmured.

Rebecca stared into the depth of her large blue-green eyes and almost stopped breathing as she waited for this wise old woman of eighty-six years to speak.

"You're a bit younger than I was when I went through this, but still…" Her voice trailed off as her eyes slowly traveled over Rebecca, before she said, "And how are you feeling over all?"

"Well, I … meaner than a black snake some days, but…." She stopped, as Elizabeth's eyes lowered. Rebecca's stomach fluttered, uncertainty touching her mind.

"Well then, Rebecca, squaw's root is plenty good for the change," Elizabeth said.

They ate slowly and talked of other things, then

finished another cup of tea.

"It has been good to visit with you, but I must rest now," Elizabeth said as she rose.

Without anything further, the visit was over. Elizabeth walked her to the door, kissing her goodbye before saying, "I miss Starlyn so. Please bring the children next time you come."

Rebecca left without enough knowledge of what she sought, wondering if 'squaw's root' would take care of her problem. Uncertain thoughts loomed deep in her mind. What about the look on Elizabeth's face?

Rebecca arrived home, vowing to work harder. She would not ask for help—even refuse offers of assistance from the children. She did not want the added weight the change caused some women. She flitted from room to room, doing more than before. She looked in the mirror often, searching for evidence a mustache already grew.

She paid more attention to the herbs and medicinal plants, knowledge learned from Mother over the years. Rebecca needed their healing to take her through this trying time in her life. At times the children needed medicinal cures. She must have those plants ready for use, too.

If she did not pay attention to the plants in season, then use them, there would be no chance for a contented home. Not that she ever expected to meet a man like Starlyn had been. In truth she only envisioned loneliness and uncertain days in her future.

CHAPTER FORTY-ONE

Some said Malcolm West had 'the smoke of hell fire' drifting up from below as his heels worked the floor, and during a good sermon they could smell it. Others said he had the light of God's glorious Holy Spirit flickering around his temples, and when he brought the truth home to his flock, they could see it.

Rebecca had almost stopped attending Blackwater Valley Presbyterian Church, where she had met Starlyn after he returned from war. They continued to attend there after marriage. Blackwater Valley had been started by a few Scotsmen, along with Scots-Irish, around the year 1750. Thomas and Sophrona, Starlyn's parents, became charter members. William and Mary Thompson, Rebecca's parents, joined shortly after arriving in Starlight from Ulster.

The church was made of good local brick. It was just a plain, simple square church like most Presbyterian churches were. It was built for worship, not for admiration like the Anglican Church across the valley. Rebecca's church included many hardworking people who loved God Almighty.

Some of the members were still friendly with her, despite plenty of gossip giving reasons not to be. It was a difficult time for the church. The members had adjusted to both factions of the Craighead family who struggled over their problems.

One friend Rebecca never worried about losing was Sarah. Preacher Malcolm, Sarah's husband, was a man of

God. It was because of his sermons, and her friend, that she continued to attend.

Rebecca needed to hear one of Malcolm West's sermons. He was always hard on his flock. Emphasizing control, he reminded them how much each held over their own destination. Malcolm was a preacher who strongly believed anyone leaving the church for a life of sin, who did not turn back and repent, was surely destined for hell.

Today her family entered the church. Rebecca started to close the big oak door when a sudden draft slammed it shut. Sconces on the walls flickered as her three children went forward to sit with Malcolm's family. Rebecca slipped into an empty pew across the aisle from them. She had not planned to be there today, but a strong desire to attend services changed that.

"Thank you, Lord," she whispered.

The old Anglican Church had sold their pews to her church, replacing worn out simple benches. The maple pews were stained deep brown with a carved armrest on each end. The backs reached to an average man's shoulders. Some of the congregation thought the Anglican pews too fancy for their modest church.

"Next thing ya know we'll be bowing to the king, again," Old Frederick McFarland had said, reminding everyone he remembered how it was before the Revolution.

Eight wide pews ran up the middle of the church with the communion table and baptismal font separating them and the pulpit. Five more pews on the left of the pulpit, along with five on the right gave every person a reasonable view of Preacher West.

Rebecca lowered her head. "Lord, be merciful to me, Your servant." She looked up as Malcolm stepped forward.

He prayed over the congregation, making Rebecca grateful it included her.

"Today my sermon is on new beginnings." Malcolm stood tall, his broad shoulders level and feet slightly apart. His penetrating scrutiny seemed to dare the congregation to look away. Then within a minute he was on fire for the Lord.

"What if you lost everything?" His hand shot into the air, palm up, before it crashing down flat on the pulpit. "You would be looking for another start. There are many ways to begin anew in this world!"

Then he was out of the pulpit standing in front of the congregation. Almost in front of Rebecca.

Malcolm's hazel eyes flashed more green than golden brown. Wavy, honey colored hair, tied at the nape of his neck, streamed out behind him with every turn, a few tousled strands loose at his temples. A black jacket over a white shirt stood in stark relief to his heated face. Wrinkles etched between his eyes and on his forehead stood out.

"You had better be careful how you conduct yourself if you must start new—whatever you do—wherever you go!" Malcolm's eyes blazed as he shook his Bible high over the congregation and declared, "God is watching you!" The man of God mopped his face with a linen handkerchief then slowly righted himself.

Suddenly, Jeremiah Smith leaped out of his seat and hollered, "Amen! Keep us on the straight path, Brother Malcolm!"

Jeremiah punctuated his demand with a fist to the air and hollered again. Next to him, his small wife Effie waved a lace-trimmed handkerchief in front of her face, bony little wrist working fast.

Malcolm continued awhile before his long legs inched back toward the pulpit.

"Don't struggle with God," he declared. "He might have something for you to do!"

After the sermon wound down the congregation slowly shook itself from the grip of Malcolm West. Rebecca suspected he was not done, though.

Back in the pulpit, Malcolm laid his hands flat on the wooden top he had pounded earlier then assumed a solemn stance. The way he swiped at his face it looked to Rebecca like he had something in his eyes. Feet shifted as a few cleared their throats.

"We have been asked to start up a new church in the young state of Tennessee," he said, voice thick with emotion. "I have decided to go there for the Lord."

A hush fell over the congregation before gasps of shock broke the silence.

"Tennessee is six years old, and it is in need of strong new churches with godly people to shepherd them. I, for one, am answering my Master's call." Malcolm lifted his hands from the pulpit, swiping them along the sides of his breeches before stepping back. Something like relief showed in his face.

Rebecca's head snapped up as she straightened in the hard pew. What did he say? Tennessee? She shook her head. Oh, no. What will I do?

The congregation sat there in silence. No one made a sound, until the children grew loud.

Malcolm shrugged, groaning before he continued. "We plan to leave in late summertime, if all goes well. We will be traveling with a few members from church. Maybe even some of the community will come along." He hesitated, as if at a loss for words. She could not remember seeing that before, or the congregation so quiet.

"A friend at a Presbyterian church in Nashville has asked me to go there and help start new churches. Moses Bryant will remain behind to assist a new pastor when he arrives, much as Moses has worked with me. You see—the Good Lord's given us an explosion of churchgoers due to revivals in the new territories. Some folks believe the immediate dangers in the underpopulated regions are starting to worry people about where they stand with God." He paused briefly.

"An agreement has been reached, folks. The Congregationalists who migrated west and south are joining Presbyterian churches. Those churches need God-fearing ministers. If the Lord our God is calling you to make this trip with us, better get ready to go."

Malcolm cleared his throat then started again.

"You're welcome to help us start these new churches in Tennessee. Deacon York is handling this. If you're interested, speak with him."

Malcolm paced the floor then gave his forehead another swipe.

"Are you deaf out there? Can you hear me talking?"

Suddenly the church erupted with noise as everyone tried to speak at once. People rushed out of their seats, streaming toward the pulpit, where Malcolm stepped down to greet them. Sarah and their children took a place by Malcolm's side. Rebecca joined them, hugging her best friend.

One young man reached the pulpit just ahead of the crowd. "How rough will the trip be? How long does it take?" It was well known that he and his bride were looking to get off her father's land to start somewhere new. He looked at her and smiled before adding, "Is there any land available in Tennessee?"

"Yes," Malcolm said. "There's land for sale, homesteading in certain areas. Also, some patriots from the revolution are selling their bounty land warrants. With a warrant you can pick out your land."

There was silence as Malcolm spoke.

"It will require about eight to ten weeks travel, depending on what we run into." He continued. "The journey will not be easy. If that puts you off, best stay in Virginia where you are settled. But if you're looking for a new life or to own land, it is a good place to go."

"What about Indian trouble?" another person said.

"Well, there have been Indian problems. I won't deny that, but these are somewhat cleared up."

The pressing questions were soon answered, but the congregation seemed reluctant to stop. It was as if they did not want to turn loose of Malcolm West or his family, whom they had come to trust, including Rebecca. Finally, though, when the last comments were made and the last pieces of advice given, there was nothing left for the congregation but to leave. They started home sure to mourn the loss of the best preacher some had ever known.

* * *

It was a windy day. Ransom struggled with the team as they rode home in silence. Rebecca could hardly believe her best friend was leaving Virginia to live in a sparsely populated wilderness. Remembering a change was coming for her family, she shook off the tingle starting up her spine to wonder just what that might be.

She worked with the girls readying the house for the evening while Ransom took care of chores. The fires were blazing hot with supper on the table when the four sat down to eat.

"Why must they leave?" Janey demanded.

"Miss Rebecca—Miss Rebecca—" Rosie started. Then, pushing hair away from her face, she started again. "What'll happen to 'em so far from home?"

"I do not know the answers to your questions, girls. I can hardly believe they are going."

They ate until Ransom interrupted with his own observations.

"It's going to be a hard trip. I think we'll do well to stay right where we are."

Caught up in their thoughts, they finished in silence.

"Janey, let's make something good," Rosie said.

"Do not bring anything upstairs for me," Rebecca said. "I am so tired."

The girls cleared the table and went to the sideboard. They were deciding what to bake. Ransom went to join them. Rebecca suspected sweet molasses or some other cookies would be on the table in the morning.

She went to her room, starting a fire before changing into a warm gown. It was not long before she was on her knees, praying for guidance for her family. She crawled under the covers dropping off to sleep, when it crossed her mind she must speak with Tomson.

* * *

Malcolm laid his Bible aside. Turning to Sarah, he said, "Go into my office. There's something on the desk for you."

The children were in bed and the house was quiet. The wood in the fireplace crackled as little spurts of flame leapt off the logs, flickered in the air, only to be replaced.

Sarah picked up a lamp and started down the hall. She spotted the cloth upon entering the room. Her heart beat faster as she hurried to examine it.

She held the bolt of cloth in the crook of an arm, unrolling a portion for a better look before dropping a length from her waist to the floor. The color took her breath away. It was a lovely dark blue with lavender paisley. Cotton was too expensive for them to afford. So far, they had done fine with homespun. Sarah sat at Malcolm's desk, smoothing the material between a thumb and forefinger. Her thoughts went to Rebecca, someone she would most certainly miss.

Sarah liked Rebecca Craighead better than anyone she knew. There was a quality about her friend she could not put her finger on, except it was soothing to her. She admired the way Rebecca stood up to the problems seeming to flood her family after Starlyn's death. Sarah wondered if she could be as strong, under such a heavy load.

She considered the way Jack had interpreted Starlyn's will. Did he really believe it was what Starlyn had wanted? There had been talk among their congregation, but the Craigheads were longstanding members of the church. Gossip about Jack had run into opposition.

Sarah had asked Malcolm if they were really going to Tennessee.

He simply said, "Whatever God wants is the way it will be. It is up to Him."

How she loved her husband. It was no wonder the congregation did not want him to go. Malcolm heard the call of his Master long before anything else. If he said they were going, they were going.

Sarah thought about what they would leave behind. She had grown accustomed to their position in Starlight, and to living in a comfortable home in an established community. She dreaded the hardships she envisioned waiting for them in this new land.

Back in the summer she met travelers headed for Kentucky, Tennessee, even a few to Ohio.

"Why did they take their families so far?" she murmured as she fingered the pretty cloth. "Because we had our land, not leaving enough here for others. They must have wanted land, too."

Saying it aloud helped her understand more clearly.

Malcolm had encouraged the church members to extend their hospitality to these families with food, assistance repairing their wagons and shoeing their teams. She remembered the smiling faces of the children they helped when they sat down to supper along with the sweets she had baked. Sometimes they were barefoot with their clothing in tatters. When their parents spoke of a home in a new land, their hopes and dreams had been reflected in the faces of the meagerly dressed children looking back at them.

She already grieved the family and friends they must give up for her husband to answer his Master's call. Sarah prayed that their journey would be easy. Malcolm's father, Doctor West, would be traveling with them. He was in frail health. What if something happened to him? They could not leave the grandfather of their children some strange place along the way.

What if she was with child again? Deep in her heart Sarah suspected Malcolm would not change his decision.

"I might have to give birth to our child somewhere between here and Tennessee," she complained softly. Instead of worrying, though, she should be thankful Martha Taylor was traveling with them. Everyone knew she was the best midwife around. Sarah was suddenly ashamed of her thoughts.

Several families in the congregation intended to make the trip with them. Whoever went, it would be better than traveling alone. Her heart was broken that Rebecca would not be among them.

Sarah shifted her legs and yawned, looking to gauge the level of oil in the lamp. Realizing she had been in the office for a while, she carefully rolled the material and put it away. She went to find Malcolm, one thought still lingering in her mind.

What would the move really be like?

CHAPTER FORTY-TWO

Jack sat in his office working on claims due against Starlyn's estate. He felt a smile spread across his face as he thought about his attorney. It seemed Morris Whitley knew people who could do just about anything, if a person wanted it badly enough.

The magistrate had accepted the will, and the no appraisal clause, though he might have to account for the sale of some assets. It was a simple enough matter for him. Reputable people could suggest an amount for the estate's items they chose to purchase. Jack would subtract the debts from the assets and, if there were sufficient funds, this could also include the land note. He had not truly decided, though, how to handle the note just yet.

The last time Jack had seen Ransom in Starlight, he felt the urge to tell him the truth about his plans.

"I'd like to speak with you, Rance," Jack had said, in that confident way he always addressed his brother's son. "When can you come by for a visit?"

"You have the nerve to ask me this, after what you are doing?"

"Wait—hold on! I want to speak with you." Jack placed a hand on his shoulder.

"I'll have to think on it." Ransom shrugged off his hold and walked away.

He remembered when his nephew's face showed admiration. Jack sighed, wishing it were still so and that none of this had happened. He stood and stretched, crossing to the window before gathering up the claims. He would take them by Morris' office in the morning.

He should straighten everything out with Rebecca. There was no reason not to do the right thing, especially since Clayton Baxter left town. Now there was no need to worry about him making off with what belonged to Starlyn. The man was gone.

The news had finally reached Jack. Clayton's departure had been unexpected. Some said he left in a hurry. There was even talk that he claimed Rebecca was in love with him, and that Polecat ran him off in a jealous rage.

"He left in the middle of the night," they said. "Just up and left real quick-like."

One of McClutcheon's fiddlers had run into Clayton heading out of town. He said Clayton acted peculiar, looking over his shoulder all the while he talked. That was the last time anyone in Starlight laid eyes on Clayton Baxter.

Jack put this aside as he saddled up and started the ride to the cemetery. He had the strong urge to go. It seemed like a long time since he was there, having missed the previous week. He tied the horse to a tree limb before entering the graveyard Starlyn had kept up the years since their father passed on. His brother did that job faithfully until his death.

After Jack discovered Felix had taken over that chore, he offered to pay him for his trouble. Felix had reacted as though Jack struck him, saying in that Irish brogue, "You ain't got enough money to pay for Thomas or Starlyn. For them, I do it free."

Jack shook off the thought and went to Granda's grave to talk. He moved on to Father's and Mother's site, crying by the time he reached Starlyn's. "Brother, I am sorry for breaking the promise I made to you. I intend to do the right thing for Rebecca. For your children."

His Granda, father and brother each had been honorable men. The Craighead word was as good as gold until he broke the promise to Starlyn. How could he have done that? Never mind he was worried about Clayton Baxter getting Rebecca, then possession of his family's land.

Jack's shoulders shook as harsh sounds erupted from his throat to echo in the still air. He should not have let anything keep him from helping Starlyn's family. He grieved again over losing his brother, and for the family. It was like they had died, too.

The grief subsided as the cold air stung his raw face. He mounted, starting down the hill, passing Father's house where Felix now resided. He traveled over the land the two had played and worked on as young boys. Happiness stirred as he crossed onto Starlyn's land. Rebecca now owned all the property except the five acres Felix's house sat on. Making things right with her had pressed on his heart. Soon it would be done.

* * *

Rebecca stood on the back porch, clutching a shawl closer against the cool air. The bright sun gave some warmth. Her gaze raked over the hill. She could almost see Starlyn turning back toward the porch the day he hauled freight to Charlotte Town. She turned to see Jack riding from the direction of his parents' old home and hurried back into the house. He most likely came from the family graveyard, now on land Starlyn had inherited. Land she now owned.

The girls had gone with Ransom to Starlight. She began to gather what was needed to prepare supper when she heard footsteps coming toward the common room. They must have returned early.

"Janey, will you fill the flour bowl for me? Hurry, I need…"

"It's me, Rebecca. I came to see you." Jack's face was pale, strained, unlike he usually looked.

"What are you doing here? Get out. You are not welcome." She swept hair from her face, hands coming to rest on her hips.

"I implore you to just let me talk. I know the way I have acted toward you is not what I promised Starlyn. I want to make it right."

The tremor in his voice caught her attention. Something was different about him.

"Oh? How do I know you will finally do what is right since your word, so far, has been worthless?"

"I want to buy my brother's property, to keep the graveyard in our family. That is very important to me." He rubbed the back of his neck. "Are you content with staying here?"

Picking up a mixing spoon, she ran a finger along its edge, recalling Clayton was out there somewhere. Did he already spread his lies about her?

"Well, the place is awfully big without Starlyn." She did not tell him how it broke her heart.

"I just heard that Mr. Ewing is selling a small farm for an acquaintance, not far from here. He is handling it through correspondence from Tennessee. If you are interested, we can look into it."

"Will I have the funds to pay for it?"

"More than that. You and the children have quite a bit coming."

"Where is that farm?" Rebecca said.

"About thirty miles, I believe. It is across the river in Bedford County."

"Then we will cross over Hale's Ford to get there?"

"That's the best way." Jack scratched his head. "Do you want to think about this?"

"No. I believe you can contact Mr. Ewing to let him know I am interested. You know, Starlyn knew his father-in-law, General Davidson. " Rebecca gripped the spoon before putting it back. "Jack, could you do that soon?"

"Yes. Right away." Jack looked down. "When you move, can I have first chance to buy your property?"

Jack was contrite and more humble than she could remember. It softened her opinion of him. "Yes, we will come to an agreement on this land."

"I shall make the arrangements then take you to see the house." He gave a soft cough. "I will let myself out."

He was not gone long before the children arrived home, bursting through the door.

"Uncle Jack passed us down the road," Janie said.

"Yeah, he waved at us," Rosie added.

"Did he stop here?" Her son fixed keen blue eyes on her.

"Yes, he did," Rebecca said.

"Well then, what did he want?" Ransom had a defiant look on his face.

"We discussed the outcome of your father's will." Rebecca hesitated to talk about the full extent of Jack's visit. She handed Janey the bowl. "Rosie will help me start supper while you get the flour.

Ransom rubbed his belly. "I'll poke up the cook place. After we eat I expect to talk about this."

She nodded, not surprised her son wanted to pursue Jack's visit.

* * *

The family finished supper. After the evening's chores Rebecca boiled water for tea. Ransom came in and sat at the table.

"Shall I fix you tea?" she said.

"No. No, I want to talk about Jack's visit."

"Oh, yes. What would you like to know?" Her stomach tightened.

"Everything he discussed with you."

"He has promised to act on our behalf in pursuit of a small farm across the river, in Bedford County." Rebecca must get away from the memories of Starlyn's death soon as possible. Her anchor was gone.

Worse, she could not forget what Clayton Baxter had done to her in the home Starlyn had built for them. She must protect their children from the lies he would tell should he return. Moving was the only way to do that.

"Mother, how do you know he will keep his word?" Ransom said.

"Because he is remorseful for the way he has treated us."

"Remorseful? Is he remorseful for trying to starve us out, or calling Father a thief in court?"

"Many lost their temper that day, Ransom."

"He attacked me, as I tried to defend you and Father. He struck me—slapped me in the face!"

"Can you forgive him for what he has done? He truly has changed."

"I could forgive him if he has changed, but he has not." Ransom struck the table with enough force to shake her teacup. "Why do you not believe me?"

"He really is a different man. If only you had been

here." How she hoped her son was wrong about Jack.

"Mother, you are going to be sorry. Just you wait." He jumped up, arms stiff at his side. "I'm going to bring in more firewood."

* * *

The following afternoon Rebecca took a walk. She pulled her coat closer while avoiding the patches of snow.

Ransom was level-headed most of the time, hardly ever losing his temper. The evening before, though, he was adamant about not trusting his uncle. She just could not believe Jack would go back on his word this time.

Soon their children would be far away from Clayton Baxter, where his lies could not hurt them. With her and the children gone, Clayton would have to contend with Jack.

She glanced at the trees down by the spring and missed Starlyn.

The End

ABOUT THE AUTHOR

Patricia Fay Reece lives in Washington state, along the Columbia River. A native of Tennessee, she enjoys researching the past history of her ancestors and the times in which they lived. The historical novels she writes have been inspired by that.

Patricia has a love for history, people, and details. She especially enjoys history connected to her family's genealogy. There is a hunger for exploring the lives of individual people she meets through intense interaction and thorough conversation.
The roots of her writing go way back in the hills and hollows of her youth, all moved along by the descriptive verbs of her father and the deep love and understanding of her mother. Along with experiences made possible by interaction with eight siblings and multiple cousins, Patricia's confidence was gained by the exploration of the deep woods countryside they all called home.

Patricia looks forward to any and all comments or questions from readers. Please do not hesitate to contact her at:
patriciareecewrites@gmail.com

Patricia Reece

www.ingramcontent.com/pod-product-compliance
Lightning Source LLC
Chambersburg PA
CBHW051330250626
47155CB00007B/2536